THE LAST ACT

DEBORAH KLÉE

Print book ISBN: 978-1-8380804-7-1 First Printed 2023

Published by Sherman House

OTHER BOOKS BY THIS AUTHOR

The Borrowed Boy

Just Bea

The Forever Cruise

For Laura-Jade

PROLOGUE

The Victorian theatre was already ablaze. It illuminated the sky as if turning a spotlight on the pink, green, and lavender doves that swooped in circles, as bewildered as the onlookers.

Fifteen minutes earlier, Howdy! magazine's junior reporter had been sitting in the front row between an enthusiastic man from The Evening Standard, and a talkative lady from The Tatler, wondering at her fortune about being asked to cover the prestigious Golden Globe Easter Gala. The press had been invited to witness a new talent that would change the face of theatrical magic. Top producers had already offered contracts, there was talk of a TV series, and film rights.

When flames leapt from the stage floor, she had sat on the edge of her seat, intrigued. There had been a murmur of approval. The audience was gripped.

'Fire! Fire! Evacuate the building.' It took a few seconds for her to register – this wasn't an act. The theatre was on fire.

Outside, a fluffle of bunny girls huddled together, men's jackets draped over their shoulders.

'Do we know how the fire started?' the Howdy! reporter asked, as she edged her way into the circle of puff ball tails.

'We were in the bar. You probably know more than we do.'

In the distance, a siren wailed. The theatre was crackling now, reminding her of bonfires and fireworks when she was a child. A parrot's squawk pierced the night, another refugee from the burning building.

'You can't stand there. The assembly point is in the Strand.' A man in an orange tabard tried to shepherd them.

An explosion. Screams. People were running towards the theatre. Blue lights flashed.

'Keep away from the building. Make your way to the Strand.'

She watched the chaos and felt sick. If anyone was still in the theatre, they wouldn't have survived. The man from the Evening Standard was taking photos. Damn, she didn't have a camera – only a notebook and her ears. Listening and observing were what she did best. Nobody seemed to notice her as she wove in and out of groups, eavesdropping on conversations. This was how she came to discover a much bigger story than the fire which destroyed the Golden Globe Theatre.

Now, nearly a year on, she had interviewed everyone concerned. It was the perfect time for Howdy! to publish this compelling story. The scribbled notes blurred and danced before her tired eyes. She took a slug of strong coffee and turned the page.

'I don't care what anyone says; it was the curse of Molly May. It had been going on for years – unexplained accidents and the like. If you were alone in the theatre at night, you'd hear her, a horrible moaning and rattling. I only stayed once on my own, never again. There were mice too, and rats. They'd run over your feet when the lights went out. Well, I thought they were rats, now I'm not so sure.' *Sly shivers, then lowers her voice, leaning in.* 'I reckon Molly May had something to do with that other girl's disappearance. It was only a matter of time before something really bad happened.' **Sly Fitzgerald, Hocus Pocus dancer.**

'The Golden Globe was a beauty, that's for sure. Everything preserved, just as it was in her day. They don't make them like that anymore: the mechanics, the pulley systems, the workings under the stage. Before Peter Walker took it on, there was talk of turning it into a museum of Victorian magic. It would have rivalled the set up they have at The Magic Circle, by all accounts. But he had big ideas. Wouldn't be told about what needed doing to make it safe. I swear I tried. Maybe I should have tried harder. Don't write that down. It was an accident waiting to happen.' **Pedro Lopez – Caretaker and Front of House.**

'It started with a bit of kit falling from the gantry. That was no accident. Someone or something must have meddled with it for that to happen. I'm not saying nothing like that happened before, it did. But that was when it got me thinking. I started watching out for things and when you do that, you see things that others don't.' *Lenny points to his eyes.* 'You know what I mean? Well, I saw, and I saw things weren't right. I just wished I'd said something sooner. Before it was too late.' **Lenny Charles – Stagehand.**

. . .

She had read and reread the stack of notes. Circled and underlined. Now, the truth was clear. The story to be told. It had started when Nico walked into The Hawley Arms and, on meeting the beautiful Jojo Evans, conjured three white doves to fly out of her handbag. Because from that moment on, Jojo was under his spell.

1

FEBRUARY 1980

The stage was partly lit, casting a pearly blue mist around Jojo's feet. A spotlight shimmered centre stage, a ghost of the last performance. The seats empty now. Sometimes, she had to hug herself to affirm that she was really here. Everything about her life was different. She was a professional performer – paid a proper wage to do what she loved best. Magician's assistant was the first rung of a ladder – Jojo knew she could be more. But this – *everything*, her life with Nico, the flat they shared... Where was Nico? She was meeting Annie in fifteen minutes. Jojo strode across the stage to stand in the spotlight. If he was in the auditorium, he would see her.

'Nico? You there?' Her voice sounded loud. With no audience to absorb the noise it bounced off the walls. She held up a hand to shield her eyes. 'Nico, I'm going now. To meet Annie.'

Something moved. A scraping sound and then a squeak, like a lazy gate swinging on its hinges. Jojo shivered. The ancient mechanics that swung above the stage and turned noisily beneath gave her the jitters.

'Nico?' There was something out there moving in the shadows.

'Watch out!' Nico seemed to come out of nowhere. He pushed her with force and before she could yell in protest, there was a resounding thump on the stage behind her.

She tried to turn around to see what had happened, but he held her tight. Too tight. 'I'm okay.' Still, he held her, his body rigid, unyielding as though she were clamped in iron. Jojo could barely breathe. 'I'm okay. I'm okay.'

He relaxed, and Jojo took a few seconds to steady herself. His arms were still around her but no longer trapping her movement. She turned to see a shaft of metal lying across the stage. It was in the spotlight where she had been standing. Jojo's knees wobbled, and she grasped Nico for support.

'Oh my god. It could have killed me.'

Nico hugged her, more gently now. 'Don't. I can't bear to think about what might have happened.'

Charlie joined them on the stage. 'I don't know how that came loose. I checked it myself. Are you okay Jojo?'

She felt Nico's body tense; his attention now on the stagehand. Like a cat arching his back. 'I'm fine Charlie. I'm just glad Nico was there to save me.'

'Yes. What good luck,' Charlie said, with an attitude that did nothing to diffuse the growing tension.

Not this again. Not now. Why couldn't the two of them get along? Nico charmed every woman, young or old; he was popular with the other magicians and stagehands. Likewise, Charlie was everyone's friend. A joker. One of the hardest working stagehands and a good friend to Jojo. When Nico had introduced her to the Golden Globe as his assistant, she had been overwhelmed. It was an enchanting place to work, but there was an undercurrent born from ambition, jealousy, and fragile egos. If Charlie hadn't come to her rescue in that first difficult week, when the showgirls were eyeing her with suspicion, and Nico was preoccupied talking prop design with the technicians, then Jojo may not have been accepted so quickly. She had been reading a DC comic in Cake Presto, the Golden Globe's café, when Charlie joined her table. They discovered a shared love of comic books, although Charlie favoured Marvel. From there on they adopted an easy banter and to the rest of the performers it was as though Jojo had always been one of the troupe. Unassuming, funny, and down to earth, Charlie created calm in a storm. Nobody was threatened by him, and so under his cloak of protection, Jojo had slipped into the life of the Golden Globe without creating many waves. Nobody that was except for Nico. Charlie and Nico were facing one another now, like a showdown at high noon.

Exasperated, Jojo broke away. 'I'm going to be late.'

'Surely you're not still going to meet your friend? Not after a shock like that?' Nico said.

Charlie rolled his eyes before leaving them alone on the stage.

'It's fine. I'm over it now. Nothing happened. You saved me.'

'Let's have a quiet night in.' His warm breath tickled her ear. 'If you go home now and run a bath, I'll join you when I've finished here. A couple of sirloin steaks with salad. A bottle of Beaujolais.'

It was tempting. They had been rehearsing for ten or twelve hours every day that week and she was exhausted. Jojo checked her watch behind his back. 'Mmm. But no. I can't. Annie will be waiting.'

Nico pressed against her, and she felt him grow hard. 'If

you're sure that's what you want to do.' He had mischief in his eyes.

Damn him. No wonder she couldn't concentrate on anything else. Jojo backed away from 'essence of Nico,' the unique scent of his warm skin, a lingering scent of olives, and a delicious cedar aftershave. 'No. But it's what I *have* to do.'

Nico shrugged and raised his palms in defeat. 'Go then. Give Annabelle my regards.'

When Jojo glanced back at the stage, Nico had already left. The spotlight died. One stagehand called to another. Then all was quiet. And dark. Jojo stood still, waiting for her eyes to adjust. Someone else was there; she could feel their presence pressing against the darkness. A chair squeaked. Jojo scanned the balcony boxes. 'Who's there?'

It would be easy to let her imagination run away with her. There was bound to be creaking in a place that old. The rows of seats were visible now, and she made her way towards the illuminated exit at the back of the theatre. A voice startled her.

'I saw what happened. Freaky.' It was Bobbi, one of the showgirls, who was sitting in the back row, her long legs slung over the seat in front. She blew out a plume of smoke. 'Don't tell.'

'Jiminy Jillikers. You scared the life out of me.' It did not surprise Jojo that Bobbi was smoking in the theatre. Bobbi was the kind of girl who had probably been breaking rules all of her life just for the hell of it, but why was she lurking back there in the dark? 'Funny place to chill. Sitting here with the lights out.'

Bobbi laughed. 'It's perfect. Don't you love this old theatre when it's quiet? You can sense its magic. A place absorbs everything — good and bad. I bet this theatre holds a few secrets. Like who, or what, pushed that lump of metal just now?'

Jojo shivered. 'It was an accident. Unless you saw something we didn't?'

Bobbi shrugged. 'I saw Nico save your life. Lucky, he knew it was about to fall.'

Jojo didn't have time to gossip. Everyone in the Golden Globe would know the story of the falling kit by the following morning, exaggerated beyond recognition. Theatre folk loved embellishing the truth. 'He did. My hero!'

'It's not the first time something like that has happened,' Bobbi said, flicking her ash onto the threadbare carpet.

'What do you mean?' She had to ask. Bobbi would not let her go until she had told her story.

'Unexplained accidents. Things falling from the gantry. Objects flying across the stage as though they had been thrown. Restless spirits. Ghosts.'

The hairs prickled on Jojo's neck. It was nonsense. She laughed under her breath. 'Spooky.'

Bobbi stood up and stretched, arching her back. 'A double scotch is what you need, darling.'

She did need something strong, but it would have to wait until she was with Annie. 'I can't I'm meeting a friend.' Jojo checked her watch; she was already fifteen minutes late.

As Jojo ran the best she could in her clumpy boots, it felt as though she was being pulled in opposite directions: Nico willing her to stay, Annie claiming the friendship of a lifetime – her neglected friend. Jojo stopped to catch her breath. Nico had seemed disappointed. Maybe he had forgotten she was going out. If he had planned a special meal perhaps, she should go home to be with him. Annie would understand. When Jojo imagined explaining to Annie, telling her about the near miss, she guessed her friend's reaction. She would be outraged on Jojo's behalf. Since they were little kids, she had taken on the role of her protector. Jojo smiled to herself. Dear Annie. She set off again for Lee Changs. Somehow, between rehearsals and being with Nico, she would find more time to see her friend.

2

Annie had ordered a bottle of Liebfraumilch and nearly finished her first glass of wine, when Jojo blew in like a colourful whirlwind, in a psychedelic mini dress of purples, pinks, and green, her auburn hair in a high ponytail. Today it was a 1960s look, but it could have been any outfit from the 1920s through to the 1970s. Pleasure at seeing her dearest friend was tempered with annoyance. It was the first time they had met in weeks, and Jojo was forty minutes late. Annie resolved not to ask about the theatre or Nico; that's all Jojo wanted to talk about. No, let Jojo ask about *her* life for a change. Annie poured Jojo a glass of wine.

'Oh, I need this!' She held up her glass and grinned. 'Annie Apple Cheeks. It is so-oo good to see you. Cheers!'

Annie smiled at Jojo's irrepressible energy and joy for life. 'So, what kept you this time?' Her voice was playful, disguising any lingering resentment.

'Same old. Rehearsals. You know what Nico's like.'

Annie wanted to talk about something else, like her parents' announcement that they planned to sell up and move to Scotland, but this was a red flag. 'No, Jojo. I don't know what Nico is like. I've never met him.'

'You will, I promise. In fact, come to the Golden Globe on your day off and we'll meet for a cream tea in Cake Presto.'

Annie pursed her lips, unwilling to let Jojo off that easily.

'A nice bit of Battenberg,' Jojo coaxed. 'I know! Mrs Brew does a fabulouser Black Forest gateau.'

'Okay. Okay. It's a date. But don't leave me sitting there like one of your forgotten props. Tell me a time and I'll be there.'

'Promise.' Jojo said this softly and reached for her hand.

Annie wanted to cling tight. To beg Jojo to come back. To be the way they were a year ago, before she met Nico. Instead, she smiled. 'It's a date. Now let's order.'

The waiter had been hovering by their table since Jojo's arrival. Lee Chang's was busier than usual, with it being a Friday night and still early enough for pre-theatre diners. Some office workers – men in suits and girls in heels – were raucous, celebrating the start of the weekend. They had probably been drinking since lunch time.

Annie ordered more than she could eat, because Jojo never ordered enough and always ended up eating everything in sight.

'When's your next public performance? It's about time I saw you in this act with the Amazing Nico.'

'The *Incredible* Nico.' Jojo did jazz hands. 'In four weeks, but it's a really important one. The Starlight show attracts some of the top talent scouts and decides who will be the last act at the Easter Gala.'

As dishes arrived at their table, Annie organised them. She topped up their glasses, emptying the bottle. 'Is it important, who does the finale?'

Jojo dropped a spring roll from her chopsticks. 'Jiminy

Jillikers! Of course, it's important. The press know that the last act is the one that's attracted the attention of the talent scouts. You've no idea how many famous magicians made it to the big time because of Easter Gala. Yes. It's important. It's a *really* big deal.'

'Okay,' Annie said with care. She did seem to have lost touch with Jojo, but she would visit her for tea at Cake Presto, and go to this important show. Envy? Jealousy? A little green worm had been eating at her soul and Annie was ashamed. 'Then I wish you success.' She raised her glass. 'To the Incredible Nico and his even more incredible assistant, Jojo!'

'Are you going to eat the rest of those pork balls?'

'No, help yourself.' Annie smiled as she watched Jojo checking with her before finishing up everything on the table, just as she had predicted.

'Jessica's getting married,' Annie said.

'Really? Your little sister. When did she get old enough to even have a boyfriend?'

'I know.' There must have been something in her voice, because Jojo stopped eating and gave Annie her full attention.

'That's good, right?'

'I guess.' But it wasn't. Everyone was moving on in their life except her. 'He seems a nice bloke – Gary. They met at a bowling alley.'

Jojo scooped some rice from the bottom of her bowl. The meal was over. Soon, Jojo would leave, but Annie wasn't ready to say goodbye.

'Do you remember when you first started at our infant school — Brookfields? You would stand on your own in the playground and be so absorbed in your game, I was afraid to talk to you. It was as though imaginary friends surrounded you.'

'I probably was. I got used to being on my own at home. I

remember you beating up Simon Pugh because he was calling me names.'

'I didn't beat him up. He was making fun of you. Simon wasn't known for *his* imagination.'

'Whatever you said, or did, it worked. With Annie Apple-cheeks as my friend, nobody messed with me again.'

They both laughed, although this was a story frequently told. It reaffirmed the bond between them, but that evening Annie sensed their ties weakening.

'How are your parents?' Jojo asked.

It felt as though Jojo was checking she had covered all that was expected of her before she returned to a world that Annie knew nothing about. 'They're talking about moving to Scotland.'

'Oh,' Jojo said, and Annie was pleased that she had saved this important news. 'Does that mean they will sell your house?'

'Yes. Once Jessica's married. Dad wants to return to his Highland roots and Mum's ready for a change.' Annie sighed.

'What about you? Where will you live?'

Annie wanted to wail, *I don't know. I'm lost. I'm scared. I'm lonely.* 'I'll find somewhere,' she said.

'Shall we get the bill then?'

So that was that. Annie had dropped her bombshell, but it barely made a ripple on the surface of Jojo's world. Annie knew her friend had already disconnected and was mentally making her way home to the Incredible Nico.

Whilst Jojo was digging around in her bag, Annie said, 'What about Monday?'

'For what? I can never find anything in here.'

'Give it to me.' Annie reached out a hand and Jojo passed her the battered leather bag. 'I've not seen this before. Did you get it from Portobello Road or Camden market?'

'No. It belonged to a magician — a Gladstone bag. I found it in the props room and Charlie said I might as well take it because it would only get thrown away.'

'Well, it's ridiculous. You can't find anything in here.'

'It is a magic bag,' Jojo laughed. Annie rummaged and then held aloft Jojo's green purse.

'So, Monday? For afternoon tea?'

'Oh. Okay. I think that's alright, but we're really busy with rehearsals for the Starlight show.'

'Fine.'

'But I will be there. I promise. About four?'

They hugged each other goodbye. Jojo said she would get a taxi and offered Annie a lift, but they were going in opposite directions.

It was still light, and the streets buzzed with anticipation for the weekend as girls with big hair, dressed in animal print and silks strode with meaning and young men with attitude gave them the eye. Everyone was going somewhere except for Annie. Before Jojo moved in with Nico, they might have met up on a Saturday in Camden to scour the market stalls looking for old clothes for Jojo. *I'll spend the evening with Mum for a change. Buy her a box of orange Matchsticks, her favourite, and we'll watch Dallas together.* But Annie's heart was heavy. She knew that one day Jojo would meet someone, that their lives would take them in different directions. It was just that Jojo knew where she was going, and Annie had no idea. It was as though she had been waiting for the right bus to come along, watching everyone else leave. Then, when she was alone at the bus terminal, the news that there would be no more buses. Her bus had come and gone without her.

. . .

Annie only worked at the travel agents on Saturday mornings and so by mid-afternoon, she was back home. When she popped her head around the kitchen door to say hello, the comforting smell of baking greeted Annie. 'I thought I'd stay in tonight, Mum. Have a bit of a girls' night. We haven't done that in a long while.'

Janet Daley wiped her hands on her apron. 'What a good idea. We haven't seen Jojo for ages.'

Jessica joined them. She leaned against the kitchen counter and eyed the warm fairy cakes. 'Isn't she shacked up with some Italian stud in the West End?'

How could Jessica be her sister? They were so different? Annie sighed. 'Jojo is living with her boyfriend, Nico, who also happens to be her stage partner.'

'That's what I said. And he's Italian, right?' Jessica reached for a cake and Mum swiped her hand with a tea towel.

'At least wait until they've cooled down. This batch is for the freezer, and they're not for you. They're for the WI Spring fayre. Margaret told me that Jojo hadn't been home in a while, but I don't think she knows Jojo's living with an Italian.'

'We don't even know if he is Italian.' The sharp tone in Annie's voice caused her mum and Jessica to throw questioning looks. She softened it. 'Jojo's mum and dad know nothing about him because he makes no effort to meet with her family or friends. *I've* not even met him.'

'But he is Italian,' Jessica said. Somehow, she had sneaked a cake unnoticed and was talking through a mouthful.

'So, he would have us believe, but as far as I can make out, he hasn't told Jojo anything about his life or upbringing. I tried to warn her about moving in with a man she knows nothing about, but you know what she's like. Anyway, Jojo's not coming over. I thought you and I could watch Dallas together, Mum.'

'Hmm. Why don't you sit down, Annie love? I'll make a pot of tea and we'll sample this bake. There'll still be plenty for the Spring Fayre.'

'Why does she get offered one and not me?'

'Because you've already helped yourself.'

'Ha! Sounds like you're in for a mother daughter chat.' Jessica stole two more and scurried from the room before she was caught.

Annie unpacked a Radio Times and the Matchmakers from her bag. She flicked through to Saturday evening's entertainment. 'Perfect. Love Story is on straight after Dallas.'

Her mum fussed around with plates and tea things, then sat down heavily opposite her. 'That would be lovely, but your dad and I are having dinner with the McIntyres. I'm sure we told you.' She cocked her head. 'You've been a bit out of sorts. Is something troubling you?'

'No. Not really.' Annie sighed. She didn't know why she felt so lost. It wasn't Mum and Dad's plan to move to Scotland, or Jessica getting married. She missed spending time with Jojo, but it wasn't just that. 'I'm probably tired. A quiet night in is exactly what I need. It's been busy at work with everyone booking their summer holidays. It's okay, I'll watch Love Story and eat all the Matchsticks.'

Her mum poured the tea. 'Meanie. Save a few for me. I know you miss Jojo. You've been a good friend to her. Poor kid had a hard time of it at home; just as well she had you.'

'And her imagination,' Annie added.

Her mum smiled. 'Yes, she has plenty of that. But what about you, darling?'

A lump formed in Annie's throat. That was it. She had no imagination. If she had a smidgen of Jojo's creativity, then she might see a life beyond the family home in Fenwood and working as a travel agent. But she couldn't. Her horizon was bleak. Empty. 'I'll think of something,' Annie said.

'You're a born carer. Jojo doesn't need you to look after her now that she's a grown woman. What you need are children of your own.'

Jessica stomped into the kitchen, hauling a bag containing her bowling ball and shoes. 'She'd have to find a man first, and that isn't going to happen.'

Annie wanted to throw the ball at her sister. Knock her down like a bowling pin. 'There are plenty of men who are interested in me.'

'True. But none of them survive beyond a first date with the ice queen.'

Mum shook her head in exasperation and started to clear away the plates.

'Just because I'm discerning.'

'Nobody's good enough. You know that you're going to end up living on your own with a load of cats.'

'Fine. I'd rather share my life with cats than get married for the sake of it. I don't need a man.'

Later that evening, when the house was quiet, Annie relaxed in a warm bath sprinkled with Radox salts and breathed in the scent of pine. Finding a man of her own was not the answer to her problems, but maybe she should be a little more open-minded. Nobody was perfect, including herself. Perhaps she did set her expectations too high and was a little quick to judge. It was a big commitment getting involved with someone. If she was too cautious, then Jojo was the opposite. Jojo was fearless. She took risks trying out new things as though selecting an outfit from her dressing-up box.

Annie was happy to be led by Jojo: discovering Camden

market together, helping Jojo set up her street performances – collecting the money thrown into a hat. One Saturday, they had hired roller skates and taken them to Hyde Park. Life without Jojo was like champagne with no bubbles. Annie sighed and hauled herself out of the cooling water. The bath salts had almost completely relaxed her, but one worry would not be washed away. It niggled like a burr beneath her skin. She was afraid for Jojo and didn't understand why. Was she being overly suspicious or just a teeny bit jealous of Nico? Maybe, but there was something else. Jojo seemed distracted – entranced. It was as though she was watching her friend, but an invisible screen separated them. She couldn't reach her. On Monday, she would meet Jojo at Cake Presto with an open mind. She would reach into Jojo's world and reassure herself that all was as it should be.

3

'Don't you have a leotard from your days as a dancer, bella?' Nico watched as Jojo tossed garments out of an old trunk, a pained expression on his face.

'Those horrid lycra things with legs cut up to the waist? No, thank you. Ah, my polka dot 50s skirt. This'll do if I wear it without the petticoats.'

Jojo threw open the lid of a vintage hatbox, which was stuffed full of ribbons, evening gloves, silk stockings, and other accessories to complete her outfits, and chose a matching red ribbon.

Nico groaned. 'We should have left by now.' He squatted alongside her and screwed up his nose as he peered into the trunk. 'There must be something more suitable for climbing in and out of props.'

A wing of black hair fell across one eye, and Jojo gazed at him in wonder. He was so perfect. So beautiful. She let the ribbon slide from her fingers and draped herself across his back.

'What on earth is this?' Nico held up a fur stole with a fox's head.

'That's Freddy. He looks real, but he's not. I found him in my granny's attic. He was all alone, curled up in the bottom of that very trunk. Which is *now* my dressing-up box.'

Nico dropped Freddy and shivered. 'It's disgusting.'

'Don't be mean to Freddy.' Jojo rescued the faux fur from Nico. It was one of her most precious acquisitions, not just because of the family history her grandfather had saved for months to buy it for her grandmother but because it was a collector's piece being in such good condition.

'Come on, find something. Anything. We're late.'

'You don't mean *anything*, otherwise you'd be okay with my polka dot skirt. But I'll find something else.' She sighed.

'Just something a bit more...'

'Debbie McGee? Nico, I don't want to look like every other magician's assistant. I want to look like *me*. The day you wear a high cut satin leotard I will, but until then...'

'Okay. Okay. Five minutes and then we've got to leave.'

Three teenage girls and a gawky boy brandishing autograph books greeted them at the Golden Globe. Nico gave his pseudo shy smile and Jojo witnessed the melting of at least two hearts. Always the showman, he pretended to search for his fountain pen, flourishing silk handkerchiefs from a pocket, and then a bouquet of paper flowers which he presented to the prettiest girl, a tall blonde. Nobody was interested in Jojo. 'I'll go ahead then,' she said.

'Okay,' he said without looking up. 'Room three.'

The rehearsal and prop rooms were on an extension to the theatre. There was a back entrance, but Nico and Jojo always arrived at the front of house and walked through the theatre.

Nico to please his fans; Jojo because she liked to stop at the altar of her dreams - the stage with its velvet curtains. One day, she would be the star act. The audience would hold their breath in awe and disbelief as she performed an illusion that defied expectation.

'Miss Jojo?' Pedro, the caretaker, interrupted her daydream. 'Someone left this at the box office for you.' Her heart lifted; she had a fan. But no, it was addressed to Nico's assistant. Not Jojo Evans. It was just another way for one of Nico's fans to get his attention. Jojo hoped it wasn't a pair of panties. The last ones, revolting pink kami knickers, she had thrown with a pincer grip into the bin. And to think Nico had the affront to turn up his nose at Freddy the Fox.

Hocus Pocus had just finished a workout and the changing room was fragrant with peach, apple, and cucumber gels melding in the steam of showers. Jojo unzipped her white boots - a buy from Oxfam. They went well with the bibbed 60s hot pants she had worn that day as a compromise, as well as the psychedelic dress she had worn the previous day. Besides, Nico couldn't resist them. She remembered his passion last night when she returned from dinner with Annie.

'A good night?' Bobbi smirked, interpreting Jojo's expression correctly.

'I'd better learn to be less transparent if I'm to become a magician,' Jojo laughed.

Bobbi finished wiping her face with a cotton wool ball - the almond scent of Anne French cleansing milk, familiar and comforting. She paused, watching Jojo's reflection. 'Is that what you want? To be a magician in your own right?'

Why had she said that out loud? Jojo felt her cheeks flush. 'No. I mean, I don't know. Maybe.' Was she greedy for wanting more when she had all this? 'I just think I could contribute more to our act.' Now she felt disloyal.

Bobbi released her hair, and it fell about her shoulders. She swivelled around to face Jojo. 'Even if Nico's ego allowed it, I doubt Peter Walker would. This place is stuck in the 50s. Haven't you noticed all the women performers are dancers or assistants? It's fine when you're starting out, but when you get to my age, you need a bit more security. This face and these,' she pushed up her breasts, 'will not be enough when I turn forty.'

Apart from the trickle of a shower, they were alone in the changing room. It was a rare moment for Bobbi to share something so personal with her and Jojo was both surprised and honoured. 'That's a long way off.'

'Unfortunately, not. I wanted to star in West End shows and look at me now.'

Jojo did, and she saw the Golden Globe's most talented and successful dancer, a woman who possessed effortless grace and worldly sophistication. To say this would give away her inferiority and Jojo wanted to hang on to the feeling of being Bobbi's equal for just a little while longer. 'What about the classes you teach at Mango? Couldn't you set up your own dance school?'

Bobbi gave a half-hearted chuckle and stood up. Dressed in a luxurious velour leisure suit, she was on her way out. 'Saturday Night Fever started something of a craze, but how long will that last? Anyway, we were talking about you. What is it you think you could introduce to Nico's act? And I warn you, for all of his sexy charm, our Nico is a bit of a chauvinist.'

Jojo didn't like to hear Bobbi speak badly of Nico, but she suspected Bobbi was right. 'I don't know. Aerial acrobatics. Juggling. I can do more than contort my body. I trained as a dancer too.'

'Wow. You can do aerial acrobatics?' Bobbi seemed

genuinely impressed. 'Could you teach me? Nothing complicated. It would be perfect if I added that to the Hocus Pocus routine. Just something simple for the matinee which starts in three weeks. I've put Adele Pearson, owner of Mango, on the guest list. I doubt she'll show up for any of the shows, but if she does, she'll be so impressed. We have a harness and the wires.' Bobbi was almost jumping up and down in her excitement.

Jojo glowed with pride. Bobbi wanted her, Jojo, to teach her something. 'Of course, I can.' She hoped Nico would release her from their gruelling routine to work with Bobbi.

'And you know the world is changing? Peter Walker might be a bit behind the times, but he can't hold back the revolution in entertainment.' In response to Jojo's frown, she continued, 'Monty Python transformed the comedy scene, The Sex Pistols, music. Maybe it's time Jojo Evans transformed the world of magic.' Bobbi winked, and Jojo felt as though she had been accepted into Bobbi's exclusive club. An outsider at school, she had just become the confidante of the most popular girl at the Golden Globe.

'I'll start work on Nico. Try to persuade him to let me improvise.' Already her mind was racing ahead with possibilities. There wouldn't be time to change their act before the Starlight show, but there was no reason they couldn't work together to create something unique. Bobbi was right – everything was changing in the world of entertainment. Traditional cabaret acts would soon be passe. They could be at the leading edge of change. New wave magic.

'Late afternoons are good for me if you could find some time this week,' Bobbi said, slinging a pink leather duffel bag over her shoulder.

Jojo nodded eagerly. Nico wouldn't like it, but she would just have to make up the time by starting rehearsals earlier.

It wasn't until she was alone that Jojo remembered the letter passed to her by Pedro. There was just one typed line.

If you value your life, keep away from him.

She turned the paper over, looking for an explanation. Nothing. Then she searched the envelope, but it was empty. Was it a warning or a threat? A deranged fan? Surely, it wasn't a threat to her life. Jojo's instinct was to tell Nico, but she knew what he was like. He would become obsessed by the note when, in reality, it was probably nothing. There was no point winding him up, especially with the Starlight show fast approaching. He was already on edge, driving them both relentlessly, and over-reacting to any imagined threat. Take the falling gantry, for example. Jojo was tired of hearing about Charlie's incompetence and how she could have been killed. Nico would be unbearable if he saw this note and it would affect his performance. She didn't want him throwing knives at her, if his mind was elsewhere. She pushed the note deep into her bag, thankful that it would get lost in there.

4

When Annie stepped into Cake Presto, the scent of freshly brewed coffee, cinnamon, vanilla and hot sausage rolls greeted her. Annie had visited the café with Jojo before she started working at the Golden Globe. Every week there was another trendy place recommended in Time Out that Jojo would drag her to. The Golden Globe had been there for years, but the tourists, theatre folk, and creative types queuing up to get a table believed they had discovered a secret gem. Annie had hoped that Jojo had reserved a table, or would get preferential treatment, but apparently not. Afraid to lose her place in the queue, Annie ordered two cream teas and, by a stroke of luck, was hovering near a table when the occupants, an elderly man and younger woman, left. Annie tidied away their empty plates to make room for her tray and waited for Jojo.

'Is she a real genie?' a child exclaimed, pointing to a door at the back of the café where many of the visitors' eyes were trained, hoping to see one of the Globe's performers emerge.

It did not surprise Annie to see her beautiful friend, who

today did indeed look like a magical genie. Jojo knew how to pull it off: a shimmering top that stopped above her midriff, harem pants, and ridiculous embroidered slippers that curled up at the toes. Annie laughed and waved her over. 'You look like something out of Aladdin.'

'I know. Crazy, isn't it? Nico wants me to dress appropriately for work. I thought this was perfect. The pants work for yoga. Good, you got cream teas. Didn't you want a slice of Black Forest gateau or a Rum Baba?'

Annie laughed and poured the tea. 'I wish I could eat as much as you and stay slim. It's no wonder the amount of exercise you do. What does Nico mean by appropriate? I have no idea what a magician's assistant should wear.'

Jojo threw the end of a silky scarf over her shoulder. 'No trailing scarf. Or – she tapped her turban, headwear. Nothing that can get trapped in the equipment.'

'And the curl toed slippers?'

Jojo stretched out her legs and waggled her feet. 'Aren't they cute? A bit small, but so pretty.'

'Well, he does have a point,' Annie said. Nico would have his hands full trying to get Jojo to conform.

Jojo shrugged and helped herself to cream and jam. 'So, day off. What have you been up to, Annie Apple cheeks and what have you got in those Topshop bags?'

It almost felt as though she had her friend back. Annie told Jojo about the change to her hours as she now worked Saturday mornings and had every Monday off work, and the plans being made for Jessica's wedding. Jojo said all the right things, but Annie sensed her attention was elsewhere. Questions about Nico were deflected by, 'You'll meet him soon and then you can see for yourself.'

It was after four and the café had emptied when a young man wearing dungarees came in through the back door.

'Sit down, Charlie boy, and I'll bring you a slice of apple pie. It's fresh from the oven.' The woman behind the counter kissed her fingers.

'Mrs Brew, you are an angel. I *love* your apple pie.'

He headed straight for their table and joined them, sitting astride a chair with the back facing him. 'Hi Bat Girl. Did you get to recharge your superpowers on your day off?'

Jojo laughed. 'I did. Recharged and ready for action.' She did a superhero pose. 'What's new to the world of superheroes?'

Charlie grinned. 'Spiderman! There's a TV show in the States. Oh, and I found an ace comic book. Spiderman is my new hero. He could out smart Bat Man any day.'

'Ooh, do you have it with you? I'd love to take a peek.'

'I'll bring it in and show you.'

Annie followed this back and forth of banter, bemused. Until now she had thought Jojo one of a kind, but this Charlie was as cookie as her friend.

'Oh Charlie, this is Annie Daley. We've been friends since she joined forces with me against evil.'

Charlie seemed unfazed by Jojo's explanation, but Annie interpreted anyway. 'We've known each other since infant school when I stood up for Jojo on the playground.'

He looked impressed and Annie felt a warm glow. 'Wow. Now that is the sort of friend to be treasured. Does Bat Girl treasure you Annie Daley?'

Jojo was helping herself to the other half of Annie's scone, intent on spreading jam. Charlie caught Annie's eye and grinned.

'What?' Jojo looked up. 'Sorry, did you want that, Annie? I'll order some more.'

Mrs Brew arrived with warm apple pie and cream for

Charlie. He jumped up and returned with another fork. 'Annie can share my pie.'

It was good to be sitting between the two of them, feeling as though she was part of their world. Jojo seemed relaxed and happy. She had been imagining problems that didn't exist. If Nico was as carefree and warm as Charlie, then there was nothing to worry about.

Jojo looked as though she was about to sample the apple pie, but Charlie slid the plate away from her. It turned into a game with Charlie and Annie passing the plate between them as though they were playing football with Jojo on the opposing team.

'Jimminy Jillikers. I promised to meet Bobbi at four to teach her some basic aerial acrobatics.'

Annie was disappointed. 'That's a shame. I had hoped you would show me around and maybe introduce me to Nico.'

Jojo bit her lower lip and frowned. Annie hadn't meant to put pressure on her, and now she was sorry for sounding needy and demanding.

'It's okay. Of course, you're busy with the Starlight show. Another time?'

'Hey, I could show you around if that's cool with Jojo,' Charlie said.

Annie watched Jojo's face closely. She would know if Jojo wasn't happy with his suggestion. Although she was intrigued to get a glimpse into Jojo's new life, she didn't want to intrude. When Jojo smiled broadly and thanked Charlie, Annie relaxed.

'But I'm afraid Nico will be busy with rehearsals, so I'll introduce you to him another time,' Jojo said.

When they parted, Annie felt at peace. She had all the reassurance that she needed. Jojo was happy, and their friendship was as strong as ever. Charlie's offer was a bonus. Annie was itching to peek behind the scenes of the Golden Globe.

'Ready for your tour?' Charlie said, when Jojo had disappeared through a door back into her magical world.

They started with the little theatre. Annie gasped in delight at its faded splendour. It was perfect: a lavishly decorated ceiling, balcony boxes, gilt adornments and velvet seats. No wonder Jojo loved performing on that stage.

'Is it real?' she asked. Charlie frowned, and she felt foolish. 'I mean, is it really Victorian?'

'Yup. With all the under-stage mechanics, trap doors and pulleys. That's why it's ideal for performing magic.'

Annie's blood stirred. This was what she had missed. Excitement. Adventure. Discovering new things. She followed Charlie onto the stage. A couple of stagehands looked at her curiously as they went about their work rigging up lights.

'I haven't got to the bottom of what happened with the falling kit,' Charlie said.

Annie thought he was talking to a man who was reeling an electric cable across the stage. 'If Nico hadn't seen it coming down, I dread to think what might have happened.'

Annie's skin prickled. 'Was Jojo on the stage?'

Charlie faced her. 'Didn't she tell you? It was a near miss. I know everything was secure moments before. It makes little sense. Nico had some kind of second sense and threw himself at Jojo just in time.'

'When was this?'

'Friday. Jojo was about to leave to meet you for dinner. Nico tried to persuade her to cancel.'

Annie and Charlie exchanged a look. She didn't know what he was thinking, but she was wondering why Jojo didn't mention it to her. There could only be two reasons: either it was so unimportant to Jojo that she forgot, or it rattled her and she didn't want to worry Annie.

Charlie pointed above the stage. 'Up there is the fly tower

and grid. This theatre has more space above the stage than a modern theatre as it was designed for lifting and lowering props and sometimes people. Nico's going to be lifted and then lowered into a water tank for his escape act. We'd just been up in the fly tower talking through the logistics and checking the pulley systems the night the gantry came loose. Nico was with me. He knows everything was secure.'

'So, what do you think happened?' Annie said.

'I don't know.' He sounded worried.

'Can we go up and take a look?' Annie asked. Partly because she wanted reassurance that the equipment was safe and properly maintained, but the real reason - it was fascinating. When would she ever have another opportunity to see behind-the-scenes mechanics of a theatre?

'Are you sure you want to climb up there and stand on the scaffolding?'

'Is it safe?'

'Absolutely, but I'm used to it. If you're scared of heights?'

Just looking up into the never-ending space with its mysterious pulleys and grids made Annie a little breathless, but if Jojo had taught her one thing, it was to try everything once. 'Lead the way,' she said with more confidence than she felt.

They didn't climb too far, just enough for Charlie to point out the different systems for lighting, electrics, and special effects. There were so many technical terms, she wondered, that he could remember them all. When they had safely climbed down, Charlie showed her the trapdoors on the stage floor.

'All theatres have trap-doors,' he explained, 'but this one has more than most, as it has a long history of being used for magic acts. Come on, I'll show you under the stage.'

It was a wonderland of hidden tunnels, compartments that

opened on to the stage or into a room beneath, and others that had trap doors with elevating platforms.

'There's a tunnel that goes from under the stage to the back of the auditorium, but I won't take you through there because it hasn't been used for years and I dread to think what might lurk in there.' Charlie opened a door, releasing a damp and musty smell. They peered into the darkness.

'Is there any lighting down there?' Annie could just make out some wooden steps.

'There is somewhere. Hold on.' He fumbled and then there was a dim orangey glow.

Annie marvelled at the light switch, a round brown fixture with a cream switch. 'Is it Victorian?'

'I should think so, or at least the original light switch from the days when electricity was introduced to the theatre. All the pipes that service the Golden Globe run under there – water and electricity. They used the old gas piping to house the cables.'

There was a loud and long rumble from the belly of the cavern. Annie jumped and instinctively shrunk against Charlie for protection.

'That's our resident ghost,' he laughed. 'So, the theatre folk would have you believe.' He shut the trapdoor and dusted off his hands. 'Nah, it's just a build-up of pressure in the water pipes.'

'Shouldn't there be some kind of inspection to make sure everything meets with the new health and safety guidance? I know it's a quaint little theatre, but the safety of the public shouldn't be compromised.'

'You're probably right. I'm sure the management wouldn't put anyone at risk. Now, what else do you want to see?'

Annie had so many questions. This was no longer about Jojo. She was just enjoying the experience of seeing backstage through Charlie's eyes. He sounded passionate about the theatre and his work. 'Did you have to train to be a stagehand? There seems to be so much to learn?'

'I trained as an architect, but I've always loved the theatre. My mum is a costume designer – well was, before she had children and gave up work, and my dad a keen amateur dramatics actor. Outings to the theatre, whether it was to see my dad perform, or a London show, were part of family life.'

They had wandered into the auditorium and so Annie settled herself in one of the worn velvet seats. 'How many siblings?'

'Just me and my sister. How about you?'

Annie didn't want to talk about her family life. She was much more interested in Charlie. 'Same. But why work as a stagehand when you're a qualified architect?'

'This is just a temporary job. I want to work as a set designer for a big London theatre. Working with a magic theatre is fantastic. I'm learning so much about special effects and what can be achieved with props. I might not get along with Nico, but I have to admire his genius.'

His disclosure discomfited Annie. Maybe her initial instincts about Jojo's infatuation were right. Charlie was so inoffensive. He was warm, gentle, and obviously cared about Jojo. In fact, he was the perfect partner for her friend. 'I didn't know that you didn't get on with Nico.'

Charlie gave a hollow laugh. 'It's not a big deal. I guess we're just different.'

'I wouldn't know,' Annie said. 'I've not yet met him.'

'That doesn't surprise me.'

Before Annie could question Charlie further, he stood up. 'Phillipe's waving to me from the stage. Looks like I'm needed. It was really good to meet you, Annie. I hope I get to see more of you.'

'I'm sure you will. Perhaps when I come to see a show?'

When Annie left the theatre to travel home, she was buoyed up with excitement. An adrenalin that had her blood pumping. Charlie's enthusiasm must have been infectious. He had that same sparkle Jojo possessed. What a shame *he* wasn't Jojo's partner. Charlie seemed perfect in every way. For Jojo.

5

'Don't you find those clothes restrict your movement?' Bobbi said as she and Jojo warmed up in a dance studio.

'Maybe not great for a dance workout, but they're fine for a magician's assistant. In fact, the genie look is quite fitting.' Jojo did a little pose.

'Did you talk to Nico about updating your act?'

Jojo wished she hadn't confided in Bobbi. It made her feel disloyal. 'I didn't say it needed updating. I just wanted to contribute something more than being a decorative prop.'

'Maybe, but you've got to admit it's a bit old school. Nico's popularity is all about his sex appeal. It sells tickets, but that's not enough to compete with some of the innovative acts coming on the scene.'

Mention of Nico's fans made Jojo's stomach dip. The anonymous note was buried in her bag, but it might as well be pinned to her forehead because the words were ingrained there.

'I know Nico has a lot of fans. Are there any you would

consider being a bit deranged?' She made a goofy face, so as not to seem too serious.

'Not that I know of. Meryl left because she had some sort of breakdown, but I wouldn't call her deranged, despite the rumours.'

'Meryl?' It was the first time Jojo had heard the name.

'Nico's last assistant. They were in a relationship, too. I don't know what happened to her. She seems to have disappeared from the scene.'

Nico hadn't mentioned Meryl. He had mentioned none of his past girlfriends. Jojo knew there would be several. He was older than her and bound to have a history, but he was evasive about his life before meeting her. 'My life started when I walked into that dingy pub and discovered the girl of my dreams,' was his stock response when Jojo pushed him for answers. This glimpse into life before Jojo fascinated her.

'What was she like?'

'A bloody good assistant. Very talented. Beautiful too. Quite stunning, in fact.'

Of course, she was. Jojo suspected that all of Nico's girlfriends had been more attractive than her – prettier, wealthier, and more sophisticated.

'So, did you suggest to Nico that you update your act?' Bobbi did a side stretch, watching her reflection and then Jojo's face.

'No. I was going to wait until after the Easter Gala. There would be too much pressure if we tried to change things now.'

Why was she feeling deflated and a little sad? Maybe it was because she felt like an imposter. How could a street performer compare to the legend of Meryl? Maybe Nico was too heart-broken to mention her name. He had aimed lower with Jojo. He obviously expected little of her, but she wanted to prove herself, to show him she could do more than juggle a few hoops, and ride a unicycle.

'You don't have to change *everything*. Why not sow a few seeds? If you handle things right, Nico will think it was his idea.'

'Do you think he would be open to change?'

'You just have to pick your moment.' Bobbi winked at Jojo. 'Ready to go?'

Phillipe and Charlie had released the harness from the fly tower and were checking it was safe and ready for use when Jojo and Bobbi joined them.

'You just missed Annie,' Charlie jumped down from the stage.

Jojo was relieved that Annie had left, but then felt guilty. It was just that Annie represented her life before Nico and, if she was going to transform to fit into his world, it was easier to do it alone. 'Thanks for showing her around, Charlie.'

'A pleasure. Okay. It's all set. I'll leave you with Phillipe.'

Jojo stepped into her role as Bobbi's tutor, not quite believing the honour bestowed on her. 'We'll practice using the harness today. Just up and down, and back and forth. It sounds easy, but you have to use your core strength to stabilise. If you relax, not only do you look a mess, you can start to spin and go lopsided.'

Phillipe fitted the harness on Jojo and raised her slowly until she was high above the stage. This had been her favourite class at stage school. Up here, she felt weightless. The voices below faded and Jojo took flight. Her peers had been afraid, but Jojo was afraid of returning to earth. The terraced house littered with her father's medical equipment and medication, a mother who was too depressed to notice her daughter, and the knowledge that she was an outsider who would never fit in. She would have swapped the ties of her limited existence for those of the aerial wire any day. Jojo ran through the routine she had learnt in class, holding her legs in the splits, then a 360-degree turn. She soared across the theatre holding a pose, experimented with a few somersaults and then glided back.

There was a cheer from below and applause.

'How far back in the auditorium does the cable go?' Bobbi shouted.

Jojo tried to see in the dark. 'Not sure.'

'It should go right to the back. Have a go. We'll see if we can lower you that end,' Phillipe said.

Jojo gave the thumbs up. It was easy. When she reached the back of the theatre, Lenny came out of the projection room to help her down.

'That was amazing.' Bobbi climbed the aisle steps to join her. 'How long would it take you to teach me that?'

'I can teach you the basics, but you'd need professional tuition to do some of those moves.'

'You're wasted as a magician's assistant. Why don't you come and join Hocus Pocus?'

It felt as though she had been invited to join the school netball team by the most popular girl. For a split-second Jojo wanted to accept, but the exhilaration of flying above the stage had given her a new perspective. Joining the Golden Globe Theatre was her opportunity to prove herself. She knew she could accomplish more. 'It's tempting – but honestly? I want to give this idea of combining my skills with Nico's a chance. I really believe we can create something special if we work together.'

'I've yet to see what else you can do, but that was pretty impressive.'

Jojo beamed. For the first time in what felt like a long

while, she believed in herself. 'Now, what were you hoping to learn in time for the Hocus Pocus matinee?'

Bobbi wanted to fly from the back of the theatre onto the stage. It sounded simple and Bobbi obviously thought she would learn it in minutes, but Jojo knew it would take a lot of practice.

Lenny helped Bobbi into the harness and secured all the straps. 'How does that feel?'

When Bobbi nodded her approval, Phillipe worked the controls from backstage to lift her a few feet. Immediately, she spun around, out of control. Her arms and legs flayed, and she swore loudly.

'Hold your body still. Use your core. It's all about balance,' Jojo called out, but Bobbi didn't seem to hear.

'Get me out of this bloody thing.'

When her feet were back on firm ground, she blamed Lenny. 'You couldn't have put it on right. The straps must have been twisted. I want Phillipe to strap me in.'

Lenny shrugged and then sloped off to confer with Phillipe.

Jojo wasn't sure what to say without making matters worse. 'Just as well Phillipe and Lenny are making sure everything's working properly after the falling gantry incident.' It seemed to do the trick because Bobbi's attention was diverted.

'That was freaky. Hold on and I'll get my ciggies. I need one after that.'

Bobbi collected her menthol cigarettes from her bag by the side of the stage and returned to sit in the back row with Jojo. Phillipe seemed in no hurry to assist with the harness and so they settled down to continue their chat.

'What did you mean when you said it wasn't the first time that there had been unexplained incidents?'

Bobbi blew out a long stream of smoke. 'I've not witnessed

it myself, but there's been talk of strange happenings in the past. Some people have seen the ghost of Molly May crying in the forbidden tunnel. No wonder. A magician cut the poor girl in half.'

Jojo was horrified. 'Did that really happen? Oh my God. I always worry that Nico might put a sword in me if he loses concentration.'

'Are you two-timing him? Having an affair?'

'Certainly not.' Jojo was affronted. Surely that wasn't one of the rumours going around.

Bobbi laughed. 'Don't look so serious. I was joking. Apparently, the magician thought Molly May was being unfaithful, and he intentionally sawed her in half. She walks up and down the tunnel wailing and rattling chains.'

'That's a bit far-fetched, and gruesome. Anyway, I don't think Molly May was responsible for the falling gantry,' Jojo said, but she was a little spooked.

'Who knows? I'm just saying – not everything is easily explained. From what I heard; Charlie had checked things were secure. So, what happened? You tell me?' She took another long drag.

'When I find out, I'll let you know. Now, here comes Phillipe. Are you ready to give it another go?'

This time, Jojo surreptitiously steadied the harness and wire as Bobbi was lifted, and she got Bobbi to practice her posture first so that she could hold a position. This worked, and Bobbi held an elegant pose for at least twelve seconds before she wobbled, and Jojo nodded at Lenny to lower her down.

'Let's practice again tomorrow,' Jojo said, so that they could end on a high.

'I know that I'll never be as good at this as you, but I'm sure I'll improve with practice.'

'You can do plenty of things that I can't and you're right, you'll learn this in no time.'

'If you could just teach me how to swoop across the stage without looking like a flying hippo, I would be happy. Hey, who is that gorgeous man?'

Jojo followed her gaze to a man with an athletic build who had wandered into the theatre and seemed to be lost. Bobbi fluffed up her hair and then slinked across the auditorium. 'Can I help you?'

He had the bone structure of a film star, square jaw and defined cheekbones. Curious, Jojo followed Bobbi, keeping her distance so as not to cramp her style. When they got closer, she noticed his startlingly blue eyes.

'I was looking for Mr. Peter. He is expecting me.'

'Peter Walker?' Bobbi said. 'Let me take you to him.'

She looked over her shoulder and raised her eyebrows, a wicked gleam in her eye. 'Thanks, Jojo. See you later.'

Jojo loved Bobbi's pizzazz. If only she could be that confident and self-assured. As she turned into the corridor leading to the changing room, she met Nico coming the other way.

'Perfect timing. Are you ready?' he said.

Jojo was well and truly ready to go home. She wondered what they would have for dinner, whether they would pick up something instant, or maybe Nico was in the mood to cook one of his fabulous Italian dishes. 'Absolutely,' she said, stretching her back and rotating her shoulders.

'Good. We still have studio three.'

Her heart sank. 'But it's nearly six. I'm starving.'

Nico laughed. 'You are always hungry. It wouldn't hurt you to miss a meal or two. I bet you ate cake this afternoon with your friend.'

'That was hours ago. Since then, I've been doing acrobatics

and so anything I ate has burnt off. Can't we go home and relax? Buy a takeaway?'

'The Starlight show is in four weeks, bella. Four weeks. We haven't even decided on our acts. I've got an idea, but it needs more working up. While you were eating cake, I was in the resource library planning. So now, my little genie, we need to do some magic. Can you do that?' He kissed her cheek, her neck, her ear, tickling her with his breath.

'Okay. But I would like to talk to you about our act.'

'Talk.'

'Maybe not now. Tonight? When we get home?'

'Now you have aroused my…' he clasped her buttocks and pulled her to him, 'interest.'

Jojo giggled. 'Later.'

'Spoil sport. Come on then, genie. Grant me my first wish and get your sexy little arse into studio three.'

Jojo didn't approve of manipulation – it was underhand, but she wasn't sure how Nico would respond to an outright suggestion that she took an active part in planning their act. They had just finished eating a takeaway Tandoori mixed grill with a big home-made salad when Nico said, 'You wanted to discuss our act. Are you finding it too challenging bella? You can be honest with me. Maybe I expect too much from you.'

Jojo had been rehearsing in her head what to say. Now that it was time, she was losing her nerve. 'Not at all. If anything, our act doesn't challenge me enough. Maybe we need to up our game. The Starlight and Easter Gala shows could bring amazing opportunities. I really want our act to be the best it can be. If that means I have to do more, then I want to. Well, nothing is too much trouble or too hard. Okay, I know I whinge sometimes…' This last remark was in response to Nico's raised eyebrows.

'Bella, you are the perfect assistant. I can trust you one hundred percent. I know you will not let me down and that means a lot. It is because I have your support that I'm able to give my best. I have more ideas and I will share them with you when I'm ready. I'm sorry that I have asked you to work so hard, but it's only for a few more weeks.'

Nico's expectations of her were so far removed from what she felt she could contribute; Jojo didn't know how to bridge that gap. 'I impressed Bobbi with my aerial acrobatics.'

'My clever bella.' He took her hands and wiped them with a napkin as though she were a small child. Jojo was about to object when Nico shook the napkin and a tub of ice-cream rolled across the table.

Jojo never got used to his tricks. She caught it. Made with fresh strawberries and cream. 'I've heard of this new American ice-cream chain. I wish you had said. I would have gone with you to choose. They have thirty-two flavours.'

'Then we have thirty-one more to sample.'

Jojo would have happily eaten the whole lot from the tub, but Nico measured out a scoop each and put the rest away for another day, reminding Jojo that she had already had one sweet treat and needed to watch her figure.

'Nico. What would you think about me contributing a little more to the act? You have taught me so much; it seems a pity to waste my talent.'

'It is true. You are quick to learn. Let me have a think about it.'

That was all she needed for now. Bobbi was right to suggest that she sow the seed. Now she would just have to wait and see if it would germinate.

6

A rainy Tuesday in February was guaranteed to bring in punters yearning for a summer holiday in the Mediterranean. The travel agents where Annie worked had a steady stream of customers waiting for her attention. Her visit to the Golden Globe had done her good because she felt light of heart, buoyed up with what could only be described as happiness. On her way to work, Annie had tried to pinpoint what had caused this change. A rest from work. It was true, what she had said to Mum, she was tired. Seeing Jojo, certainly. They had enjoyed a laugh and a catch up just like the old days. But there was something more. It was the excitement of seeing the workings of the theatre, the trap-doors, and the hidden tunnel. The enormous space that stretched high above the stage. How Charlie had taken her hand as she stepped off the scaffolding.

'Do you think that's the man from head office talking to Lisa?' Sarah leant across the space between their desks to point out a man in a suit who was opening a briefcase.

'Looks like it. How long is this training session?'

'Don't know, but we're closing from twelve until two and I doubt it will be for a long lunch break.'

Lisa turned a sign on the door to closed. 'If anyone needs to pop out to buy a sandwich, go now. We are going to start in twenty minutes.'

'That answers your question,' Sarah whispered.

Annie collected her lunch from the fridge — Mum insisted on making her sandwiches as though she were still at school — and put on the kettle for a coffee. It was worrying what Charlie had said about the falling gantry. In the old days, Annie would have phoned Jojo to ask what was going on and why she had said nothing, but she didn't like to phone Jojo at Nico's place. It felt as though she was intruding. Charlie was sensible. He would make sure something like that didn't happen again. If only Jojo were involved with Charlie, life would be simpler. He was easy to be with and had included Annie. He had gone out of his way to make her feel welcome at the Golden Globe, unlike Nico, who had made himself scarce when she visited. Annie shook herself; she was being unfair. Jojo was in love with Nico and so Annie had to accept him and stop finding reasons to dislike him. So long as Jojo was happy, that was all that mattered. If she was missing the excitement of being with her friend, then she just had to make her own magic.

'What are you doing at the weekend?' she asked Sarah, who had joined her at the little kitchen counter.

'Me and Rick are going to a custom car show. Why?'

How could she have forgotten about the infamous Rick? Sarah started nearly every sentence with Rick said, or Rick did. 'No reason. Just wondered what you were up to.'

The man from head office, Henry, was waiting at the top end of the office as the staff drew their chairs into a circle around him. He looked directly at Annie, and she wondered if they had met before. A slim build, neat hair, wire-framed glasses. She didn't think so. He was still looking and so she dabbed her cheek in case there was a blob of mayonnaise, and he looked away.

Lisa clapped her hands, and the room fell silent. 'Henry. Mr Clarke. Is going to tell us about an exciting new development for the travel industry, and the resorts that we are promoting this season. So, over to you Henry Clarke.'

Annie sat up in her seat prepared to be wowed, but as the man from head office started describing the technical detail of the Bulletin Board System which was meant to revolutionise how holidays were booked, her mind wandered. Outside, the rain was relentless. She didn't want to spend another weekend at home watching Dallas. Before Jojo met Nico, they had gone to parties and met friends in the pub. The invitations had been from friends of Jojo's – actors, students, artists. Colourful creative types. She knew that they only tolerated her because she was Jojo's friend; her plaid skirts and Laura Ashley dresses, not really fitting with the arty scene. Now that Jojo was living with Nico, these friends seemed to have dropped off Jojo's radar, just as Annie had.

There was a bit of activity as the projector was set up. Annie opened her Tupperware box, releasing the scent of tuna. It mingled with the other food smells circulating the room.

'That was a waste of time,' Sarah said. 'We've only just been supplied with a fax machine. I doubt we'll even be working here by the time we get one of those bulletin things.'

Lisa clapped her hands. 'Could you switch off the lights, Annie?'

The projector whirred and images of white hotels against cerulean skies and azure blue seas transported them to the Greek islands. 'We have three new destinations, Santorini,

Mykonos, and Naxos,' Henry said. Now there was genuine excitement in the room. New resorts meant an opportunity for a few lucky members of staff to have a free holiday — work trip — to experience what was on offer to customers.

Henry, the man from head office, was suddenly popular as three of Annie's colleagues assisted him with packing away the projector. Lisa could recommend staff for the working holiday, but head office made the final decision.

She was returning to her desk when Lisa said, 'Would you mind collecting some brochures from Mr Clarke's car, Annie?'

Grateful for some fresh air, despite the rain, Annie left the store with Henry. He held a briefcase over his head, refusing the offer of a shared umbrella, which was just as well because it was always awkward, especially with a stranger. They headed for an underground car park by Trafalgar Square.

'I didn't know there was a car park close to the office,' Annie said. 'Not that I would drive into work.'

'Where do you live?'

'Fenwood.'

Henry stopped in his tracks. 'You're kidding? I live in Fenwood too.'

Maybe that was why he had been staring at her. He must have recognised her, maybe from the train into London that she took every day. 'Small world,' Annie said.

His car was a Jaguar. When he opened a rear door to haul out a box of brochures, Annie breathed in the scent of new upholstery.

'I'll help you carry them back,' Henry said.

'No. There's no need. I'll manage.'

'Well, if you insist, but please let me give you a lift home to Fenwood when you finish work. It's the least I can do after dragging you out of a warm dry office to help me.'

Now that he was relaxed and not standing in front of an

audience wittering on about developments in technology, Henry was personable. He removed his glasses to wipe away the condensation, and the milky blue of his eyes struck Annie. A lift home in his luxurious car was tempting, but Annie didn't know him and she wasn't one to take risks.

'That's kind, but I don't know. I won't finish until six and I don't want to hold you up.'

Henry deposited the box of brochures into Annie's outstretched arms. 'If you won't accept a lift home, then I'm escorting you back to the store.' He lifted her upturned umbrella from beside the car. 'You need me to hold the umbrella, otherwise the brochures will get wet and, as area manager, I would not approve.'

Annie acquiesced and together they dodged puddles as they made their way back to the store. She felt Henry's hand lightly on her back as he struggled to keep her and the brochures sheltered from the rain. Breathless and laughing, they burst through the shop door, causing several heads to turn.

'Mission accomplished. One box of brochures safely delivered and completely dry, which is more than I can say for me. Have I convinced you I'm not a mad axe man?'

Annie grinned sheepishly. He was right. She had been a bit nervous about accepting a lift from a stranger. 'I would love a lift home, but I don't want to inconvenience you.'

'In that case, it's all arranged. I'll swing by at six. Be ready to jump in the car as I can't really park outside.'

The journey home was luxurious compared to Annie's usual commute on a crowded train. As the car purred along Victoria Embankment, commuters battled with umbrellas, and girls glared at drivers who splashed through puddles, sending spray over their tights and shoes. Annie wriggled deeper into the soft, buttery leather. 'Do you always drive to work?'

Henry slowed down and changed gear as they approached some stationary traffic. 'Not if I'm in the office all day. It's easy to get to Barbican by train.' The traffic started to move. Annie enjoyed watching Henry drive. His movements were economical — slow and precise. 'I was visiting a few London branches today to do the same spiel.'

'Maybe that's where you recognised me from,' Annie said. 'The train.'

'I don't think so, but I'll look out for you next time I take the train.'

It was easy to be with Henry. He didn't seem to have any need for conversation and so Annie relaxed and enjoyed the journey.

'Where do you live?' Henry said as they approached Fenwood.

'Oh, it's okay. Drop me where it's convenient.'

'No, I insist on driving you to your door.'

It was still raining and so Annie accepted his offer. When they drew up outside her house, Henry said, 'Have you been to the new wine bar in the High Street, Wine and Roses?'

'No. My sister Jessica says that it has a great atmosphere.'

'Want to give it a try?'

He was asking her for a date. Annie hadn't seen that coming. Henry was so quiet on the ride home she had decided he wasn't interested in her. Was she interested in him? He ticked all the boxes: sensible, good job, intelligent. 'When were you thinking?' Annie stalled.

'This weekend? Saturday night?'

'That would be perfect.' She hadn't meant to sound so enthusiastic, but the relief of having something to do at the weekend made up her mind.

The living room curtain twitched as Annie approached the front door. She took her time divesting herself of coat and boots, knowing that her mum was desperate to find out who had driven her home.

'How was your day?' Mum looked at her expectantly.

'Okay,' Annie said and, hiding her grin, disappeared upstairs. She would make her wait a little longer.

7

'Is the wire and harness ready for us?' Jojo asked Phillipe, as he passed by with a trolley that spilled a bounty of jewel-coloured scarves.

'Charlie's assisting you this evening.'

Jojo couldn't resist plunging her hand into the silky kaleidoscope of scrumptiousness. She marvelled at how the silks caught the light, cerise, turquoise, and jade. An idea nudged at her imagination – turning the little silk squares into a sari. If she got something made up in similar silks then she could do a quick change in the hidden compartment under the stage.

Ideas were still buzzing around her head when she joined Bobbi in the dance studio. Bobbi was at the barre doing a classical ballet warm up. Jojo remembered the moves from her days at stage school and the witch of a teacher who berated her for a lack of discipline. She couldn't help it if her feet wanted to chasse when they should have been still, or a dance sequence cried out for a spilt leap — a ciseaux, which was not scripted. Now, she positioned herself alongside Bobbi and mirrored her movements.

'Where did you train?' Bobbi said without removing her eyes from a focal point.

'Camden School of Performing Arts. I didn't finish the course.'

Bobbi turned to work the other leg and Jojo wandered from the barre to face her. 'Why did you leave?'

Jojo sighed. It had been easier to blame the school at the time, a rigidity that didn't allow for self-expression, but inside Jojo had felt the same pain she had at school — of being a misfit. 'I don't know, maybe something that they call artistic differences. Some classes were great, but I didn't get on with ballet or tap, and you don't want to hear me sing. I was better off making my own way.'

'Good for you. I'm regretting my limited vocational skills. In fact, I can only spare an hour today as I've started teaching at a health club. That's four more paid teaching classes a week.'

'Can you fit them in? You're already working all hours.'

'To be honest, darling, I have little choice. My rent's going up next month. I know the landlord is trying to get me out so that he can let or sell to Arabs. It's going to be the same story all over Chelsea, so I want to hang on to my flat.' Bobbi rolled her shoulders. 'Are you ready?'

Jojo stretched her arms above her head. She was still warmed up from contorting her body in the magic tricks. 'Yup. Let's go.'

'Did you talk to Nico about your act?' Bobbi said as they made their way to the theatre.

'I may have planted a seed. Oh Bobbi, I have so many ideas. I know I said that I would wait until after the Easter Gala, but now I'm impatient to see what Nico and I could do together. If only he wasn't so set in his ways.'

'Bide your time. Men like Nico need careful handling and they must never suspect that is what you are doing.'

Annie's mum had shared the occasional pearl of wisdom with them. Don't go to bed without resolving an argument. Save a little each week from the housekeeping for a rainy day. Handling a complex, sensitive man was beyond Jojo and Annie's experience.

Charlie was waiting for them on the stage. 'You've got me tonight. Phillipe explained what you want me to do.'

Bobbi raised her eyebrows. 'Did he? How did Phillipe know what I wanted you to do to me, Charlie?'

Jojo watched as a blush crept from Charlie's neck to his face. He was beetroot. And that was why Bobbi and the Hocus Pocus girls loved to tease him. She went to his rescue. 'Good, you can witness my super powers. Come on, harness me up and I'll show you what I can do.'

Charlie busied himself strapping Jojo in and as he did so, she made sure that he knew exactly what to do so that he was confident when it came to securing the harness on Bobbi. Once lifted from the stage, Jojo did her stuff. She twisted and twirled. Turned herself upside down, and contorted her body as though it was made from pipe cleaners.

'And now…' Jojo did a Superman pose. 'I am going to fly to the back of the auditorium. Ready?' She held the pose as she glided across the seats. Today, there was no Lenny to help her down and so her feet dangled as she waited for Charlie to release her.

'Way to go, Bat Girl. Impressive!'

'You haven't seen half of what I can do.'

'Then you're going to have to show me and the rest of the world.'

Jojo was shaking with an energy too big to contain. Up there, her mind had been soaring and cartwheeling beyond the limits of her body. There was so much she could do using the aerial wire. Nico had said he was open to Jojo being more involved in their act. She couldn't wait to tell him her ideas. They would be the chosen last act for Gala — hands down.

It was hard to settle her emotions and concentrate on Bobbi who had glided part way across the auditorium. 'Well done. Good posture.'

Bobbi relaxed her body and instantly slipped sideways in the harness. 'Fuck.'

Jojo stood up and willed herself to give Bobbi one hundred percent of her attention. 'It's okay. I put you off. Let's try again. This time, I won't say anything until you've completed the move. You were almost there.'

They tried a couple more times and then called it a day.

'That's a big improvement on yesterday. A couple more practices and I'm sure you'll be ready for the matinee,' Jojo said.

Bobbi's eyes sparkled. 'It's pretty cool. I can see why you love aerial acrobatics. If I had the time, I would take classes myself. I would love to be as good as you.'

Jojo's heart swelled with pride. 'I would love to dance like you.'

They got changed quickly as Bobbi had a class and Jojo was looking forward to a night in with Nico, who had left early with a promise to prepare an Italian meal.

'Who was that man? The one looking for Peter Walker?' Jojo said as they walked through the theatre.

'Kai Keisler. Haven't you heard? He's big in Germany and Walker has high hopes that he will be the Golden Globe's next big star.'

Nico would not like that.

8

An aria from Madam Butterfly and a wonderful garlicky smell emanated from the kitchen when Jojo opened the front door. She crept in undetected by Nico and took delight in watching him stir a pot, singing at the top of his voice. He had the voice of a tenor. A gorgeous, passionate man who was devoted to her. How had she got so lucky? Last year she was living in a squat, her bed a mattress on the floor of a damp room. Nico had rescued her, transformed her life.

He spun around, and the wooden spoon he was using to conduct an imaginary orchestra stilled. 'Bella, you're home. This is almost ready.'

It smelled divine. Jojo took the spoon from him and tasted the sauce on the tip of one finger. 'What is it?'

'Polpette Sorpresa. Italian meat balls. Open that bottle of Beaujolais. I think we deserve to spoil ourselves after all of our rehearsing.'

Jojo poured them both a glass and then settled herself on a high stool to watch him as he measured spaghetti and then tipped it into a pan. 'Have you heard anything about this new German magician?'

'Kai Keisler? Yes. Peter Walker introduced us today. He might be successful in Germany, but that doesn't mean he will experience the same here.' Nico was adjusting the heat and so Jojo could not see his expression.

'Do you know where he will be in the lineup?'

He turned. 'Where's my wine?' Jojo handed it to him. 'Walker would not put an unknown top of the bill. I am confident that it will be the Incredible Nico and his glamorous assistant.'

Jojo was bursting with her news. Nico was going to love her ideas. Working together, they would absolutely nail it. Kai Keisler would be history.

'What's making you so happy?' Nico kissed the corner of her mouth.

'Oh, a gorgeous man preparing a delicious meal for me, and a little idea I have for our act. You said there might be room for me to contribute more.' She remembered Bobbi's advice and instead of blurting out her vision for their own 'Flying Circus,' breaking the traditions of magic the way Monty Python's had for comedy, she tamed it down. 'I was just thinking, working together we could create an amazing act.'

'We *are* good together, aren't we? I've been thinking the same thing.' He sipped his wine and Jojo had to bite her lip to stop herself from interrupting.

He raised an eyebrow, and she realised her face must have given her away. 'I'm going to give you your own spot.'

Jojo threw up her arms to hug him and sent a spray of red across the worktop. 'Oh Nico. Thank you. You won't be sorry. I'll really have the stage to myself?'

Nico dampened a cloth, squeezed it out and then wiped

the work surface. 'Red wine can stain. Is there any on the floor or wall?'

Jojo jumped down from her stool and checked for spillage. Nothing. 'I'm sorry. It's just that I'm so excited. This is the best news.'

'You are wrong there. The best is yet to come.'

Jojo's heart couldn't take any more. Nico had no idea what this meant to her. He was giving her the opportunity to perform as a professional acrobat in front of a theatre audience. A dream come true. She must have been six years old, legs crossed, as she sat on the floor in assembly. They were listening to a record of classical music and Jojo had imagined herself flying above their heads, dancing inches from the ceiling. She knew nothing about aerial acrobatics then, but the feeling of being free, inspired by the music, had stayed with her.

'Nothing could be better than this, Nico.'

'You will have to wait until after dinner to see my surprise.'

Madame Butterfly was still playing as they ate their meal. 'Ah, this aria is magnificent. She is pining for her husband, who has gone away to sea. Listen,' Nico said.

The music was powerful, and so Jojo closed her eyes and surrendered to its beauty. Before Nico, she had never listened to opera music. He teased her about her lack of sophistication. Jojo didn't mind. She loved the way he enriched her life.

She had heard grown-ups whisper she was a menopause baby and learnt, as she grew up, that meant unexpected and Jojo believed unwanted. She had tried to be forgiving and generous, to understand her parents' neglect and disinterest in her life. Her father had always been unwell; the medical equipment he needed to breathe and the other paraphernalia made the tiny terraced house feel claustrophobic. Mum had never seen Jojo perform, not once – not even her first nativity play, when she was cast as the innkeeper. Jojo understood now she must have found it difficult to leave the house with no-one sharing the care of Dad. She imagined herself on stage at the Golden Globe, her parents in the audience. It would never happen, but a part of her that had never grown up still wished for the impossible – just once.

'I love seeing you like this. Happy.' Nico twirled spaghetti around his fork.

'It's because of you.' Jojo watched his long, slender fingers and felt a rush of love and desire. If he wasn't so proper, she would abandon their meal and make love to him there and then — on the floor.

'What are you thinking?' He gave a lazy, sexy smile and Jojo was tempted to tell him, but she knew he would not approve of such wanton behaviour.

'That I'm very, very lucky. You are making all of my dreams come true. I love you so much.'

'I love you too, my little butterfly.'

She should have enjoyed the moment. Everything was perfect. But like a self-destruct button, an image of the goddess Meryl invaded her thoughts. A memory of herself tangled in the bed sheets between Nico's legs was replaced with one of Meryl, who in Jojo's head now resembled Bianca Jagger.

'Bobbi was telling me about your last assistant, Meryl.' Jojo watched his face closely.

There was the tiniest flicker around his jawline. 'What did Bobbi tell you?'

'Not much. Just that she left suddenly.'

Nico put down his fork and gave a long sigh. 'Meryl was the love of my life. My partner in all things.'

'Oh.' She wanted to run from the table, to take back her question — anything that would save her from hearing Nico was still in love with this goddess. 'Why didn't you tell me about her?'

'Because Meryl is dead to me. It is as though she never existed. Poof. Gone.' He waved a hand and Jojo half expected to see his plate disappear.

'How long ago was this? When did she leave?'

'Not long before I met you, bella. You are everything that Meryl was not.'

'I hear she is beautiful and talented.'

'I gave Meryl everything, but she betrayed me. This is what I am always telling you bella. There has to be absolute trust between a magician and his assistant. I trust you one hundred percent, but Meryl she was deceitful. If things had gone according to her plan, I would not be here today.'

'What did she do?' Jojo had visions of the mad woman in Jane Eyre roaming the corridors at night holding a lighted candle.

'I have protected her for old time's sake, but Meryl tried to kill me. Don't look so shocked bella, she failed, but this is why I prefer to forget that woman.'

'What happened to her? Where is she now?' Jojo was afraid that Meryl might be responsible for the anonymous note. Was she watching Jojo, jealous that she had taken her place? Biding her time to make a move? Jojo shivered.

'Don't worry bella. That woman will come nowhere near me. I prefer not to hear her name. Now that you know, can we forget about her? Put her back where she belongs in the past?'

Meryl was out of the box and there was no way Jojo could squeeze her back in and close the lid. 'Does anyone else know she tried to kill you?'

Nico frowned. 'Please Jojo. I prepared a special meal because I have a surprise for you. I do not want memories of that woman spoiling our evening.'

'No. You are right. Sorry. This is delicious.'

They ate in silence. Nico seemed completely at ease. He topped up Jojo's wine and gazed at her through half-closed eyes. He seemed to be lost in the music. She ought to be relieved that Nico was no longer in love with Meryl, but she had so many questions. The woman had taken up residence in her head and was now occupying more space than before when she was just a past love. Now she was a potential murderer. What if she was watching them; jealous of Jojo's involvement with Nico? Jojo forced herself to finish the meal.

When his plate was clean, Nico stood up and wiped his mouth on a linen napkin. Jojo recognised his body go into magician mode. It was how he stood, relaxed but alert, his stare hypnotic. He waved a hand around the napkin, as if he was sprinkling fairy dust. Then he frowned and slowly lifted the napkin to reveal a white baby rabbit. Its little pink eyes looked startled as it sniffed the air over the safety of Nico's hand.

Jojo was completely disarmed and thoughts of Meryl vanished. 'Oh, he's so cute. Let me hold him.'

Nico dropped the soft bundle into her lap and grinned as she lifted the rabbit to her face.

'Are there anymore meatballs?' Nico sat down and reached for the serving dish.

'Yes, of course. Here.'

Jojo settled the rabbit on her lap and opened the lid. A tiny white head with floppy ears popped out of the dish and twitched its nose.

'Oh, you poor little thing, you're covered in sauce! Did you think we were going to eat you?' Jojo lifted it out with one hand. 'Is this my surprise? They're adorable. Can I give them names or do they have them already?'

Jojo snuggled them in the napkin on her lap. Soft and

small, she could feel their fragile bones beneath her touch. She stroked their long, silky ears.

'It is part of your surprise.'

Jojo looked up expectantly. 'There's more?'

'This is the best bit. I am going to teach you a trick to perform on your own whilst I change for the escapist act. You will have the stage to yourself. Well, almost because those two cuties will be your assistants.'

Nico scooped up one rabbit and held it in the palm of his hand. Then he brought his hands together. Clap. The rabbit had disappeared. 'I will teach you the trick that I want you to perform.'

'Oh. You have a trick that you want me to do alone? When you said that I would have my own spot…'

'What?' Nico's face darkened.

'I just thought I would have to make something up.'

Nico laughed. 'You're a funny little thing. As if you could invent a magic trick fit for the Starlight show.'

'No, of course you are right. I'm not even sure I could do a solo magic trick. Perhaps if I showed you some of the other things I can do?'

'You are sweet but juggling batons whilst riding a unicycle might entertain bored shoppers at Covent Garden market but the Golden Globe?' He laughed and Jojo's face burned with humiliation. His image made her sound ridiculous. 'Don't worry, I will teach you the trick.'

'I'm grateful for the opportunity. It's just that I don't think I'll learn it in time. Maybe if you teach me the basics and I improvise a little?'

'Absolutely not. No improvisation. I am trusting you to deliver this trick exactly as I say. Can you do that?'

The word trust had a loaded meaning since Nico revealed the breakdown in trust between him and Meryl. Visions of her ballet class returned to Jojo, how she had ruined a performance by getting carried away, putting too much energy into her moves so that her head bobbed up and down when she should have merged into the background. She had to learn to conform, to stop showing off.

Jojo nodded. 'Will there be enough time for me to learn?'

'It's a simple trick. You will have to work hard. No swanning off for Black Forest gateau with your friend Annabelle.'

'No. Of course not.' Jojo took the rabbit from Nico and hid behind her hair as she stroked it. He wouldn't see her tears if they escaped. 'I'll call this one Muffin.' She cleared her throat and tried to sound more upbeat. 'Where's the other one?'

'Look under that top hat.'

Jojo composed herself so that she could smile at Nico. He must not see her disappointment and hurt. 'Over there? On that shelf?'

He laughed. 'Go and see.'

The tiny rabbit looked startled when Jojo discovered it beneath the hat. She held its beating heart to hers. 'I'll call this one Pixie.'

'We'll take them into the Golden Globe tomorrow and I'll show you the trick. Don't look so worried. So long as you follow my command, all will be well.'

9

Wine and Roses had only been open a few weeks and so it was still attracting a crowd. Mostly couples wanting a romantic night out or women who were attracted to the laid-back atmosphere as an alternative to the male dominated pub.

Henry found them a table tucked away in a corner. 'I hope you haven't eaten,' he said. 'There's a decent menu of bistro food — quiche, salads, a cheese board and desserts.'

Annie hadn't known whether to eat first and so she had eaten half a sandwich, intending to eat the other half on her return home if she was still hungry. 'Quiche sounds good.'

Henry went to the bar to order a glass of Liebfraumilch for her and a white wine spritzer for himself as he was driving. The music, *My Sweet Lord,* was playing. Candles in flask shaped wine bottles on each table, and giant Yucca plants strategically positioned to afford some privacy created a pleasing ambience. Henry's choice of venue was perfect.

They sat in silence. Henry gazed into the distance and seemed lost in thought. Annie took a few sips of wine. It was refreshingly cool and slipped down easily. 'Have you had a busy day?'

Henry brought his attention back to Annie. 'I went into the office this morning, but got away by midday. How about you?'

Annie took another sip of wine. 'Unlike head office, we don't finish on a Saturday until four. I needed this.'

Henry frowned. 'Maybe you had better slow down or you won't have any wine left when the food arrives.'

Annie put down her glass, feeling as though she had made some kind of social faux pas. Henry hadn't started his spritzer. 'The new holiday destinations on the Greek islands are going to be popular.' Afraid that Henry would think she was after a free holiday, she added, 'Not really my scene, though. I prefer somewhere with a bit of culture: Florence, Rome, Paris.'

'Then you haven't read the brochures.'

Wrong-footed again, Annie reached for her glass and, remembering Henry's last comment, her hand wavered and then dropped back into her lap. 'They look amazing.'

'There are six thousand Greek islands in the Agean and Ionian seas. Not all of them inhabited. Each island has its own characteristics. Why do you think we chose the Cyclades?'

Annie was saved from having to reply as the waitress arrived with a quiche and salad.

'That looks delicious,' Annie said, wondering what Henry had ordered for himself.

Henry slid the bowl of salad towards him and peered closely at its contents. 'There's red cabbage in this salad. Please take it away and bring me another with no red cabbage. Not the same one with the cabbage removed, mind. A fresh one.'

Thank goodness she hadn't started to eat Henry's salad. This was why she didn't date. There were so many things that could go wrong. Maybe it was because she didn't date that she had not acquired the skills. Henry was a decent man: sensible, intelligent, a hard worker, nice looking. She just had to relax and stop trying so hard. The waitress returned with another salad.

'Indigestion. Red cabbage gives me indigestion.' Henry looked embarrassed now. Annie decided to stop thinking about herself and instead put Henry at ease. He was probably as nervous as her. 'Tell me about the Greek islands. You're right, I haven't had a proper look at the brochure but with the colour of the sea and those beautiful white houses against a clear blue sky, I'm sure the posters will draw in lots of customers.'

Henry's shoulders seemed to drop and his face became animated. 'I love culture too and the Cyclades islands have it all. Not only are they close to Athens, which as you know is steeped in history, but they are known for their architecture: little white houses, blue domed churches, paved paths, and flowers everywhere — reds and deep blues.'

'It's certainly picturesque.'

Henry munched on the last of his salad. 'Piracy. That's why those pretty villages are up in the hills, away from the sea. It means they have incredible views.'

'Why are all the houses white?' Annie found she was enjoying their conversation. She just had to get Henry onto a topic that he was interested in.

'Absorb less sun. Would you like a coffee?'

Annie would have preferred another glass of wine, but if Henry couldn't drink because he was driving, it would be polite to follow suit.

Now that they had both relaxed, they found other common interests, like the theatre.

'What did you last see?' Henry asked.

Annie racked her brains, but in the past few years she had

spent weekends caught up in the whirlwind that was Jojo and Annie didn't think Henry was referring to fringe theatre. 'It's hard to remember. I haven't been to a West End production for some time. My friend Jojo is a performer and I support her by going to all of her shows.'

Henry's eyes widened. 'Would I have seen her? What's she been in?'

Annie doubted Henry would have caught Jojo's walk on part in the Camden Players production above the Bull pub last year, or her one woman show in Covent Garden market. 'Possibly not.' Annie hesitated, but then plunged straight in. She had to stop sitting on the side-lines and give whatever this was a chance. 'Have you heard of the Golden Globe?'

Henry frowned. 'Should I? TV or play?'

'It's a tiny Victorian theatre tucked away in a side street off the Strand. Would you like to see my friend perform in a magic show?'

'Top hats and white rabbits? I've not seen one of those since I was a kid and my dad thought it would entertain us at my ninth birthday party. The memory still makes me cringe. It was not cool.'

'This is different. Jojo is amazing. I promise you will be impressed. It's in three weeks' time – The Starlight show. A variety show but mostly magic acts with some dancing — kind of Vegas-style, I think. I'm going and just thought if you would like to join me, I could get two tickets.' There, she had said it. A second date. Jessica would applaud her.

'I would be honoured, but in return you must let me take you to a West End show.'

Annie had just turned out her light when Jessica landed heavily on the end of her bed. 'Well? What was he like?'

Annie sighed and made much of turning the light back on and sitting up in bed, but secretly she was glad to have Jessica's company so that she could reflect on the evening. 'He was okay. We've got a lot in common.'

'Like?'

'We both enjoy travel.'

'Duh. You both work in the travel agents.'

'Henry is cultured. He loves the theatre, art galleries, museums.'

'Boring then?'

'Not at all. As I said, we've got a lot in common. In fact, I am taking him to Jojo's next show.'

Jessica curled up her knees and then flipped the end of the duvet to cover them. 'A second date? Wow. He must be something.'

'I think I've committed to two more dates. Henry's going to buy tickets for a West End show.' Saying it out loud filled Annie with terror. What had she done? 'Do you think that was a bit rash?'

Jessica shook her head. 'I don't get you. Why are you so afraid of a second date? How can you know if you like someone when you never give them a chance?'

'I know you're right, that's why I suggested taking him to the Golden Globe, but I didn't expect him to suggest another date. It seemed rude to say no. Now we are going on two dates and so he will read something into it. I like him, but I don't know if I want to marry him.'

'Oh my God. Who's talking about marriage?'

'Well, go steady.'

'Two dates are not going steady.'

'Three actually. But then it will lead to another one and another. Once things start, how do you stop them without someone getting hurt? I'm not like you and Jojo. I don't want to go out with lots of men. I want to find the one and then commit.'

'Bloody hell. Don't tell Hooray Henry that or he'll run a mile. You've really got to lighten up, Sis.'

When she had kicked Jessica out of her room, Annie thought some more about the evening. She had enjoyed Henry's company. That was a good start. He was an excellent match in every way. If she had made a list of requirements, then he would have ticked all the boxes. If she fooled herself into thinking that the nebulous thing called love was real, then she might wait all of her life and find herself at that empty bus terminal. *Like* was probably as far as she would get to fulfilling that ideal. All the talk about love was just something to sell films and songs. Jojo bought into it because she was a romantic and wanted to believe in fairy tales. No, Henry was a decent man. Besides, he might just be the last bus.

10

Jojo hated giving up her one day of rest, but she had been practising the rabbit trick all week and unless she mastered it soon, she would have to come clean with Nico and admit defeat. Nico thought she was going in on a Sunday to assist Bobbi with her aerial act and this was partly true, but had served as a cover.

All she had to do was make Muffin disappear – she was using the top hat – and then reappear elsewhere. Nico had said the details weren't important as this was just the basis of the trick and they would refine it. Simple. But it wasn't.

Pixie, tucked into the wide sleeve of her woollen wrap, dug her claws into Jojo's arm as she tried to scramble out. Jojo would wear a glamorous version of a magician's jacket the night of the show. 'You only have to stay still for a few seconds,' she pleaded.

Nico had discovered the leotard and soft woollen wraps in the furthest depths of Jojo's wardrobe. Stuffed in a plastic bag on the top shelf, she had forgotten they were there – a relic from her days at stage school.

'I knew you would have something like this,' Nico said, holding up the shiny pink lycra.

Jojo cursed herself for forgetting to donate them to a charity shop. It had been bad enough when the dance tutor insisted on students wearing leotards for dance. The leg-warmers and wrap over cardigans made the costume a bit more tolerable, as Jojo had chosen brightly coloured woollens, but they could not be worn in class as they disguised form.

Nico had similar ideas to her dance tutor. 'If you want to be taken seriously as a performer, then you must dress and act like a performer,' he said, inspecting the kit. 'These are entirely suitable for rehearsing. Nothing to get caught in equipment.'

In the end, Jojo had agreed to change into the hated garb when she arrived at the Golden Globe, on the condition that she wore what she chose to and from work. It would, at least, save the daily arguments.

Whilst Pixie was scampering up her arm, Muffin was refusing to drop into the hidden compartment beneath the top hat. When she thought he had finally settled, she lifted the hat with a 'Ta da,' to find the rascal clinging onto the lip of the hole, his back feet frantically trying to find purchase. 'You are meant to drop through!' Jojo lifted him out and ruffled his fur.

When Bobbi walked in a few minutes later, Jojo was lying on her back fiddling with the door to the hidden compartment, whilst Pixie pummelled her belly and Muffin nibbled her hair. Jojo giggled. 'Can't you behave yourself for one minute?'

'Now what fun would that be?' Bobbi drawled. 'I never behave myself.'

Jojo went to sit up and banged her head. 'Ouch. Sorry, am I late?'

'No, I arrived a bit early. What are you doing under there?'

Jojo explained the difficulty that she was having mastering

the act. 'If I get this wrong, I could ruin Nico's chances of success. You know how important the Starlight show is. I might just have to confess.'

Bobbi gathered Muffin up and tickled him under his chin. 'It seems a pity to give up the opportunity of a solo performance. I thought that was what you wanted.'

'It was. It is. But not like this. I have no idea what I'm doing. It's going to be a disaster. I know it is.' Jojo hugged Pixie to her and the rabbit poked its nose into the scooped neck of her leotard. 'Hey come out of there.' Too late, Pixie had decided this was a game and was burrowing down between her breasts, his tail just visible.

'You know that's pretty funny,' Bobbi said as she watched Jojo wrestling with the errant rabbit. 'Lots of magicians use comedy in their act, Tommy Cooper, for example. There, that face you just made, it's hilarious.'

At last, Jojo had liberated Pixie. She took Muffin from Bobbi and deposited them both in their carry basket. 'Nico would be furious if I turned a serious trick into a comedy routine.'

'What's the alternative? If you turn down the opportunity to do a solo act because you lack the confidence to pull it off, will Nico ask you again? You've got one foot in the door. If I were you, darling, I would make damn sure that I elbowed my way in.'

Jojo knew Bobbi was right. If she backed down now, then her role as glamorous assistant would be forevermore. Nico considered this a simple trick — and it was. If she couldn't get this right, he would give up on teaching her anything else. She had to try to conform. Her independent spirit and refusal to follow the rules had resulted in her being asked to leave stage school. Only Annie knew the truth. 'I'll just have to practice more.'

'You've got less than three weeks. Good luck.'

Charlie was assisting them that afternoon. They could fit the harnesses themselves, but needed him to operate the wire. First up was Bobbi. There was nothing for Jojo to do, as Bobbi could now glide effortlessly from one side of the theatre to the other.

'Teach me something more challenging,' Bobbi said when she came in to land.

Jojo needed little encouragement to take her turn on the wire. At first, she was trying things out to decide what to teach Bobbi, but then she got experimental. If she had a length of strong material, then she could free herself of the wire and be much more fluid. Bobbi clapped as Jojo descended.

'I don't think I'm ready for those moves. That was pretty impressive.'

'Let's just try a pirouette.'

Bobbi was practising turning 180 degrees whilst maintaining her posture and so Jojo wandered over to Charlie. 'Do we have a long length of material, like old stage curtains in storage? Something strong but smooth and silky?'

Charlie rubbed his chin. 'Hmm. I'm not sure. Why?'

'I just had an idea of using it with the wire to incorporate more acrobatics.'

'It would have to be very strong. What about parachute silk?'

'Perfect, but where are we going to find that?'

'It just so happens that a friend of mine knows someone who is disposing of the silks from a parachute factory. I could get a length on loan, but we would have to make sure it was safe before you do your spider-man thing.'

Jojo's imagination was off again. She could visualise twisting and turning, wrapping herself up and then down a silk banner, twisting it around her feet to free her arms. The possibilities were endless. 'You could make it safe, couldn't you?'

Charlie winked. 'Let's see first if he has anything suitable. Don't go trying anything out without a proper safety check. I'm serious, Jojo.'

Jojo turned her attention back to Bobbi. 'That's great. A bit more practice and you'll have it.'

'Have you seen Kai Keisler's act?' Jojo said as they walked to the changing room.

'Why? Is Nico getting nervous about the competition?'

'A little competition is healthy. It keeps us on our toes, and I'm sure Nico has nothing to worry about. It's just that he seems so mysterious.'

'I may have had a sneak preview. He's talented.'

Maybe Nico did have something to worry about. Nico's good looks had helped push him up the popularity charts. Now that Kai Keisler was on the scene, he had serious competition. 'I expect Kai Keisler has a lot of women fans, like Nico.'

Bobbi pushed open the door to the changing room. Today it was empty and from the smell of pine had just been cleaned. 'I don't think Kai encourages them. Not like Nico.'

It surprised Jojo that Bobbi seemed so familiar with Kai, but it shouldn't. Bobbi was single and quick to notice a good-looking man. Her comment about Nico stung a little, although it was true Nico did flirt with his fans. It was mid-afternoon on a Sunday. They would be back at work again tomorrow. Jojo loved her job, but sometimes it felt as though she spent every waking hour at the Golden Globe. She peeled off the sweaty lycra. Bobbi had already stepped into a shower. Jojo wrapped a towel around herself and then, after some thought, retrieved the anonymous note from the depths of her bag. She had not looked at it again since the day she opened it.

'What's that?' Bobbi said, when she emerged in a cloud of lime scented steam.

Jojo handed her the note.

Bobbi's eyes scanned back and forth, as if she was reading and then rereading. 'Who gave you this?'

Jojo sighed. 'I don't know. Someone left it at the front desk and Pedro handed it to me.'

'Is there an envelope?'

Jojo passed it over.

'Nico's Assistant.'

'Do you think it's from one of his fans?'

Bobbie turned the note over and then back again. 'Must be. Don't let it worry you, darling. Some fans might be a little crazy, but they're harmless.'

'That's what I thought. So, I shouldn't worry?'

'You get your share of drama. The mystery of the falling gantry. An anonymous letter. I wonder what the third thing will be?'

'What do you mean?' Jojo wanted no more scares.

'They say everything happens in threes.'

'Oh right.'

She wanted to feel reassured but, in the shower, as hot water washed over her, Jojo was uneasy. It was the concern on Bobbi's face. Bobbi said the right things, but Jojo could tell that the letter had spooked her. The near miss was not so easy to pass off as an accident, now that she knew about Meryl. She wished Nico would go to the police. He thought he was being kind to Meryl, but he could put both of their lives at risk.

11

Annie had read somewhere that a person transforms every seven years. There was a famous saying, 'Give me a child until he is seven and I will show you the man' or woman in this case. It kind of said that your aspirations and characteristics at seven would be the ones that would shape you into an adult. Annie tried to recall herself at seven. Serious. Sensible. The bookshelf in her bedroom had to be organised in alphabetical order by author, then title, and series number: Malory Towers, The Secret Seven, The Chronicles of Narnia. Annie's bedroom was always tidy, Jessica's was a mess. It was no different today. School was okay, even before she met Jojo. As milk monitor, register monitor, and any other responsible role that needed filling, Annie had gained a senior status amongst her peers. They didn't have prefects in infant school, but if they had, Annie would have been chief prefect. 'Thank goodness we have one sensible daughter,' her parents were always saying.

Being organised meant having some control over your life. If you thought ahead, weighed up risks, and made careful choices, then you were less likely to be surprised or disappointed. Protecting Jessica and then Jojo had come naturally. They were oblivious to danger and as she had well-honed instincts; it was easy to step in and minimise risk. Maybe she had put her own life on hold. Now Jessica was getting married, Jojo was happy living with Nico, and her parents were planning a move to Scotland, it was time to do some serious thinking about the next stage of her life.

'How much longer are you going to be?' Jessica hammered on the bathroom door.

Annie was in no hurry to get out; the bath was where she did her best thinking. 'What do you want?'

'My toiletries. I'm staying at Gary's.'

'Give me thirty minutes.'

Jessica groaned. 'You spend half your life in there.'

Annie slipped under water to block out Jessica's voice. When she emerged, she could hear Jessica talking to Mum downstairs. It would be good to get a place of her own. Maybe rent a house share with other young professionals. She would look in the local paper. It was time to apply for a more senior role at the travel agency, maybe consider moving to a different branch.

'Ha! You'll have to shift your arse now,' Jessica shouted up the stairs. 'Looks like Hooray Henry is about to pay a visit.'

Annie couldn't have got out of the bath faster. Water dripped over the floor as she rummaged through the airing cupboard in search of a big towel. She wasn't expecting Henry. Who turned up uninvited at four fifteen on a Sunday afternoon? 'Tell him I'm out,' she shouted.

Too late, she could hear his voice from the hallway. 'Annie, Henry is here,' Mum called in her posh voice.

As Annie threw potential outfits onto her bed, she cursed Henry for his unannounced arrival. The Victorians had got it right with their rules about visiting. Her hair was damp and looked a mess. If she took her time making herself presentable, Mum and Jessica would interrogate Henry; Lord knows what they would say. She could imagine Jessica running through a relationship CV with him: What was his best attribute? How many women had he dated? Reasons for leaving them or being dumped? Helpful as a manual or review would be, she couldn't risk Jessica and Mum ruining this relationship before it had been given a chance. Annie paused, and surveyed herself in the wardrobe mirror wearing just her undies, body still flushed and steaming from the bath. *Relationship.* Was she actually committing to a relationship? Find a house share. Get a promotion. Start a relationship. It was what everyone else her age was doing – had already done. Oh heck, she was taking too long. Mum would have sat Henry down for a good natter by now. Annie wrestled with a cotton top to wear over jeans, but it got stuck like a wet swimsuit and she could peel it neither up nor down. When Jessica gave a loud and lewd laugh Annie almost tore the damned thing off trying to free herself. Then in her desperation to rescue Henry, she grabbed a floral sprigged dress that was loose fitting, secured her hair on top of her head and looking decent, if not presentable, charged down the stairs.

They were sitting in the conservatory, Jessica, Mum and Henry. Mum leaning forward in her chair to get as close to Henry as she could without sitting in his lap, and Jessica perched on the arm of Mum's chair, working her way through a handful of Ginger Snaps.

'Oh, there you are, darling. Henry is perfectly happy to wait until you've finished getting dressed. Have another biscuit, Henry.' Mum proffered a china plate on which an assortment of biscuits was artfully arranged. 'If Annie had told me about your visit, I would have baked a cake. Would you like some cake, Henry? I have some fairy cakes in the freezer. It won't take long for them to defrost.'

Jessica snorted and sent a spray of biscuit across her mum's shoulder.

The March sunshine magnified in the conservatory and Annie, not yet cooled from her bath, felt uncomfortably sticky. She sat in an upright chair, rather than share the two-seater with Henry in her half-dressed state. Her hair fell out of its clip, her usually neat bob flicking up at awkward angles. 'I'm sorry I wasn't expecting you, Henry.'

Henry leapt to his feet. 'No, I'm sorry to have intruded and caught you unawares. I was going to put this through the letter box, but your sister opened the door.'

Annie guessed what had happened next. Mum would have intercepted with the guile of an SAS officer, the best china on standby for special operations. He wouldn't have stood a chance.

Henry handed her a glossy magazine. 'It's the trade one. I thought you might be interested in an article on the Cyclades and their growing popularity. It's very interesting, tells you about the history and geology of the islands.'

Annie took the magazine, relieved that Henry would soon be leaving.

'There's no need to rush away, Henry. Stay for supper.'

'I'm sorry, Mum, but Henry really does have to go. I was getting ready to go out myself. Perhaps another time.'

'You didn't say you were going out. Where are you off to?'

Jessica intervened, 'Mum, please could you get that article about bridesmaid dresses you found in the hairdresser's magazine?'

'I didn't tear it out of the magazine in the hairdressers. I'd never do such a thing.'

'Whatever. Can you get it please?'

'Now?'

'Yes. I should have left for Gary's, only Annie was hogging the bathroom.'

The way was clear for Annie to steer Henry to the front door. 'I'm sorry about all of that,' she said when he was safely on the doorstep.

'No, I'm sorry for interrupting your Sunday afternoon.'

They had an awkward goodbye. It was only the third time they had met and so far, they had not even attempted a peck on the cheek. Now was not the time to start, although Henry did start to lunge forward before Annie ducked away and closed the door saying, 'Okay. Thank you. See you soon.'

'That was a total car wreck.' Jessica was standing behind Annie.

'Why on earth did you open the door?'

'Yeah, sorry about that. Why did you come down dressed like that?'

Annie glanced up to see a mad woman in the hall mirror. Her face was beetroot, hair manic and you could see her knickers clearly through the skirt of her dress. 'Why didn't you tell me my dress was see-through?'

'Where would I start? Your hairy legs, visible panties, gross toe nails?'

Annie covered her face. It was a disaster. 'If I had intended Henry to see me semi-nude, I would have made my body beach-ready. This hasn't been on display since my September holiday to Majorca.'

'Well, now Hooray Henry has had a sneak preview. Let's hope you haven't scared him off. Frightened the horses.' She snorted.

'But a see-through dress?' Annie was mortified.

'It's all the rage since Lady Di flashed her knickers in that shot with the sun shining through her dress. Don't worry, Sis.

I'm sure Hooray knows when he's onto a good thing.' Jessica winked, and Annie felt a surge of love for her.

Later, when she had recovered from the ordeal, Annie thought about the inevitable. Next time they dated, she would be expected to kiss Henry. Would he initiate, or should she? What kind of kiss? Jessica and Jojo presumed she was as worldly as them, but how could she be with so little experience? She wasn't entirely innocent. As a teenager she had been groped at parties, and on one occasion she had allowed things to progress, partly because the boy was intent on having his way, and then she had thought why not? She might as well find out what all the fuss was about. After that dismal experience, Annie had been waiting for the right man. Was Henry the right man?

12

Charlie wheeled in a trolley of silver boxes, cylindrical tubes, and curtained cubicles; it was going to be a busy day. Jojo wondered if Nico had remembered her lunch with Annie, but she daren't mention it. Word of Kai Keisler's impressive act was circulating the Golden Globe, and comparisons were being made with Nico. All of this extra equipment was Nico trying to up their game. He was always focused and intense, but today she could imagine smoke coming out of his ears.

'Charlie, could you fetch the rabbits from the pets prop?' Nico said, and Jojo's heart sank.

'I'll get them, Nico,' she said.

'Okay, but be quick. We don't have any time to waste.'

When they were out of earshot, Jojo turned to Charlie. 'I can't do it. I've practised and practised, but it's impossible.'

'Do you want me to say that I can't get them? That there's a prop blocking my access or something?'

'No, then Nico would be mad at you. I'll just have to hope that they behave.'

'I've seen you do it perfectly. Have faith. You just need more practice and then you'll be confident.' They were at the door to the pet prop room.

'What if it goes wrong on the night? Maybe I should back out now. I really want this solo, Charlie — I just don't want to screw it up.'

Charlie gripped her shoulders firmly as if channelling positive energy. 'You are capable of so much more than that stupid trick. Why don't you show Nico what you can do on the aerial wire? Incidentally, I can get some parachute silk for you.'

'Thanks Charlie. Don't mention the parachute silk in front of Nico. It may not work, but I'd like to try something out. Bobbi said I should adapt the rabbit trick, making it a kind of comedy act.'

Charlie held his chin as if giving this some thought. 'I don't know about a comedy act, but I agree you should make it your own. Talk to Nico. You are not an incompetent assistant Jojo, you are a performer in your own right. If Nico just wants someone to look pretty, he could find a thousand replacements.'

'But none prettier?' Jojo pulled one of her faces.

'Plenty prettier. But he doesn't. Nico knows you are talented and original. You just need to persuade him to let go a little. Now go Bat Girl. Good luck.'

The pep talk from Charlie boosted Jojo's confidence. He was right. Nico valued her experience and skills. He hadn't seen her aerial acrobatics, only her street performance routine. Of course, he thought them unsuitable for the Golden Globe and she agreed. When she got the chance, she would demonstrate, but not now. He was stressed and tired preparing for the shows. Jojo wanted to do everything that she could to help him. After all, being the top act was important to both of them. She hurried back to the studio with the basket.

'What's that?' Jojo said when she opened the door to see Nico assembling what looked like a big doll's house.

'This is the next part of your trick?'

Jojo was relieved that Nico didn't want her to demonstrate the first part, but there was more? 'Before we over-complicate things, maybe I should just perfect the basics.' *Try to hold the rabbits for two minutes without them wriggling out of my hands,* she thought.

'You are being modest, bella. When I show you the next part of the trick, you will be amazed. This has to be special. It is not enough to just use the hat and the magic table. That is alright for a children's party but not for the Easter Gala. I designed this little house. The audience will see the rabbits in the different rooms. There are four rooms: a bedroom, a bathroom, a kitchen and a library. Two downstairs rooms and two upstairs. You see these mirrors dividing the rooms? I will show you how to make it appear the rabbit has disappeared. The floor slides back if we want to use the under-stage compartment.'

It was adorable. It reminded Jojo of the White Rabbit's house in Alice in Wonderland. She peered into the rooms and imagined Pixie sitting in the study with tiny spectacles on his nose, and Muffin in the kitchen wearing a chef's hat.

Nico lifted the rabbits from the basket by the scruffs of their necks, and Jojo flinched. They looked as though they had been hung from a butcher's hook. 'So, you will produce one rabbit from your sleeve. Then you turn one rabbit into two rabbits. Now bella, make sure you give the audience time to applaud you and they will. I know you will be magnificent.'

She couldn't even produce rabbit one — Muffin, from the

top hat she'd been using. Trying to make it look as though Muffin had turned into two rabbits was beyond her.

'Um Nico, that all sounds wonderful, but...'

'That is not all bella. We now use the doll's house to show the rabbits transported from one room to another by magic. They are there and then they disappear. Maybe we should introduce more rabbits — five or six.'

Jojo gulped. 'Oh, I don't think so. Two are plenty.'

'Let me demonstrate how to make two rabbits into one. You will have to use Muffin as he is a bigger than Pixie. If you hold him flat on your palm, you can make him look fatter, as though he has absorbed Pixie, who, of course, will have disappeared into the hole in the table or behind a mirror. Get the rabbits. I'll show you how.' Nico dropped the silky bundles of rabbit into Jojo's arms.

She lifted Muffin to her face and kissed him. *Behave for me.* Then Pixie.

'No, no, no, that will not do bella. They are working animals. We use rabbits because they are docile. Baby rabbits because they are easy to manipulate and hide. If you treat them like pets, they will want to play. They will get excited and run about when you want them to stay still and hide. Believe me, it will make your job much harder.'

Jojo knew from experience that he was right. Nico arranged the equipment with one hand, the other expertly holding Muffin and Pixie. She glared at them. Traitors. Acting all docile with Nico when she knew they would wriggle and squirm when handed to her.

Nico was going through each step of the trick as though it were easy enough for a child to perform. It looked simple, when he did it.

'Now you bella, show me what you can do.'

Jojo wrestled the rabbits from him. She could hold them in

her arms, but had not yet mastered how to contain them in one hand. There was a knock on the door, and Charlie popped his head around. 'Annie's waiting for you in Cake Presto.'

Nico rolled his eyes. 'Really? You're going to take time out now?'

'I'm sure I mentioned it.' Jojo was torn. Nico was right, with the Starlight show fast approaching, and now this complicated trick to learn, it was bad timing. 'I'm sorry I won't take a long break, but I have to eat.' It was true, she needed something for lunch.

'Okay. But remember to go steady on the carbs.'

'Why don't you come and meet her, Nico? Annie's always asking to be introduced.'

'You know I can't. It's less than three weeks until the show. Walker still hasn't decided whether Kai Keisler is going to be the top act or me.'

'You're not worried?'

'A little.'

This was the first time Jojo had glimpsed a chink in Nico's confidence. Maybe she should send a message to Annie and concentrate on trying to learn the trick or persuade Nico to simplify it. But if she stood Annie up, then she would hurt her friend, and they had just got back into being okay. 'I'll only be gone half an hour. You have nothing to worry about, Nico. You are going to be the absolutely toperoony act.'

'You look like a professional dancer,' Annie said, commenting on the lycra catsuit beneath soft wraps and legwarmers. 'It does seem more practical, but you don't look like you.'

Jojo pulled a face.

'Now you do.' Annie laughed. 'Cream teas?'

'No. I'll just have a salad or something. But stay there and

I'll get you a cream tea with Earl Grey. Did you want a sandwich?'

'Yes, please. Ham or cheese. No, Charlie today?'

'I saw him earlier. He might well pop in. Why? Is there something I should know?'

'Absolutely not. He's a great guy, but not my type. If you weren't with Nico, I would say he was perfect for you.'

'But I am. There is something though, isn't there?' Jojo couldn't help a little smirk —she knew Annie so well.

'Maybe. Go and get our lunch and I'll tell you.'

The queue was longer than Jojo would have liked. She looked back at her friend of fifteen years. They had been inseparable as children, but as she got older, Jojo felt the need for more space to spread her roots. Annie looked happy, and Jojo hoped that she had met someone special.

His name was Henry, and he worked for the same travel agency as Annie. 'Nothing serious, but I have agreed to a second date.'

'A second date! Annie Apple cheeks you little devil. That is virtually going steady for you. I don't know of any other man who has been granted a second date. So, when am I going to meet him?'

Annie gave her a steady look. 'It's important to me you meet Henry because I value your opinion and if he doesn't get on with my best friend, then he can walk.'

Jojo hid behind her mug of coffee. It was awkward. Nico had to meet Annie; she couldn't keep them apart any longer without seeming weird. 'So, how about a double date? You and Henry, Me and Nico?'

Annie clapped her hands. 'Really? Oh Jojo, I would love to meet Nico.'

Jojo's heart was on a seesaw — joy at pleasing her dearest friend and apprehension for delivering this news to Nico.

13

Annie was so pleased with the news that she would finally get to meet Nico; she almost forgot the purpose of her visit. 'Charlie told me you had a near miss with a piece of equipment which dropped to the stage from the fly tower.'

'*The fly tower*? Hark at you an expert on theatre architecture.'

Jojo had finished her salad, but had not reached for Annie's ham sandwich as Annie had expected her to. It sat untouched on a plate that Annie had nudged towards Jojo. 'Half each?'

Jojo shook her head. 'There's nothing else to tell you. A piece of gantry fell from the *fly tower,* and if Nico hadn't pushed me out of the way, it might have hit me. But he did, and it didn't.'

Annie could tell from her expression, that despite making light of it, Jojo was worried. 'Charlie says that it's a mystery how it happened. He had checked that everything was properly secure just moments before. Nico had been up there with him, checking something out for his act. It doesn't seem very safe, Jojo. It's a beautiful little theatre, but the mechanics are Victorian. Does the management comply with health and safety law?'

Jojo bit her lower lip and looked away. When she turned back, Annie saw the anguish in her eyes. 'There's something else. It's probably nothing. In fact, I'm sure it's nothing.'

'Go on.'

Jojo sighed. 'The next day, I received an anonymous letter. I thought it was fan mail, but it was something a bit more sinister.'

Her instincts had been right. Jojo was in trouble. 'What did it say, and why didn't you tell me before?'

'It's not a big deal. Not really. The note was probably from one of Nico's fans. It was warning me to leave him alone. I don't think the two incidents are connected. A fan couldn't get into the theatre to mess with the equipment.'

'Are you sure? Charlie showed me an underground tunnel that isn't used anymore. Maybe it leads to outside the theatre. Or, it could be a fan who is working as a member of staff.'

'Maybe. The only person who knows about the letter is Bobbi, one of the dancers. I don't want Nico to find out because he's already wound up about the Easter Gala and because it's probably nothing. The falling gantry was just an accident. I know Bobbi is spreading a rumour that it was the resident ghost, but that's just theatre folk amusing themselves. They have to have some sort of drama.'

'Can I see the note?'

'It's in my bag in the changing room.' Jojo checked her watch. 'I've got to get back to Nico. We are so busy with rehearsals I shouldn't really have taken time out. If you follow me, I'll nip in and get it. Then I have to concentrate on learning a trick with live rabbits. It's a nightmare; they keep escaping from me and run amok.'

Jojo led Annie into a part of the theatre that she had not explored with Charlie. 'Wait there, I won't be a mo.'

Five feather headdresses atop five glittering dancers bobbed past Annie as she waited in the corridor outside the changing room. A rotund man with an extravagant curling moustache called out to someone who replied, 'Bon chance.' There was laughter. The distant sound of cymbals.

'Here. It's probably nothing, but keep it to yourself. Don't worry about returning it; I don't want to see it again. Now I really have to go.' Jojo gave Annie a hug and Annie wondered again at Jojo's dress. It was so unlike her. She was used to Jojo's outlandish wear; she always wore outfits that turned heads, never something that was sensible and normal. Maybe she was just growing up.

The note didn't say much, a couple of lines that looked as though they had been typed on a word processor. That might serve as a clue. Not everyone had access to a word processor. *If you value your life, keep away from him.* It could be a threat or a warning. What if someone knew something about Nico and they were trying to tell Jojo? The sooner she met Nico, the better.

'Are you auditioning as a dancer?' Charlie said, when he came across Annie, who was trying to find her way out of the maze of corridors.

Annie stuffed the envelope into her jacket pocket. 'Do I look like a dancer?'

Charlie stood back and pretended to be giving this some consideration as he looked her up and down. 'More a leading lady. Certainly not chorus line.'

Annie laughed. 'If you haven't had lunch, would you like a ham sandwich? It's from Cake Presto.'

'Great. I'm starving. I was going to take a break once I'd delivered a cage of doves to our new magician, the infamous

Kai Keisler. Want to see where the animal performers hang out?'

Annie wasn't sure what Charlie meant, but was happy to find out. She was mesmerised by the glamour of the Golden Globe and by spending time with Charlie, she might unravel the mystery surrounding Jojo's anonymous letter.

'I'll just peek around the door, make sure they're all decent. Ready for a visitor, ladies?' Charlie stood back and Annie stepped into the room. There was a cooing and fluttering of wings, a parrot squawked. He lifted two baby rabbits from a hutch. 'These little beauties are Pixie and Muffin.' Charlie passed one to Annie and held on to the other.

Annie could feel a tiny heart beating beneath her touch. 'Which one is this?' She lifted the little twitching nose to eye level. 'You are beautiful. Yes, you are.'

'I don't know. Jojo named them. She's performing a rabbit trick, but from what I've seen, it will be more of a comic act.'

Annie settled the rabbit back into its hutch. 'Have you seen Jojo perform her own material? She's incredibly talented and hilarious. Maybe she should improvise. I bet the audience would love her.'

Charlie cocked his head to one side and looked thoughtful. Annie was expecting him to respond with a suggestion, but whatever had been going through his mind, he kept it to himself.

Another stagehand burst into the room. He hesitated for a second, as if he might be disturbing something. 'Lenny, this is Annie, a friend of Jojo's. I was just showing her around.'

'Cool.' He nodded at Annie and stalked over to the doves.

'Are they for Kai Keisler?' Charlie said.

'Yup.' He expertly transferred the doves into a wire cage and wheeled them away.

'Okay, doves sorted. So, I am now available as a tour guide, unless you would just like me to show you how to get out of this madhouse.'

'Could I have another peek at that hidden tunnel? It's so mysterious.'

Charlie laughed. 'The myths surrounding it are more exciting than the tunnel itself. I expect there are a few rats down there. I hope you don't want to go inside.'

'No. I'm just intrigued where it leads to.'

'Come on. I'll show you.'

Annie followed Charlie past the rehearsal rooms. A door opened and a tall dancer in lycra and woollens similar to Jojo's stepped out. She stood like a dancer, her toes turned out and head held high. 'Charlie! You've been neglecting me. I have had to massage my own feet.' She pouted and, with a condescending look at Annie, slunk off. Charlie seemed unaffected by her behaviour and continued to lead the way. They entered the theatre from backstage. The same dancers that Annie had seen earlier passed them in the wings. Spangled bosoms, ridiculously long legs, and feathery plumes — they trooped past like a parade of peacocks. Each one of them had a word, gesture, or caress for Charlie.

Annie saw how his blushes encouraged them. They were naughty schoolgirls.

When they had gone, leaving an aroma of fresh sweat and perfume, Charlie collected himself. 'They were just showing off for your benefit.'

Annie guessed that her presence backstage was causing a bit of a stir. All the women, even Mrs Brew in Cake Presto, seemed to treat Charlie like a favourite brother, or in Mrs Brew's case – son. The dancers were marking their territory like cats. Annie wondered how they had taken to Jojo and guessed that her close friendship with Charlie had helped.

Charlie took Annie's hand and led her down the stage

steps into the theatre. 'They're having a dress rehearsal, but it's okay. Just stay close to me.'

His hand was warm and dry. When he let go, Annie felt the memory of it imprinted on her palm.

'We can't go through the tunnel, but I'll show you where it comes out. This way.' Annie followed Charlie as they climbed past tiers of seats towards the back. On stage, the rotund man Annie had seen earlier was sitting at a table with a checked cloth, behind him, the backdrop of a Parisian café. Annie was entranced and forgot that she was meant to be following Charlie. 'Psst,' he hissed.

At the top of the tiered seating, Charlie pointed to a gossamer curtain. Annie was about to ask what was behind it when a man emerged. He swept back the curtain and stepped into the dark theatre. Charlie gasped at the same time as Annie attracting the man's attention.

'For once, you're in the right place at the right time,' the man said to Charlie, not bothering to keep his voice down. Annie didn't like his tone. 'We need to get this tunnel operational before the Starlight show.' Then he noticed Annie and scowled.

Charlie jumped in. 'I'm guessing you two have met.' When the man did not respond, but continued to glare at Annie, he introduced them. 'Annie, this is Nico, Jojo's partner and Nico, this is Annie, Jojo's best friend.'

'A pleasure to meet you, Annabelle.' Nico kissed her hand and Annie had to force herself not to snatch it away. His hand was cold and clammy.

'Likewise. Charlie was just showing me out as I got a bit lost after leaving Jojo. I'm looking forward to getting to know you when we meet for dinner.' Annie knew she had surprised him and took pleasure in seeing him discomfited. He was far too sure of himself and his charms, but he didn't fool her.

'Of course. I am looking forward to it.' He bowed his head a little and Annie whipped her hand behind her back. When he raised his head, he handed Annie a red rose. Then he glided away as though a spotlight was following him back to the stage.

'I take it you two hadn't met before?'

Annie shuddered. 'No.'

'That doesn't surprise me.'

'Why?'

Charlie shrugged. 'I dunno. Just a hunch, I guess. Anyway, that is the other end of the tunnel.'

'Can you get to outside the theatre through the tunnel?'

'I've heard a rumour, but it seems unlikely. I suspect I'm going to be clearing it out, so I'll let you know.'

'Doesn't it bother you having to do things like that when you're a trained architect?'

'Can't say I'm looking forward to it, but we're a small company; everyone has to multi task. Have to take the rough with the smooth. Besides, it's only until September. Hopefully, by then I'll get a job as a stage set designer. I'm aiming high. A big West End theatre or New York.' Energy buzzed from him, and Annie felt a tingle of electricity.

'You will get there. I know you will.'

When Annie emerged from the theatre into the bright light of day, she had to shield her eyes. The Golden Globe was like a hidden world. Outside, office workers commuted home, tourists consulted maps, and restaurant owners touted for business. It was a normal day. But there was nothing normal about the Golden Globe. It was exotic. Magical. And, Annie feared, a little bit dangerous. The note that Jojo had received. An unexplained incident that could have been fatal — was it really an accident? And Nico. Annie didn't like him. She wanted to, but there was something about him that set alarm bells ringing. She had caught him off guard before he had put on the magician persona. Conjuring a red rose would not win her over. Jojo was completely under his spell, and so she would have to tread carefully. An hour ago, she had been delighted that they were finally meeting for dinner, now she was dreading it. If only she and Henry were meeting with Jojo and Charlie.

14

'My finale isn't good enough.' Nico stood on the stage wrapped in a towelling robe. They were going through a dress rehearsal of their act. Each of the performers had a time slot to practice on the stage; stagehands were the only people permitted to be present.

'You were confident this morning. What's changed?'

'Captain America. I met him, Kai Keisler, upstairs. He thinks a lot of himself. Says he has something planned that will have critics talking all year. Apparently, he's going to bring magic back to the people – whatever that means. He was scathing of the traditional approach and you can't get more traditional than an escape artist routine.'

This was what Jojo had been trying to tell Nico. But it was too late to change everything now. 'I wouldn't say it was traditional. The concept, maybe, but you have modernised it with the girls in leather and chains and you look incredible. You know your female fans are going to love it.'

The tension seemed to go out of Nico's body as he

relaxed his shoulders. 'You're right. The music, strobe lights and Hocus Pocus in their S and M gear makes it contemporary.'

'Exactly. Besides, just because Kai Keisler, who is German not American, says he will transform the world of magic, that doesn't make it so.'

'It's that square jaw and white teeth. That guy looks like a Hollywood actor.'

'And so do you, my love.' Jojo nudged the towelling dressing gown off his shoulder. 'Come on, time to get wet.'

On cue, the water tank emerged from beneath the stage like a surfacing submarine. Jojo secured the chains and padlock as Nico had instructed her. On show nights Sly and Bunty would do this.

'Try to shake them loose to prove that they are securely fastened,' Nico said, twisting in his chain clad body to face Jojo.

She worried the chains trying to loosen them a little, but there was no give. 'Are you sure about this Nico? I don't see how you're going to escape. Have you actually tried whilst underwater?'

'That's the whole point. It should seem impossible.'

'Ready?' Charlie called down from the fly tower.

Jojo kissed Nico and stepped back before he was winched above the glass tank and then on the count of three lowered in. Jojo held her breath imagining that she was underwater with him. At first, Nico seemed to calmly release his hands and Jojo relaxed. He writhed one way and then the other. Jojo wanted to gasp for air, but so long as Nico was under water, she continued to hold her breath. Just as she thought she could hold her breath no longer the chains fell away. He took a key from his mouth and unlocked the ankle cuffs. At last, Jojo could breathe. He pushed himself up and Jojo prepared to greet him, but the lid of the tank was stuck. Nico pounded his fists against the Perspex.

'Charlie! Get him out.' Jojo pressed her hands against the tank as if she could save him or offer comfort. Where was Charlie? What was taking him so long?

It felt like hours although it could only have been seconds before Charlie released the electronic lock and Nico burst out of the tank sploshing water across the stage. 'What the hell happened? You could have killed me!' He swung himself out and dropped to the stage with a thud.

Charlie joined them. 'I don't know. The lock's on a timer. I'll adjust it. That's what the dress rehearsal is for, to iron out any kinks. In fact, you should keep it in the act it's more exciting.'

Nico caught a towel that was thrown to him from the wings. 'Incompetence. And not the first time. I'm keeping a note. One more wrong move and you're out.'

'You're safe. That's the main thing,' Jojo said. 'If you want to get changed, I'll practice my solo.'

It took her a few minutes to calm down. The audience never really believes that something might go wrong, but Jojo had heard enough stories to know otherwise. 'I know it wasn't your fault Charlie, but you will make sure that it never happens again?'

'Like the falling gantry?' There was a tone to Charlie's voice.

'Do you think they're connected — the two near misses?'

'Nico seems to think they are.'

'He was just in shock. We both were. As you said, the timer needs to be adjusted. Now help me set up so that I can rehearse before Nico gets back.'

At first everything was going well. Jojo amazed herself by conjuring Pixie from one room to another. Then Muffin. It was like the ball under one of three cups, only rabbits in rooms. They were there and then they weren't. Appearing and disappearing by magic. Now to turn two rabbits into one. It would have worked if Pixie had not made a dash for freedom. There were so many more places to lose the rabbits on stage and Nico would be back at any moment. She flung herself across the floor to grab Pixie's back feet.

'Here.' She almost threw Pixie at Charlie. Muffin's tail bobbed up and then he disappeared through the secret hole in the table. At least she knew where Muffin was, except he wasn't. Somehow, he had found his way under the stage.

'You are a naughty rabbit,' Jojo chastised, when she eventually caught him. She knew exactly where each piece of equipment was positioned on the stage above her and it gave her an idea. The doll's house had reminded her of the White Rabbit's house in Alice in Wonderland and now she pretended to be big Alice with her arms and head poking out of the windows, her body hidden beneath the stage.

Charlie squatted so that his face was level with hers. 'That's brilliant. Pull one of your hands in.'

Jojo withdrew a hand, already guessing Charlie's next move. It resembled a trick she had previously done with Nico. He detached one room and carried it across the stage with his own hand taking the place of Jojo's. The audience would think it was her hand.

'I'll wriggle under the stage and you move the bottom two rooms over to there,' Jojo said. There were clear makings on the stage to show performers where the under-stage compartments were hidden. Jojo giggled to herself. This was going to be perfect. She lay on her back under the stage and thrust her legs through two openings. They would come out of the two rooms Charlie had moved. It worked like a dream. Charlie pretended to pack away the house whilst Jojo's arms, legs and head appeared to be distributed between the four boxes.

Breathless and dishevelled Jojo returned to the stage with Muffin. 'What did it look like?'

'Amazing. You should turn the entire act into an Alice routine. We could use *Eat Me* and *Drink Me* labels.'

'I could use the aerial wire to somersault myself down the rabbit hole.' Jojo squeezed her hands into fists to contain her excitement.

'So are you going to show Nico?'

Jojo wanted to, desperately. Surely, if he saw this act, he would agree that it was way better than the trick he had taught her. 'I don't know. Not yet. Maybe after the Starlight show.'

Charlie tutted. 'Annie's right. You should use your solo act to show case what you can do in your own right.'

'Shh,' Jojo quietened him. She could hear Nico approaching. 'This is between the two of us. Please say nothing to anyone, Charlie.'

Nico returned, his hair damp and face flushed. 'How was it?'

Jojo edged closer to him to breathe in the warm woody scent of his aftershave. 'Not bad, but still not perfect. I've got the first half, but I'm struggling with turning two rabbits into one. Pixie is too active.'

Nico went through the trick with her again. Maybe Pixie and Muffin had worn themselves out because they were a little more docile and when it was Jojo's turn to demonstrate they were on best behaviour.

'There, I told you it was an easy trick. All you have to do is keep the audience as I left them. You are holding their attention and rapt concentration for my finale. They will not expect much from my assistant, but it is an important job because you will maintain the atmosphere that I have created.'

Jojo nodded. 'I think I can do that.'

'But I have been thinking. Maybe I should change my finale. Charlie? Where's he gone now? He's working solely with us. Charlie!'

Charlie waved from the back of the auditorium where he was talking to Lenny, then he took big strides down the steps to arrive at the stage.

'How are you getting on with clearing the tunnel?'

'I meant to tell you; it won't be ready for the Starlight.'

Nico's jaw tensed.

Before Nico could say anything, Charlie continued. 'It has to be checked for health and safety. There are electric cables running through the tunnel and –'

'– I don't care about health and safety. I need to use that tunnel in just over two weeks, so whatever you have to do, sort it. Have we got flash paper?'

'If you are going to use fire in your act, you'll have to clear it with Peter Walker.'

Nico looked as though he was about to self-combust, but Jojo had a much bigger problem. 'Fire?' Her voice was small.

Charlie used the distraction to slip away out of Nico's firing line.

'Nico what are you planning?' She was nauseous and a little shaky.

'I need something original. You will disappear in a ring of fire and reappear at the back of the theatre. I'm still planning the trick, there's more to it than that.' When Jojo didn't reply he studied her face. 'You've gone white.'

Her lip trembled.

'Come here.'

Jojo stepped into the circle of his arms and he held her to him. 'Your heart's racing. What is it, bella?'

'I'm afraid of fire. Okay. Terrified. I was a little kid, a firework hit the roof of my dad's shed and the whole thing went up in flames. He had some flammable stuff inside and it kind of exploded. It's silly, but even striking a match I feel like I did when I was four years old. My mum was screaming. There were fire engines. Nobody got hurt, but it was really scary. I'm sorry Nico, but I don't think I could stand in a ring of fire. You'll have to ask one of the other girls.'

'But it's our finale.' It was the first time he had said, our and not my finale.

'I don't see why you need to change your act. The escapist trick is good. You heard Charlie say that the tunnel won't be ready and if you've not finished planning the trick, then maybe it should wait for another occasion.'

Nico stroked her hair. 'You are always so wise. I don't want to do the finale with anyone but you. Okay, we'll stick with what we've planned. We just have to make sure that our act is perfect.'

15

'How common do you think word processors are now?' Annie said to Sarah as they ate their lunch in the staff room.

'The rest of the world will be using them before we get one here.'

'I know. But seriously, do you think most people have access to one or is it only certain professions or industries?' Annie had studied the anonymous note searching for clues. The unusual font had led her to believe it was typed on a word processor rather than a typewriter.

'Most offices have electric typewriters now, but few have a word processor. My brother uses one at his poly, but there aren't enough for all the students. He says it's much better than writing his assignments by hand. Why do you ask? Is your man from head office getting us one?'

Having finished her sandwich, Annie checked her Tupperware to find a chocolate biscuit and some carrot sticks. Mum always put in extras. When they were kids, Jojo was often sent to school with no dinner money and just a packet of crisps.

Mum always made enough for both of them. Maybe that was why Jojo still helped herself to anything Annie ordered. 'No, but my man, as you call him, Henry, is picking me up after work. Oh, that reminds me, I'd better read up on the Cyclades Islands in case he asks me questions.'

Sarah snorted. 'He sounds a bundle of fun. Does he give you detention if you haven't done your homework?'

Annie made a face. Her affair with Henry had become the talk of the office. Everyone seemed to think that she would get preferential treatment in perks or promotion. She was looking forward to seeing him after work, although she was a bit nervous about spending the evening with him in his flat. She opened the trade magazine and flicked through the glossy pages, searching for the Cyclades article. There was a jobs section for the travel industry covering several pages. This was exactly what she needed. The ones that took the most space and shouted from the page were the top executive positions with ridiculous salaries. Henry was ambitious, and Annie now understood the opportunities available to him. Maybe she should take an Open University degree and aim high too. For now, she just needed a job that paid enough money to support herself in a shared house or flat. A team leader. A manager. Then she turned the page and found a two-page advert for tour guides.

Do you have a passion for travel? Meeting new people? Discovering new experiences? Come and join our team of travel reps working in Spain where you will help holiday makers create amazing memories and collect a few of your own. Accommodation provided. Competitive salary and air travel miles. Live the dream!

There were photographs of holiday reps with big smiles, posing against a backdrop of beach heaven: blue sky, and sparkling sea, a white hotel and palm trees. Lisa joined Annie in the staff room and she realised Sarah had returned to her desk. Annie tidied away her lunch things, aware of Lisa's unspoken reproach.

Henry's flat was in a new cul-de-sac, a development of four identical apartments with attractive grey brick, and white rendering. 'Here we are.' He parked the Jaguar in his allocated spot alongside other shiny, new cars. Annie didn't think that this was the sort of apartment block that would accommodate families or old people. 'There's a pool and gym in the service block,' Henry said, as they walked along the pathway to the entrance.

Number 2A was clean, tidy, modern, and Annie thought, a little soulless. It had a new build smell, a combination of paint, carpet, adhesives, and wood.

Henry beamed. 'I was one of the first on the waiting list. Lucky to have got in.' He dropped his car keys on a bar that separated the kitchen from the open plan living and dining area. 'Want a tour?'

There wasn't much else to see, just a bedroom and bathroom. It looked to Annie like a show home, there was barely any evidence of Henry.

'I like the way you have matched the duvet cover and curtains; everything looks so well co-ordinated.'

'I paid for the interior designer to decorate and kit it out. Best leave it to the experts. Shall we get something to eat?' Henry had invited her to spend the evening at his flat, but they had not discussed beyond that.

'What were you thinking? A takeaway?'

'Don't you find takeaway meals have a smell that linger? Chinese, Indian, fish and chips?' He screwed up his nose. 'I thought it would be nice to eat in. I've lived here for two months and haven't yet shared a meal with anyone at this table.'

'That would be lovely. I would be delighted to be your first guest.'

'Hopefully one of many meals we will share here.' He put his arms around Annie's waist and looked into her eyes. 'Having you here means so much to me. Your presence makes this a home.'

Annie tilted her head and felt his lips upon hers. It wasn't unpleasant, but neither was it ground moving. She had to stop comparing real life to books and films. She kissed Henry back with a bit more passion, to seal her resolve.

'I just stocked up my freezer so I can offer you…' he opened a draw, 'Cod in parsley sauce, or a roast beef dinner, complete with roast potatoes and carrots. If we have the fish, it will have to be instant potato. And for dessert…' Henry paused to build suspense before brandishing a frosty box, 'Artic Roll.'

16

Jojo was up before Nico, with only two weeks until the Starlight show, she couldn't waste any time. Whenever she practised the trick, something went wrong. It was never the same thing, which was encouraging because it meant that she could perform each component successfully, but it also meant that there wasn't the one thing that she could work on. If only Pixie and Muffin would comply. It was her own fault for treating them like pets. If she had listened to Nico and trained them from day one, then it might have been easier. It didn't explain why they were so well behaved when he demonstrated the trick. Bewitched. That's what they were – bewitched by Nico, a bit like herself.

Nico groaned and reached out a hand to catch hold of Jojo as she sat on the bed. 'You're up.'

'I don't mind going on ahead of you, if you want a lie in.'

Nico sat up and stretched. 'We're not working today. I'm taking you shopping.'

'What for?' It had to be something to do with their act.

'Clothes.'

'Do you need more clothes?' Jojo hoped to persuade Nico to go shopping alone so that she could work.

'No, for you bella. I do not like that you have to wear old clothes. You are a beautiful woman. Classic styles. Sophisticated. I am going to buy you a collection of clothes fit for a princess.'

'That is very kind of you, but they are not old clothes. They are vintage. Some of them very valuable.'

'Like that dead fox? No. No. You must have some classy outfits. Something that you can wear to a premier or the Gala dinner. I want to be proud of you Jojo. Don't make a face. Of course, I'm always proud of you, but sometimes the way that you dress — well it's unseemly. Outlandish. We don't want to attract interest for the wrong reasons. Have people whispering behind our backs.'

Jojo's face burned with humiliation. 'Is that really how you think of me Nico? An embarrassment?' The arguments that they had each morning when she dressed for work made sense now. It wasn't because her outfits breached health and safety, it was because Nico thought her ridiculous. Did other people think the same? Maybe she had lost touch with the real world living in a squat with artists. Annie never criticised her dress. Surely, she would have told her if she had got it so wrong?

'I didn't say that bella. Just let me spoil you. I love you and I want to spend my money making you look even more beautiful than you already are. Is that such a terrible thing?'

'No.' Jojo sighed. Any other woman would be overjoyed if their wealthy partner wanted to take them shopping for clothes. She guessed that Camden market and Portobello Road would not be options. She was right. Nico took her to Knightsbridge.

The clothes were outrageously expensive and Jojo objected

on many levels. It was conspicuous consumption — a term that was freely used in her squat when discussing the greed of property developers. They were unimaginative. Most of all they were not her. She trailed her hand along a rail of silky blouses in varying shades of cream.

'Don't do that,' Nico hissed.

Jojo sighed. It was good to be doing something with Nico other than rehearsing, but this was ridiculous. She didn't need any new clothes. He would be wasting his money. 'I appreciate the thought, Nico, but you don't understand. My dressing-up box has some unique, classic items. They would have been haute couture in the day. My clothes reflect who I am.'

'Can I help you?' A saleswoman had sidled up to them and directed this question at Nico.

'You may. Thank you.' Nico flashed his stage smile and Jojo watched with detached interest at the way the woman seemed to go all melty. 'Could you help Jojo select a few classic outfits — smart/casual and evening?'

'There's no need,' Jojo bristled. This had gone far enough.

'I'll be over there if you need me,' the assistant addressed Jojo.

'What's wrong with what I'm wearing?' Jojo demanded.

Nico looked her up and down. She was wearing a navy blue 1940s tea dress with a full skirt. 'The accessories are a bit over the top.'

'What accessories?' Jojo lifted her hands to find assorted bangles on each wrist, the price tags attached.

Nico chuckled. 'The flower works though.' A silk rose was pinned to the bodice, which Jojo had to admit complimented the outfit.

She slid the bangles from her wrist. 'You're going to get us into trouble.'

'Me? What about you?'

'What about me?'

'Well, Miss Fancy pants over there will not be happy when she sees that you have purloined her keys.'

Jojo glanced over to the sales desk where the assistant seemed to be looking for something. '*Nico*. Where are they?' She jangled. Nico had somehow attached a set of keys through the belt of her dress. They giggled together as she removed her belt.

'Give the lady back her keys and we'll get out of here.'

They were leaving, arm in arm, having entertained the shop assistant and her colleagues with a few more tricks, when Nico stopped in front of a mannequin. 'Now that is what I call classy.'

Jojo folded her arms and tried to be objective. The cream shift dress was simple. A classic cut. If it made Nico happy, she would try it on. 'It could work.'

A couple of hours later, they left the department store loaded up with bags and packages. When she had stepped out of the changing room wearing the cream shift dress, Nico's reaction made her heart sing. He had that look about him of the groom seeing his bride walk down the aisle – soft focus, violins – it was Hollywood stuff. Jojo didn't consider herself a romantic, but his adoration undid her. And now she was the owner of three new dresses, a pair of wide legged pants, several silky blouses, a blazer, and a couple of pairs of kitten-heeled shoes. All the clothes were stylish and beautifully made. Just not what she would choose to wear.

'Let's celebrate your transformation with dinner. There's a wonderful little French bistro just around the corner.'

'Don't get carried away. I'm not one of your magic props. But you did just read my mind. I'm starving.'

'You are always hungry. In fact, if you were one of my

magic props then I would be getting worried that your size would make you difficult to conceal.'

If she didn't have her arms full of packages, then she would have thumped him. 'Just for that, I'm going to eat everything on the menu. At least two desserts.'

Nico topped up their glasses to finish the bottle of wine, and Jojo gave a contented sigh. 'That was delicious.' Her limbs were heavy and her belly full. 'I'm so glad you suggested this.'

'You've worked hard, you deserve to be spoiled. There's only two weeks until our big night and I know you are going to be magnifique.'

The ragout rumbled and Jojo wriggled. 'My solo. The rabbit trick. I've kind of got it, but what if I mess it up?'

'You won't. I have complete faith in you. It's a simple trick. I was nervous the first time I performed to a real audience. Every magician is. Look, if it goes wrong, just cover up. All you need to do is keep the audience enthralled and I know you can do that.'

The waiter cleared away their plates. 'Would you like to see the dessert menu?'

'No thank you,' Nico said without looking at Jojo.

When the waiter went to fetch the bill, Nico said, 'Oh I'm sorry I should have asked you bella.'

'It's okay. I'm full.'

'That is what I thought.'

They were the only customers in the bistro, as it was early in the evening and off the beaten track. Typical French music played and candles gave the bistro a soft glow. Any worries from the past few days melted away, the anonymous note, and now her anxiety about performing solo. Everything in her world was good. Last year when she was living in the squat and busking for a living, if she had looked into a crystal ball and seen herself today then she would not have believed her fortune. Nico reached across the table and covered her hand with his. She was so very lucky. If only Annie could find the happiness that she had.

'We could come here with Annie and Henry next Saturday.'

Nico withdrew his hand from hers. 'Do we have to see them? We hardly have any time to relax and when we do I like to have you to myself. I need my downtime. I have to entertain people for my living I don't want to do it on a Saturday evening.'

Jojo saw his point. It was as though he didn't know how to just be himself with other people and Annie and Henry were strangers to him. 'When you get to know Annie, it will be easier, but you never will if you won't meet her.'

'I have already met your friend.'

This was news to Jojo. How could Nico have met Annie unless it was when she left Jojo outside the changing rooms last week? 'Why didn't you tell me?'

'It was not important.' He shrugged. 'I forgot. Did your best friend not think to mention this to you?'

Jojo hadn't spoken to Annie since they last met. She didn't like to use the phone when Nico was with her, which was all the time, and Annie had said that she wasn't comfortable phoning Jojo at Nico's flat, even though Jojo reminded her it was her home, too. This was the problem. Until her best friend and partner met, they would continue to be wary of one another. 'So, what happened?'

'Nothing. I was asking Charlie to do something, and she happened to be with him. He said that he was showing her the way out. We said hello. There is nothing else to tell.'

Jojo wished she had been there. Hopefully, Annie didn't say anything to put Nico off. 'Well, I would still like you to meet properly. It's important to me, Nico.'

'If it is that important to you bella, then I will meet your friend for dinner.' Jojo held her gaze. 'Next Saturday,' he added.

'Thank you. Shall we book a table here before we leave?'

Jojo made the booking herself before he changed his mind. Nico was waiting by the door his arms loaded with shopping, dresses wrapped in tissue paper and boxes of shoes. 'Let's get a cab home. And then I have an idea of how we can end a perfect afternoon.'

17

If you value your life, keep away from him. Annie smoothed the letter flat as if by doing so she might release a hidden meaning. The stationery was unremarkable, typing paper and envelope that was typical of any office. Whoever wrote it must have done so at work. Where else would they have access to a word processor?

It frustrated Annie that she hadn't spoken to Jojo for days. They used to tell each other everything. Jojo didn't know that Annie had spent two evenings with Henry, and following another evening at Wine and Roses had stayed with him overnight. It had been okay. Conversation was easy: travel, theatre, and business. Henry was ambitious. He had talked about setting up his own travel agency and suggested that it was something they could do together. The idea excited Annie. Something inside her had opened up, letting in the light of possibility. A holiday rep abroad, an entrepreneur. With her shell of resistance prised open, Annie believed new opportunities awaited her.

On Saturday afternoon, they had used the pool and gym in

his complex to unwind after their morning at work. Lying on loungers in the solarium, he had said, 'We have to be ready to reap the rewards from technology. It's going to revolutionise the travel industry, give travel agents and holiday makers much more freedom and choice. I'm making plans, Annie. We have such a bright future ahead of us.' He had reached across to squeeze her hand and Annie felt important. Needed. As if in finding her, Henry now felt complete and ready to take on the world.

Desperate to share her news with Jojo, Annie ignored her reservations and dialled Nico's number. She would have to start thinking of it as Jojo's flat.

The phone rang five times and Annie was about to hang up when Nico answered. 'Nico Salvadori.' She could hear Jojo giggling.

'I'm sorry to disturb you on a Sunday, Nico, but would it be possible to have a quick word with Jojo?'

'Who is this?' He sounded formal. Suspicious. Didn't Jojo have any personal calls?

'Annie Daley. We met briefly at the Golden Globe last week.'

'So, we did. An unexpected pleasure. I will see if Jojo is available.' Now he sounded like her bloody PA. Annie made herself smile as she thanked him.

'Annie Apple Cheeks!' Jojo giggled again, as though Nico were tickling her.

Annie wished she hadn't phoned. They couldn't talk properly with Nico there. She would have to try to talk to Jojo at the theatre, besides she wanted to follow up on the anonymous note. Check that there was no real threat to Jojo. Wasn't that why Jojo had passed it to her? 'I know you can't really talk with Nico listening, but I have something to ask you. Would you mind if I did some snooping around to find out who delivered this anonymous note and when?'

'You sound like Velma in Scooby Doo.'

'Why can't I be Daphne, the glamorous one?'

'Because I am. You can be Scooby if you like.'

Annie laughed. 'So, is it okay?'

'Sure.' Jojo lowered her voice. 'Pedro, the caretaker, handed it to me. I doubt you'll find out anything useful, but I'm happy for you to ask around. I'm glad you called. I've booked us a table at a French Bistro we discovered. Next Saturday, if that's okay?'

'I think so. I'll check with Henry. I've got so much to tell you.'

'Okay. Can't wait. It will give you and Nico a chance to meet properly and for me to meet this mystery man. Sorry, better go. Nico's calling me.'

Annie hung up. Two minutes. That was the length of their conversation. At least they had a date. Maybe she would warm to Nico once she got to know him better.

'I'm pleased to see a glow back in your cheeks,' Annie's mum said, when Annie sat down for Sunday lunch.

'It's Hooray Henry that's stoked her fire,' Jessica said, helping herself to an extra roast potato.

Mum gave Jessica a *behave look* and then turned a *tell me more look* on Annie. Annie wondered whether there was a handbook of meaningful looks for mothers in training. Her mum's looks were very effective.

'We're going out again tomorrow evening. He's got tickets for My Fair Lady at The Adelphi Theatre. Head Office has regular booked seats as a perk for their executive staff.'

'Ooh, an executive and he has lovely manners. You must invite Henry over for dinner so that we can get to know him better.'

Jessica rolled her eyes at Annie.

Later, when the girls were washing up, Jessica said, 'I know you're all loved up with Hooray, but don't settle for the first man just because you've — well, you know?'

Annie knew where this was going and it wasn't a conversation that she wanted to have with her sister. Jessica probably thought Henry was her first. In a way, he was, because she had done her best to blot out the memory of being mauled at that party. It had been okay with Henry. Awkward. Embarrassing. For both of them. They had done it once and then when it was over, kind of acted like nothing had happened. Still, they had got it out of the way, so next time it would be less embarrassing. Jessica was annoying, but she meant well. 'So, you think it's too early to get engaged?'

Jessica's draw dropped. 'You're not?'

'No.' Annie flicked soap suds at her. 'I've got this. You can go and get ready to go bowling or whatever you and Gary have planned.'

The theatre door was open when Annie arrived at the Golden Globe; inside, a small queue had formed at the ticket booth. Jojo hadn't mentioned a matinee, and Annie was excited to be caught up in the buzz of anticipation as theatre goers exchanged greetings and chattered about the show. It would give her an excuse to talk to the staff and a reason for being there.

Hocus Pocus. Acclaimed dance troupe from television's New Faces, a poster informed Annie. She had watched the TV talent show but didn't remember the act.

'Will there be other acts performing with Hocus Pocus?' Annie asked when she reached the front of the queue.

'Not today. The next performance, with the full cast of magicians and dancers, is the Starlight show.' He handed Annie a glossy flier. Annie searched for Jojo, who she found as a tiny thumbnail in an inset, glimpsed just behind Nico who was posing for the camera — more male model than magician. 'If you want a ticket, you'd best book now, as there are only a few seats left.'

The matinee started in thirty minutes, and the people behind her in the queue seemed happy to chat. 'Yes, please. Two tickets for the best seats available and one for Hocus Pocus today.'

Whilst the assistant completed the transaction, Annie looked around her. The Golden Globe had the glamour of a West End theatre and the intimacy of a private club. People were chatting as though they all knew each other. Jojo said that Nico had a following of devoted fans and Annie wondered whether there were a few there today. She tuned into a conversation between a group of young women.

'Isn't that Adele Pearson?'

'Who?'

'She's big in the dance world. A choreographer for the stars. Doesn't she own Mango Studios? I've seen her on the telly.'

'Well, you know Bobbi teaches there? Maybe she knows Adele.'

Annie saw the woman they were referring to. She looked like a celebrity — expensive, aloof, and alluring.

'Thirty-eight pounds,' the assistant said. Annie wrote a cheque.

'Would it be possible to leave a note for one of the performers?'

A receipt was handed to her with an envelope of tickets. 'You can leave it with me and I'll do my best to deliver, but some performers don't accept fan mail unless it comes through their fan club.'

Annie nodded, and then she stepped back to allow access to the ticket booth. She found a small table with leaflets and fliers and used this to lean on as she wrote a note for Jojo. *Just testing out the delivery system. You didn't tell me there was a matinee today. Will watch the show. If you are free at the interval, meet me in Cake Presto. Annie xx.*

The foyer was empty. Ten minutes until curtain up. 'Do you have an envelope you could spare?' She asked the assistant.

He found one and some Sellotape. 'Will that do?'

Annie smiled. He was very obliging. 'I'm Jojo Evans's friend. I wanted to let Jojo know I was here so we could meet in the interval.'

'Ah Jojo. Nico's assistant. She's a live wire, that one. A burst of energy. Lights up this place. Has a good heart too. I delivered another note to her not so long ago.'

Annie couldn't believe how quickly and easily she had stumbled on this information. 'You must be Pedro!'

The man beamed. 'I am. Ticket sales. Caretaker. Occasional stagehand. You name it!'

'Then you must know, Charlie?'

He smiled broadly. 'There's another star. He might be behind the scenes, but that boy is one of the brightest stars in this place. Charlie and Jojo have between them brightened this place up. Now, if you want to see the show, you'd better get a move on. It's about to start. Don't worry about your note; I'll make sure it reaches Jojo before the interval.'

'Who left Jojo's other note?' Annie said with a mischievous smile. 'Does she have an admirer that she is keeping a secret from me?'

'Pretty girl. Must have lots of admirers. But I couldn't tell you who left the note. It was odd because I found it behind the counter here and nobody seems to know who left it.'

A bell sounded, then an announcement asking the audience to take their seats. Annie would have liked to question Pedro some more, but it would raise suspicion if she missed the show for that purpose. So, Annie found her seat and settled down to be entertained. Hocus Pocus was contemporary and sexy. Annie had been expecting something like Vegas, having seen the girls in their feathers and sparkle, but this was more a Top of the Pops act. All the girls were beautiful, but one of them stood out and Annie guessed that this was Bobbi. Jojo had spoken of her. She seemed more confident and had a stage presence which kept drawing Annie's eyes back to her. When the interval came forty-five minutes later, Annie was surprised. She hadn't expected a dance troupe to be so entertaining.

Cake Presto was quieter than the last time Annie visited. The audience for Hocus Pocus were buying refreshments from the little bar in the foyer, and the teatime rush seemed to be over. Unfortunately, that meant the scones and cakes had too. Henry hadn't mentioned dinner. My Fair Lady started at seven-thirty and they were meeting at six. To be on the safe side, Annie ordered a toasted cheese sandwich with her pot of tea. She was tackling a tricky string of melted cheese when Charlie joined her.

'Ooh.' Annie tilted her head to try to catch the errant strand. 'Sorry about that.'

'Pedro asked me to deliver a note to Jojo from her friend before the interval. Jojo's being sawn in two or having swords thrust in her and so probably best to wait until she's been put back together again. I guessed it was you.' He looked a little uncertain. 'Okay if I join you instead?'

'Be my guest. I'm afraid Mrs Brew is out of cakes.'

Charlie winked. 'We'll see about that.'

Annie watched in amusement as Mrs Brew disappeared into her kitchen and returned with a Rumbaba. Charlie shot her a look and Annie's heart stumbled.

'I guess you easily burn off calories with all of that lifting and carrying.'

'You'll share it with me?' He was already cutting the syrupy donut in half. Annie found herself gazing at the blond hairs on Charlie's forearm. The way his bones rotated as he slid a knife under one portion, the tightening of his biceps. He caught her eye, and she blushed.

'Be careful not to mark that gorgeous dress.' Charlie slid a plate towards her. He had long fingers. Neatly trimmed nails.

Annie shook herself and tried to remember if Henry had neat nails, the shape of his hands, but drew a blank. She tried to focus on why she was there. 'Charlie, when we first met, and I asked you about the falling gantry, I got the impression that you didn't think it was an accident.'

He leant back in his chair. 'You're right. I didn't.'

'And now?'

Charlie sighed. 'I don't know. Jojo could have been seriously hurt. Maybe I over reacted. It was just the way Nico seemed to know what was about to happen.'

'That makes no sense. Why would Nico want to harm Jojo?'

'He wouldn't. But then he saved her. Nico was with me when I checked everything was securely fastened. Maybe I'm just trying to let myself off the hook. I couldn't live with myself if I hurt Jojo.'

Ah, Annie thought, he's in love with her. She wasn't surprised; everyone loved Jojo.

'Are you going to eat any of this now Mrs Brew has

honoured us with the bakes she keeps hidden away for important people?'

Annie laughed. 'So, you're important, are you?'

'I am, and so are you. Jojo's lucky to have you as her friend.'

'I think I'm the lucky one. Jojo introduced me to places and experiences that I would never have considered. If Jojo's adventurous, I'm the opposite. Jojo is colourful and glamorous. In comparison, I'm a bit monochrome. Sensible.'

Charlie took a forkful of Rum baba and pushed the plate towards Annie. What had she been thinking, opening up like that? Best fill her mouth with cake to stop it from motoring on.

'I think you're very glamorous. Especially this afternoon, dressed up for the matinee. Oh, did you want to watch the second half? I forgot about the show.'

'No. I enjoyed the first half. If Jojo met me for tea, I would not have gone back in.' For some reason, she didn't want to tell Charlie that she was dressed for her evening date with Henry.

'I think you're adventurous too.' He waggled his eyebrows. 'Are you up for a dare?'

'What is it?' cautious Annie said, but before Charlie could answer she said, 'Don't tell me. Whatever the dare, I'm in!'

18

'And that is how it's done!' Jojo held a rabbit in each hand as she took a deep bow to an imaginary audience. She had been practicing alone for what felt like hours, but it had paid off. Pixie and Muffin must have become bored with their game because they were at last complying. She snuggled them to her and then lifted each one to plant a kiss on silk and settled them in their basket. Charlie hadn't popped in to see if she needed anything or to joke around, which was unusual. The matinee must be keeping him busy. Nico said that he would be in the magician's resource library upstairs, as he was developing a new trick. Only members of the Magic Circle were permitted entry to that sacred room and so Jojo hung around at the foot of the stairs, hoping to catch one of the magicians. She didn't have to wait long as Max in his dinner suit, an outfit he wore for every occasion, made his entrance as though he were hosting a show – sternum lifted, his hands momentarily held out as though waiting for the applause to die down. He hadn't even seen

Jojo. This was just Max. Like Nico, he was a full-time performer.

'Max, is Nico up there?' Jojo said, when he had descended.

'Darling. I thought you were waiting for me.' He twirled his handlebar moustache.

'I lost track of time, so he might be looking for me.'

'Then let him look. It is good not to be too available. Come and join me for a little snifter. He will find you soon enough, much to my regret.'

'Thank you, Max, maybe another time. Did you see him in the library?'

'Alas no. I have not seen him all afternoon, although I did have a little snooze. It's very comfy up there. Pink gin hour. Are you sure I can't tempt you?'

Jojo felt a bit deflated, with no Charlie or Nico to applaud her success in mastering the rabbit trick. On her way to the changing room, she met Philippe, who looked like an ostrich, as he was carrying several burlesque fans. 'Have you seen Nico?'

He puffed his lips, and the feathers rippled. 'Saw him leave about an hour ago. These feathers they get up my nose. Merde.'

As he left her, Philippe flipped one fan to cover his backside and did a little wiggle for her benefit. She forced a chuckle, but her mind was on Nico's unexplained absence.

An envelope had been pinned to her locker with one of Bunty's fridge magnets. Nico. But when she got closer, Jojo recognised Annie's writing. She tore open the envelope and checked her watch. Perfect timing. The interval was about to start and with Nico out of the way, she could enjoy a well-earned break with her friend. On cue, Hocus Pocus writhed and wiggled into the changing room as though their limbs were still charged with energy. Skin glistened. Faces flushed.

'Jojo. Thank God. Jojo's here!' Sly called from the changing room to someone on the other side of the door. 'You know how to do that trapeze thing at the end of our act? You know the finale where Bobbi is lifted from the back of the auditorium and does a few moves before landing on the stage?'

'Yes, of course.' Jojo didn't add that she had taught Bobbi the routine.

'Great. We need you to save the show.'

'Where's Bobbi?'

'She did her solo, and that was the last we saw of her. *Please* Jojo. We don't have much time. Just put on these angel wings and headdress. Your catsuit's fine. In fact, it's the perfect colour.'

'I've not warmed up. Can't you just cut that bit? Bobbi might turn up in a minute. It's not like her to miss a performance.' Jojo detected a look passing between the girls.

'We have thirty minutes. That should be long enough to warm up.' Sly gave a pleading look.

'Okay. Let me have a position towards the back for the dance routines. I kind of know them, but I may need to follow a lead.' Now the decision was made, Jojo couldn't wait to get on the stage. It would surprise Annie to see her flying over the audience.

They had been dancing for almost an hour without a break. Hocus Pocus looked daisy fresh, but Jojo was flagging. She had lost the stamina and strength gained through hours of practice as a dancer. There was no way she could have performed for the entire show.

At the back of the auditorium, Jojo scanned the audience, looking for Annie's bob. 'Ready?' Lenny had popped down from his sound and lighting box to help Jojo into the harness.

The music built to a crescendo. Spotlights danced at the back of the auditorium. Jojo took a deep breath, ready to launch herself. The biggest spotlight swung across the back of the theatre and the audience swivelled in their seats. It settled on a figure who tumbled into the light in a fit of giggles, burnished a blonde bob, then veered away to follow Jojo, as she lunged herself forward in an angelic pose.

Jojo had no time to dwell on the owner of that distinctive blonde bob as she took to the air. The simple glide that she had taught Bobbi was transformed to a breath-taking display of aerial acrobatics. The audience gasped and clapped in delight as Jojo somersaulted above their heads. This was what she had missed. When she alighted on the stage, the audience clapped and cheered as though it was the end of the show and Jojo was a little embarrassed at having stolen the limelight.

Hocus Pocus did not share Jojo's recriminations; they crowded around her in the changing room.

'That was incredible. Where did you learn to do that?'

'I've seen nothing like it. You were amazing.'

'When the spotlight fell on that woman, I was afraid she would put you off. I think we all held our breath for a moment. Of course, we had no idea that you were an experienced aerial acrobat. I didn't even know there was such a thing.'

'What have I missed? Apart from my act. I am *so sorry*, ladies.' Bobbi's entrance had gone unnoticed in the commotion, and now Sly and Bunty fell away from Jojo and busied themselves with getting changed.

'They asked me to cover for you,' Jojo said.

Bobbi put her head in her hands and then shook her head. 'Thank God you were here to step in. I didn't have a choice.'

Sly turned to Bobbi, her face set. Jojo could feel the rest of the troupe's attention as they pretended to be occupied, stealing glances at one another. 'What happened?'

Bobbi took a deep breath. 'I got a message from my landlord. He said that if I didn't pay my rent immediately, he would evict me. I asked Pedro to let you know. I took a cab and thought I would get back in time, but when I arrived, he was throwing my things into the hallway. It was ghastly.'

'Did you manage to sort things?' Jojo asked gently. She knew Bobbi would find this confession humiliating.

'For now. I'm really sorry.' Bobbi kept her eyes on Sly until her face softened, and then she looked at each girl in turn.

'You have Jojo to thank for stepping in,' Bunty said.

'I am truly grateful.' Bobbi squeezed Jojo's arm. 'Thank you.'

Nico was waiting for Jojo outside the changing room. 'Ready?'

'Where were you?'

'I told you – in the resource library.'

Jojo narrowed her eyes. 'I saw Max, and he said that he hadn't seen you there all afternoon.'

Nico laughed. 'Max? Really? If he's not half cut, he's sleeping it off. I was there. You should have popped your head around the door.'

Jojo didn't know what to believe. It was true. Max did like a drink. She decided to let it go. 'And break the magician's code? What kind of evil would befall me if I should break that secret vow?'

Nico wrapped his arm around her. 'I heard you stepped in for Bobbi. Aren't you glad that I persuaded you to wear lycra for rehearsals? An angel in hot-pants wouldn't have worked?'

'It would have been a stylish angel.'

'Seriously Jojo. Why aren't you wearing one of the outfits we bought in Hartleys? Those rags you buy from market stalls downgrade your appearance. You are a beautiful woman. You should wear classical clothes.'

Nico said nothing else about her performance and so the news of her triumph could not have reached him. When it did, he would surely agree to give her more freedom on the stage. She had perfected the rabbit trick and showed what else she was capable of. Jojo smiled and hugged to herself a feeling of success. Had Annie seen her act? Was that Annie at the back of the auditorium? It couldn't have been. Annie would laugh when Jojo told her that for one second, she thought the woman who stumbled through a curtain giggling like a maniac was her.

They were greeted on leaving the theatre with the usual band of followers wanting autographs and tricks. Jojo hung back and watched as Nico did his thing. There was one woman with immaculate makeup, salon curls, and an outfit that would look at home on Dallas, an American soap Annie was addicted to. Nico 'found' this woman's diamond ring in the fist of another woman who was dismayed. A ripple of applause. Nico took his bow.

As they walked away arm in arm, Nico said, 'Now that is the image you should go for. Sophisticated. Elegant.' He looked disparagingly at Jojo's heavily netted 1950s polka dot skirt. 'Not Minnie Mouse.'

And in those three words, Nico crushed the elation that had begun as a song in her heart.

19

Henry had stubby, bitten nails. The skin around his cuticles red and sore. Their evening at The Adelphi Theatre was not a great success. Annie put it down to being overtired after her afternoon at the Golden Globe, and hungry. When she had suggested they find somewhere to eat before the show, Henry said that restaurants inflated their prices for pre-theatre diners. He had prepared by packing an egg sandwich to eat in Victoria Embankment Gardens. Annie didn't need to go hungry. Henry offered to share his sandwich and suggested Annie buy something, but she felt like a petulant child – irritable and sulky. It wasn't Henry's fault. He tried to please her, but everything about him, the way his teeth clicked when he chewed, his disparaging remarks about some teenagers who passed by their bench, annoyed her.

When they had made themselves comfortable in the dress circle, Annie relaxed and enjoyed the show. Periodically, her mind would stray as she replayed the dare. It wasn't really a dare. Charlie assured her that the tunnel was safe and he went ahead of her. At first there was a dim light, but as they got deeper into the tunnel, it faded.

'Are you okay?' Charlie called from the darkness ahead. There was a scuffle and Annie shrieked, thinking it was rats. Charlie laughed. 'That was me, moving a crate. It will get lighter towards the other end.' He must have stayed still because a couple of seconds later, Annie drew close. Charlie smelt of soap and washing powder. The pipes jangled. 'Ooh, the ghost of Molly May. Ready? Race you!'

He was gone, and Annie lurched after him, giggling at the ridiculousness of their prank. Above them, the audience was watching the show and Annie felt like a mischievous child. There was a loud clattering behind her and Annie charged on, bursting through the hidden door in a fit of giggles. At precisely that moment, a spotlight illuminated her and Annie took a bow. Then it swerved upwards to alight on a trapeze artist. Charlie was waiting for her at the back of the auditorium. He grabbed her hand, and they slipped out of the back into the foyer.

'Don't tell me you're not adventurous or spontaneous. Annie Apple Cheeks.'

Annie was grinning so widely it hurt. 'How did you know Jojo's daft name for me?'

'It suits you, but if you don't like it, I won't use it again. Your cheeks are as red as rosy apples.'

Annie didn't know if she liked his use of her childhood name or not. 'I think I outgrew that name about a zillion years ago. But just now I felt as though I was eight years old and so I guess it's fitting.'

They had parted as friends. Maybe she had been a bit over excited when she met up with Henry. That wasn't Henry's fault.

Their evening at The Adelphi ended on a good note. Henry

bought her a glass of wine at the interval and on the way home insisted on stopping at a Little Chef where he bought her an omelette and chips. He drank a decaffeinated coffee as he watched her eat, sneaking the odd chip.

'That's better,' Annie said, contented and full, her equilibrium restored.

They decided not to see each other for the rest of that week. Henry had to spend a night in Birmingham for a conference and Annie was happy to have a bit of time on her own before they met up again on Saturday for the double date with Jojo and Nico.

The day after the matinee, Jojo phoned her at work. 'I'm sorry I didn't meet you for the interval.'

Annie could hear the low hum of traffic. 'That's okay. Where are you?'

'In a telephone box near the Golden Globe. I've got a handful of coins and there's nobody waiting outside.'

Lisa rearranged some brochures on a shelf close to Annie's desk and so she dropped her voice. 'It's okay. Charlie told me you were busy.'

'Did you see me?' Jojo sounded breathless. Excited.

Annie concentrated on trying to remember if she had seen Jojo. Why would she? 'No. I thought you were rehearsing.'

'I was in the second act! I was hoping you'd seen my aerial acrobatics. I stood in for Bobbi at the last minute. I couldn't see you in the audience, so you must have left. A woman who burst out of the hidden tunnel into the spotlight giggling looked just like you and, for one crazy moment, I thought it was.' Jojo was laughing. The memory made Annie grin, but she didn't correct Jojo.

'I only watched the first half, but I talked to Pedro and he says that he has no idea who left the note. It must be someone who has access to a word processor, but that doesn't really help. Has everything else been okay, Jojo?'

'Yes. Don't worry about that stupid note. I'm going to forget all about it. I phoned you for two things — well, three, really. First, to apologise, which I've done. Oh, and to check arrangements for Saturday night. But the most important thing — it sounded as though you had some news to share with me. Spill the beans. What's happenin'? Are you in lurve?'

It was true, Annie had been desperate to share her news with Jojo — how her relationship with Henry was progressing, but that initial excitement had quietened and on reflection she felt that there wasn't much to tell. That was the trouble with talking so infrequently. It was like missing chapters of one another's lives. They had grown used to knowing everything about each other. Now that she had a man of her own, Annie realised that closeness, sharing the details of each day, transferred to the significant other.

'You know I'm immune,' Annie whispered. Lisa was in the staff room, but a couple of punters had just come into the shop, 'but things are going well. Now, where are we meeting you on Saturday and what time?' When the pips went, Annie hung up. So, Charlie hadn't told Jojo about their silliness. The thought that they shared a secret warmed her.

The afternoon passed quickly. Feeling a little guilty for taking a personal call, Annie took the next two sets of customers. She had booked an all-girls' holiday in Ibiza, and a packaged holiday to Majorca for a family of four, when she took her break. The magazine Henry had lent her was on the coffee table. Annie picked it up and flipped through the glossy pages whilst she sipped her tea. Henry was right, the travel industry seemed to be spreading its wings with destinations further afield, and tailored holidays for every taste. She had applied for the holiday rep job in Spain, just to see what the response would be. That was almost a week ago. Since then, Annie had become less anxious about fending for herself – finding a better paid job and accommodation she could afford. Henry spoke as if they had a long-term future together and Annie could see this happening. She wasn't about to move in with him, but maybe. Mid-twenties were a good time to settle down. Annie's imagination took her to the future where she and Henry were running a family travel business. They had a couple of children, a boy and a girl. A comfortable house in Fenwood. She was deciding whether it would be a new build or something older with character when Sarah interrupted her thoughts.

'Names are going to be picked at random for the Greek Islands' holiday. I *really* hope it's me this time. Could you put in a word with your head office man?'

'You know it doesn't work like that. Here, take a look at this article about the Cyclades Islands. Wouldn't it be glorious to swim in that sea? To feel the warm sun on your back?'

They sighed in unison. It had been the rainiest March on record. Great for selling holidays, but Sarah was right; it would be good to have one of their own to look forward to.

20

Jojo had hoped that Nico would return home whilst she was relaxing in the bath. Then they could get ready together before meeting Annie and Henry at the bistro. The water was lukewarm and so she stepped out and towelled herself dry. Five-thirty. Even if they took a cab, they only had one hour before leaving. Nico would just have to do a quick turnaround. He always looked immaculate anyway.

'Now, dressing-up box, where are you going to take me today?' Jojo said, as she marched around the bedroom in a bathrobe, looking for her trunk, which had been moved from the bottom of their bed. It wasn't as if it was easy to hide. She checked under the bed, just a stray pair of knickers which she retrieved for the washing basket. 'Why does Nico have to tidy everything away?' Jojo opened the wardrobe doors. Nico had hung her new clothes up, but the contents of her dressing-up box were not there. She closed the doors firmly on this palate of blandness – shades of cream and brown. If not in the wardrobe or under the bed where would Nico have hidden her clothes? She kicked one of his handmade leather shoes.

The spare room. Of course. He had probably made some space for her in there. She was perfectly happy to dig around in the old trunk, but Nico had been nagging her to at least hang her clothes up. Fine. She would wear a beautiful black beaded 1930s dress, which she had bought at an auction. Annie had gone with her to the antique auction in Fenwood Social Club a couple of years ago. Unknown to Jojo, Annie had been bidding on her behalf, and so between them, they pushed up the price. Every outfit had a memory. They were her friends.

Since moving in with Nico, Jojo had rarely been in this room. There was no need. It was a little dark and gloomy as the one small window looked out onto the back of another building. The wardrobe was full of Nico's formal evening suits, some covered in plastic protectors, but none of her clothes. In the bottom right-hand corner of the wardrobe was a safe. Jojo glared at it, full of resentment. Nico had a secret safe, but for some reason, he thought it was okay to mess with her things. She slammed the wardrobe door shut. It had to be somewhere. Not under the spare bed. Or the hallway cupboard. Where else could it be? Her heart thumped with anger and frustration. Another round of the flat, checking every cupboard even though none of them were big enough to swallow her trunk. In the living room, she sank to her knees and hammered her fists against the floor. It was past six. Nico had promised to be home an hour ago. The door to their building opened and then closed. Jojo leapt to her feet. 'About bloody time.' He had better have a good explanation for hiding her trunk. She rushed to their door, recriminations filling her head. 'Ooh, it had better be good, Nico.'

Their door was locked. Jojo forced the handle, but it made no difference. Footsteps continued past their flat and up the stairs to the floor above. Jojo panicked. What if there was a fire? Her keys were missing from the dish on the hall table. He must have taken hers by mistake. Unless, no, she was being ridiculous, Nico wouldn't intentionally lock her in. But if he was crazy enough to lock her in the flat … what about her clothes? He couldn't have thrown them out. She would never forgive him.

Jojo stomped from room to room, burning up with fury. She didn't want to believe him capable of this cruelty. Jojo rattled the front door again. It was definitely locked. She kicked it hard and then leapt in pain. Miserable and exhausted from her rampage through the flat, she slid down the wall and, with her hands clasped around her knees, sobbed and wailed.

Soon, Annie would be waiting for them at the Bistro. The thought calmed Jojo. If Nico had done this, there was no way she could carry on living with him, but he would be home soon. She had to act fast. The caretaker must have a key to their flat. Jojo took a few deep breaths to calm herself. First, she had to get dressed and then look for the caretaker's phone number. If she caught a cab to the Bistro, arriving before Nico, then she could escape with Annie. But where would she live? She would have to leave the Golden Globe. Disappointment, anger, and disbelief battled for a place in Jojo's heart. The beige dress she pulled over her head may have been hundreds of pounds of French chic, but to Jojo, it felt like a straitjacket. A few hours earlier, she had the perfect life. Now, she felt as though she were staring into an abyss about to freefall. Jojo slipped on a pair of kitten heel shoes and piled her hair on top of her head. She loved Nico, and she loved her job. Maybe she should wait for Nico to get home, allow him to explain. There had to be an explanation that would erase this nightmare. Her breath slowed, and her heart, although broken, had a steadier beat. Whatever Nico had to say, she needed to find the caretaker and ask him to unlock the door.

In Nico's study, Jojo tried the drawers of his desk. At least he hadn't locked them. She found a collection of leather-bound notebooks in the top right drawer. Jojo couldn't resist opening one. Her heart ached as she imagined him, hair flopping over one eye, capturing his thoughts and ideas before they disappeared. She traced his scrawling words with her index finger. *O Nico.* Then she reminded herself that he had imprisoned her and disposed of her clothes collection, knowing how precious it was to her. He was a monster; she didn't know him at all. It was getting late. Annie and Henry would be at the bistro by now.

Jojo tried the top left drawer. A collection of pencils, two packs of cards, a small prism which she held up to the light. Green, blue and violet rays fell across the room. She held a rainbow in her palm. Stunned in rapture, Jojo passed a hand through its beam. Was the Incredible Nico an illusion? Her blissful happiness as transient as this rainbow? Jojo replaced the prism and returned her attention to searching the drawer.

A glossy flier for *The Incredible Nico. Celebrations. Corporate events.* And there was the goddess, Meryl. Not leggy like Bianca Jagger. Meryl was petite, more Audrey Hepburn with her elfin cut. Jojo looked closely, to see if she could detect madness in her eyes. There was nothing about the pretty woman at Nico's side that suggested she was crazy. Bobbi was right — Meryl was stunning. Brown eyes that seemed almost too big for her heart-shaped face. There was no point sitting there feeling eaten up with jealousy; she had to keep focused on getting out of the flat.

There was a slim leather-bound address book in a similar style to the notebooks. At least she could find the caretaker's number. There was just about time to get a cab if he unlocked the door for her. The number hadn't been recorded under C for caretaker, so it must be under his name. Jojo racked her brain. Had Nico mentioned the caretaker's name? He lived in the basement flat with his wife. She had greeted them in her comings and goings, but wasn't sure whether she had ever known their names. Jojo started at A to work her way through the alphabet. There were very few entries. When she got to S, there was a four-digit number under safe. Could there be a spare set of keys in the safe? Dare she look? It felt wrong, an intrusion of his privacy. Nico would be furious. *Fine. He couldn't be angrier than I am right now. Sod Nico.* Jojo memorised the number and put everything back in the drawers as she found them.

Kneeling in front of the safe, the scent of leather from Nico's shoes and a faint trace of his aftershave sat with her, chastising her for trespassing. It would probably be empty anyway, or it would hold the secrets of the Magic Circle. Jojo's hands trembled. Despite her bravado, she was afraid that Nico would catch her in the act. The version of Nico that she didn't know. What else was he capable of?

There were no keys in the safe, just a brown envelope and a reel of cine film. Jojo turned it over in her hands. What could be on a film that warranted it being locked in a safe? Her stomach lurched when she read Meryl written in capital letters on one side of the tin. Nico might have said Meryl was dead to him, but this film was proof that he was hanging onto her memory. A clock in the spare room ticked. He could arrive home any minute. The keys weren't in there. She had to lock the safe before he discovered her prying. Jojo started to close the safe door but couldn't help herself; she had to look in the brown envelope.

It was stuffed full of papers, each folded and of varying size. She placed the pile of documents down, careful not to disturb the order. The top one looked new as it had not yellowed like some others. She sat very still and listened to the silence. Then she unfolded the paper and her heart skipped a beat. Nicholas Brown, magician, married Meryl Wilson, magician's assistant on 3rd September 1978. Two years ago. Nico was married. Nicholas Brown not Nico Salvadori. His key turned in the lock.

'Bella. My bella. I'm so sorry, I took your keys by mistake,' he called from the hall.

Jojo stuffed the papers back into the envelope and threw them into the safe before closing it. She scrambled to her feet and darted from the spare room as Nico came out of their bedroom.

'Oh, there you are. You look amazing. I am so, so, sorry. It was only when I put my hand in my pocket just now that I found two sets of keys. My mind is so full of the Gala.'

The sight of her beloved Nico, his hair tussled, and eyes begging forgiveness, almost made Jojo forget his betrayal. She glared at him. 'I will forgive you for locking me in the flat if you tell me what you've done with my dressing-up box,' but already she was weakening.

'Oh, you noticed.'

'Of course, I did. Why else would I be dressed up like this?'

'Because we are going out to dinner with your friends? Do I need to change or am I okay as I am?'

'Nico. Tell me. Where are my things?'

Nico gently positioned her in front of the wardrobe mirror. 'What do you see?'

'I admit the clothes are well-cut classics and look amazing – but it's not me.'

'I see a woman who is the epitome of French Spring chic. The paparazzi will be following you instead of Lady Diana Spencer. They will know that you are a star by how you dress. You see, bella? It is not enough to be a great performer. You have to dress the part. All of your actions – how you live, must say: I am special. I am successful.'

Jojo swallowed hard. 'Please, just tell me what you've done with my dressing-up box?'

'Okay, here's the deal. Humour me by wearing the clothes I bought you for just one week. When you see the difference, how people react to you, then you will understand why it is important that you dress like a woman who has class.'

'And after one week?'

'You can have your clothes back, but I promise you, you will no longer want to wear your old rags.'

'Just tell me where they are, Nico.'

He grinned. 'I will conjour them back. Just one week?'

Jojo nodded her agreement, relieved that Nico was not the bad guy she had imagined him to be. Nico was a complex man, exciting and charismatic. He may drive her crazy at times, but she would rather live with the enigmatic Nico Salvadori than an ordinary Nicholas Brown. She could understand him changing his name for the stage, but keeping his marriage a secret was another matter. When the time was right, she would get him to confess. But not now, because Annie and Henry would be waiting for them at the bistro.

21

'Are you sure we're in the right place?' Henry checked his watch. It was seven-fifteen.

'I asked for a reservation made by Jojo Evans, so we must be. Jojo's always late.'

'Who is her partner? Remind me. The Amazing Bongo, or something?'

Annie sighed. 'You know very well that's not his name. Nico. It's really important that this goes well. I must admit I didn't take to him straightaway, but Jojo's my best friend and so I'm going to try hard to be charming and hospitable.'

Henry took her hand across the table. 'You don't have to try. It comes naturally to you. Is this them?'

Annie turned to see a woman, who initially she didn't recognise as Jojo, being led to the table by a waiter. The outfit and hairstyle were lovely, but it wasn't Jojo's usual image. Nico followed, his hand resting on the small of her back. They were a striking couple, and heads turned as they made their way across the restaurant.

Jojo made the introductions; she seemed a little subdued to

Annie. Henry pumped Nico's hand as though he was selling encyclopaedias. 'Pleased to meet you. We were wondering if we had come to the wrong restaurant.'

Jojo kissed Annie on both cheeks, a formality that was strange to them. When they had settled into their seats, Nico said, 'I apologise for being a little late. Jojo was ready on time, but I'm afraid I got delayed.' He exchanged a look with Jojo. 'Let me order some drinks. Champagne?'

'We have a jug of water,' Henry said.

'In that case,' he signalled to a waiter. 'A magnum of champagne. Merci.'

Henry scowled. 'I thought you were Italian.'

'Naturalmente, but this is a French restaurant. The waiters are French.'

Annie squeezed Henry's hand under the table because she couldn't throttle him. 'Champagne. Perfect. And what a delightful bistro. Everything on the menu looks so good.'

'Nico and I discovered it last weekend, and I knew you would love it. The food's excellent.' Jojo looked from Nico to Annie, as if willing them to get on.

'I recommend the escargots followed by steak tartare, or the ragout.'

'Yes, the ragout is delicious,' Jojo said.

Annie watched them carefully. Jojo was different. Less exuberant, but she seemed happy and from the way she kept glancing at Nico, as if seeking his approval, Annie surmised she was still very much in love. It was obvious that Nico was completely enamoured with Jojo: the look in his eyes, the way he kept touching her, stroking a hair from her face, holding her hand, smoothing a napkin across her lap.

'Are you ready for your big show next Saturday?' Annie said.

Jojo and Nico held one another's gaze, then Nico replied, 'Absolutely. I hope you are both coming?'

'Of course. We can't wait, can we, Henry?'

Henry was studying the menu. 'Fish goujons and frittes, for me.' He snapped the menu shut.

'Fish and chips?' Nico said. 'And to start?'

'One course is plenty.'

The champagne arrived and Nico poured. Annie tried to catch Jojo's eye to signal how embarrassing and awkward it all was, but Jojo seemed far away. Henry and Nico were so different. It fell upon Annie to keep the conversation going and to smooth over any misunderstandings between the two men.

Jojo and Annie both ordered escargots followed by Ragout, and Nico the escargots, and steak tartare. After some persuasion, Henry agreed to have Salad Verte as a starter but embarrassed Annie by exclaiming over the price and then he had to check that there was no red cabbage.

Somehow, they made it through the meal. The food was delicious and had Annie been sharing the meal with Jojo, or Charlie – why had his name popped into her head? Then it would have been a wonderful evening. Maybe they could revisit on their own.

'L'addition, s'il vous plaît,' Nico said to their waiter as he cleared their plates. 'I insist on paying for this meal, as we kept you all waiting.'

Henry did not object, but Annie was uncomfortable. 'It wasn't a problem at all. Let's split it.'

When Nico refused, Annie accepted graciously. 'Then we insist on paying next time.' Secretly, she hoped she would not have to endure another painful evening of Nico and Henry sparring.

When the waiter returned with the bill, Henry puffed out his chest and said, 'Grazie. È stato un pasto eccellente.'

'Ah tu parli Italiano. Come hai imparato a parlare così fluentemente?' The waiter became animated, obviously delighted with Henry.

'Lavoro nel settore dei viaggi ma il mio amico qui è italiano. I told him I am fluent in Italian as I work in the travel industry, but my friend here is Italian.'

The waiter turned to Nico. 'Sei italiano?' There was an uncomfortable silence and Annie worried that Henry might have embarrassed Nico. He might be of Italian heritage, but that didn't mean he could speak Italian. Jojo seemed unperturbed, and so Annie relaxed. Nico was composed and replied. 'Si. But let us not exclude the ladies. I am sorry my money seems to have attached itself to your ceiling.' They all looked up to see a twenty-pound note held fast to the Artex.

'How did it get up there?' the waiter exclaimed. Other waiters came over and soon they had the attention of everyone in the restaurant.

'Never mind. If you could change this twenty-pound note. I should be able to give you the right money.'

The waiter took the twenty and returned with two tens. He kept glancing up at the ceiling, trying to work out how the note was staying put. He counted one note into Nico's palm. 'It is a trick, no?' He went to pass the second note, but it was no longer in his hand.

'I can see how you make your money,' Nico said, nodding to the ceiling where the ten-pound note had joined the twenty.

'It is not possible!'

Annie stole a glance at Jojo. She was watching Nico with adoration in her eyes. Henry shuffled in his seat, signalling that it was time for them to go.

When the notes had reappeared beneath the tablecloth and

the restaurant owner was pouring them all a complimentary glass of brandy, Annie gave their apologies.

The evening had depressed Annie and Henry's ranting on the car journey home did not help.

'You know he's not Italian?' Henry said.

'Does it matter?'

'It matters that he finds it necessary to lie about who he is. *Everything* about this evening was a show. Your friend seemed okay, although a bit dull.'

'Jojo is *not* dull.' Annie would not discuss Jojo with Henry, but she was dismayed at this new image. First the dancer gear, and now she resembled a Stepford wife. However, she seemed happy, and that was all Annie wanted for her friend.

Jojo phoned the following afternoon. 'I'm so sorry we were late arriving. Henry seems nice. Not what I was expecting.'

'He is. Nico's great too. Very entertaining. Why? What were you expecting?'

'I don't know – someone with a bit more Kazaam. You've been so un-Annie-like these past few weeks I thought it must have been Henry's influence, but he didn't come across as an Annie-changer.'

'So, you think I need to change, do you?' Annie laughed. She had missed these silly conversations. 'You seemed different yourself.' This was said in a more serious tone.

'Oh, you mean the outfit? It felt like time for a change. Did I tell you Nico bought me a whole new wardrobe: dresses, shoes, jackets – the works, from Hartleys? He's so generous.'

Annie felt as though Jojo was slipping away from her. Was she wrong to hold her back? To stop her changing into a person who she didn't recognise. 'Where's Nico now?'

'Right here. It was Nico who suggested I phone you to apologise again for being late.'

'That was thoughtful of him, but there's no need. It's the

Starlight show next Saturday. What are you and Nico doing afterwards?'

'Apparently there's a party after the Easter Gala, but because the Starlight is tense with everyone competing for the last act at the Gala, I doubt the performers will get together.'

'In that case, let me buy you and Nico dinner to say thank you for dinner yesterday. You're right, Nico is very generous, and it was lovely of him to buy champagne. I think poor Henry was overwhelmed.'

'Okay. It's a date.'

The bubbles had returned, and Jojo was fizzing. Annie cursed herself for inviting another Henry and Nico experience, but if that's what it cost to keep Jojo in her life, she would just have to live with it.

'What are you doing on your day off tomorrow?'

Annie's heart soared. 'Nothing much. Why?'

'Fancy another brew by Mrs Brew?'

'When do I ever say no to tea and cake? Usual time?'

Annie could hear Nico muttering something in the background. She half expected Jojo to withdraw the invitation. 'Okay. See you tomorrow,' Jojo said.

22

'More Kazaam? Annie-like? When you talk to your friend, you sound as though you're eight years old.' Nico was laughing, and Jojo tried to push down the hurt. He was just teasing.

'Well, we have known each other since we were children.'

'Exactly.' Nico wrapped his arms around her and kissed her neck. 'Now, you are a grown woman. A very lovely, sophisticated woman of the world.'

If Nico would just tell her where she could find her clothes, then she could play his game. It was just for one week. She could pretend that she was acting a part. He would not understand that just touching those clothes, remembering how each of them had been acquired, wondering about their history, brought her comfort. Not knowing where they were filled her with dread. What if Nico had thrown them out? She couldn't believe that he would do anything so cruel.

'Just tell me that my clothes are safe, Nico.'

He smiled. 'They are safe.'

'Okay. Well, as I'm all dressed up, shall we go out?' There was no other option but to dress up, as Jojo didn't have any slouching clothes.

'How about you take them off? Dressed like that, I can't keep my hands off you. It would be torture to spend the day at your side with every man admiring you, having to wait until we got home. Did you see the effect of your entrance at the bistro?'

'We were very late. Annie looked relieved to see us.'

Nico unzipped her dress. 'And what's inside this exquisite packaging is even more sensational.' He ran a finger down her spine, and Jojo felt her body respond. 'Your skin is as smooth as silk.'

'As is your tongue.' Nico grinned, and Jojo realised what she had said. 'I meant smooth talking.' She gasped as his tongue and fingers explored her body.

Later, feeling relaxed and hazy, Nico's leg slung across her body, Jojo's troublesome mind returned to what she had discovered in the safe. She didn't want to spoil the moment but the cine film nagged her; she had to find out why he kept it locked away. And if he was still married, where was Meryl?

'Nico?' Jojo freed herself from the weight of his leg. She trailed her fingers along the curve of his back until they came to rest on the smooth incline of his buttocks. 'Tell me about your life before you met me.'

He made a sound like a lion purring but did not reply.

'Now you've met Annie, but I have met none of your friends or family.'

Nico rolled over and put his hands behind his head. 'My life is the theatre. My friends magicians. There's not much to tell. *You* are my life bella. My world.'

'What were you like as a boy? Where did you grow up?'

Nico sighed. Jojo thought he would not answer, but then he surprised her. 'Leonard and Ruth fostered me when my mother ran away to a commune. I never met my Italian father. He was apparently a one-night stand and doesn't know I exist. She would come back every so often to visit me. At first, I would get my hopes up, believing she had come to claim me. Then, after a while, I didn't want to see her. Leonard and Ruth were good parents. Leonard was — is, a magician. He taught me my first tricks.'

Jojo propped herself up on one elbow. 'I am so sorry, Nico. I had no idea.'

'There is no need for you to know. I try not to dwell on the past.'

'Are Leonard and Ruth still alive?'

'Ruth died five years ago. Leonard is in a nursing home. I visit him when I can.'

'Maybe you could take me with you one day?'

'Leonard would like that.'

'When did you last hear from your mother?'

Nico swung his legs round to sit on the side of the bed. He pulled on his boxers and then reached for a pack of cards on the bedside table and shuffled them. 'I don't want to talk about her. The two women I loved the most betrayed me — my mother and then Meryl. You are not like them bella. I can trust you.'

'I know you don't want to talk about either of them, but just one question?'

Nico was flipping the cards so fast they resembled two fountains colliding, then merging. 'Ask. I'm not promising to answer.'

'Do you know where Meryl is living now? Bobbi said that she dropped off the magic scene.'

Nico let the cards settle. 'I tried to protect her. The woman needs professional help, not punishment.'

'What exactly did she do?'

'Meryl was always highly strung. She needed careful handling. I stupidly believed that by providing her with security and love, I could keep her sane. There was nothing I wouldn't have done for that woman.'

'So, what happened?'

'Oh God, when I remember that day, my blood runs cold. Meryl went crazy with a loaded gun in the theatre.'

Jojo gasped. 'How many people were there? Was it a full house?'

'Thankfully, the Golden Globe was closed to the public. There was one witness, but I bought him off.'

'Why? You should have reported her to the police. Next time, she might kill someone.'

Nico reached for his trousers and began to dress. 'Believe me, bella. I'm acting in Meryl's best interests. She knows that at the drop of a hat, I can have her sectioned or imprisoned. So long as she gets treatment and keeps out of my way, I'm prepared to keep her secret. She fired the gun at me and if not for my quick reaction and Meryl's poor shot, I would have died.'

'What if she tries again? Meryl knows where you live and work. If she sees that I've taken her place on the stage and in your bed… what if she targets me, Nico?' Maybe now was the time to tell him about the anonymous note. It must have been from Meryl.

'I told you what happened to stop you from worrying. You have nothing to fear from Meryl, I promise. Our focus has to be one hundred percent on our performance. No more meetings with Annabelle during work hours.' He slapped her bottom. 'Tomorrow, I want you to demonstrate the trick I taught you. It has to be perfect. If we are to get the last act at Easter Gala, we can't let anything stand in our way.'

Nico's words did not reassure Jojo, but she thought better of mentioning the note.

23

They hadn't arranged an actual time to meet for coffee just late morning and Annie was happy passing the time with a pot of tea, people watching. The back door swung open and Annie looked up expectantly to see a stagehand she didn't recognise. There was a theatre magazine on the table and so Annie picked it up and flicked through the pages. There were job adverts in this one too – wardrobe assistant, theatre technician, choreographer. Jojo had always known that she wanted to perform, but Annie had kind of drifted into travel. She left school with A levels and didn't want to go to university. It occurred to Annie that she had been playing it safe all of her life by clinging onto what was familiar and predictable. Maybe Jojo did make some rash decisions, but she was creating the life that she had dreamed of, whereas Annie was being swept along with the tide. At least, she had applied for the holiday rep job. It didn't mean that she had to take it if she was successful.

Warm hands covered her eyes, causing her heart to leap. 'Guess who?'

'I didn't see you come in,' Annie said when Charlie plonked himself down opposite her.

'Ah ha, you were looking for me!'

Annie blushed. 'No. I was keeping an eye on that door waiting for Jojo.'

Charlie grinned. 'It's my college day. I popped in to pick up some books. Do you want me to find Jojo for you?'

'It's okay. She'll turn up when she's ready. Do you have time for a coffee?'

'I have all day, but a coke, not a coffee, please.'

At the counter, Annie stole a glance at Charlie. He looked different today, a cotton shirt and chinos, instead of dungarees. She approved. He looked clean and wholesome, like an advert for muesli or yoghurt. She bought a wedge of gateau and picked up two forks, hoping that Jojo would be delayed just a little longer.

'You know the way to a man's heart.'

Charlie dug straight in. He had the appetite of a Labrador but the physique of a greyhound. Annie watched him, amused. 'What are you studying at college?'

Charlie put down his fork and nudged the plate towards Annie. 'Stage design. I managed to get on a course that coincided with my stint here. So, perfect.'

Annie didn't really want any cake, but took a small forkful. Sharing cake had kind of become their thing. 'What time are you due in?'

'I don't have to go in today; I'm studying at home. Just needed a couple of books. Why don't I get my books and find out what's happened to Bat Girl?'

'Okay, but if she's busy, tell her not to worry. I'll go shopping or see an exhibition. There's plenty to keep me occupied.'

Charlie returned ten minutes later with a couple of books under his arm. 'Jojo couldn't get away and says to tell you sorry. If you have a bit of time on your hands; are you up for another adventure?'

'I'm not sure. Nothing that involves me attracting attention to myself. I thought I had got away with almost ruining the Hocus Pocus matinee without Jojo realising it was me, but somehow, I think she twigged. She accused me of being un-Annie-like.'

'That is why I am going to take you on another adventure. You and Jojo have a warped idea of what is Annie-like. I'm going to prove to you both that Annie Daley is every bit as adventurous and spontaneous as Jojo. So, do you trust me?'

'Okay, but don't be disappointed when you find out I'm not. What is this adventure?'

'A surprise. Let's get out of here and I'll show you.'

It felt strange being outside of the Golden Globe with Charlie, as if they were on a date. Annie wondered whether she had made a mistake accepting his challenge. She hadn't told him about Henry, and if this was anything other than a couple of friends passing some time together, then it was wrong of her. Maybe later she would drop into the conversation that she had a boyfriend. If she just blurted it out now, it would seem as though she was making assumptions, and if Charlie wasn't interested in her, it would just be embarrassing.

'Do you want me to put those books in my bag?' Annie said, taking them from him. There was a plastic covered book on technical drawing for stage design, and a battered paperback on magic props. 'Don't forget to remind me to give them back to you.'

'Thanks.' Charlie took hold of her hand as they crossed the busy road and a current of electricity shot through her. Was it static? It ended in her heart, and she wondered if he had felt it too. They were still holding hands a minute later.

Charlie let go to point out an Easter rabbit wearing a bill board.

'I hope you will not suggest I do that?'

Charlie laughed.

'So, where are we going?'

'Somewhere that I'm willing to bet you've never been before.'

'Don't forget, I've been hanging around with Jojo most of my life and she has introduced me to things that I would never have done.'

They weaved through pedestrians and then Charlie led her down an alley. 'It's somewhere along here.' He stood in the middle of the street and frowned. 'I usually come here at night. It looks different.'

'Just tell me what we are looking for.'

'Ah. There it is! Up there.' Charlie pointed above the shops and restaurants, but all Annie could see were flats.

'You're not taking me to a massage parlour? Or a clairvoyant? A dope den! You know I'm a clean-living girl?'

'Trust me. It will be fun.'

They climbed the steps of an iron fire escape at the back of the building. Annie giggled as her heel caught in the open ironwork and Charlie reached out a hand to steady her. 'Okay?'

At the top of the stairs there was a door with a window and in it a pink sign with Japanese writing.

'A tea ceremony with geisha girls?'

'Just wait and see.'

A middle-aged Japanese man greeted them at the door. 'It is good to see you, my friend. Is this the brown-eyed girl? Come, I will find you the best seats.'

Annie made a face at Charlie. 'I'll explain later,' he said.

The tiny bar was empty except for a couple of old men

playing mahjong, which, Charlie explained, was a Japanese version of the game. Before Annie had time to ask questions, a girl delivered what looked like a coffee pot and two ceramic tumblers to their table. She poured them each a cup, bowed, and then left.

'I haven't eaten Japanese food. Is it good?'

Charlie lifted his tumbler. 'Cheers. Neither have I.'

The drink was warm and had an unfamiliar scent. Kind of floral. She took a sip. It was good. Then a few more.

'Don't do what I did the first time I tried Saki. It slips down easily but packs a punch. I could barely stand after finishing a bottle. Fermented rice wine.'

Annie opened the gold and blue embossed cover. Inside were the names of songs in English with Japanese beneath. She turned the pages. More songs. 'Where are the dishes?'

Charlie took the menu from her. 'This isn't a restaurant. It's a karaoke bar. They're big in Japan and had taken off in the States when I was there last year. You choose a song from here, then they play the backing track for you to singalong.'

'And people do that?'

'Yup. On a Saturday night, it's packed. People fighting to be the next one up to sing.'

Annie couldn't imagine singing in that little bar. It was so bizarre; it made her laugh. Charlie poured them more Saki. 'Your laugh is like a babbling brook. Sorry, that sounded weird. It's the way it comes from deep down and then kind of escapes in giggly gurgles. Even more weird. I'll shut up.'

The waitress refilled their pot with warm Saki. A few more people had settled in the bar, all of them Japanese.

'When did you join the Golden Globe?'

'Just before Jojo. A friend helped me get a short-term contract, and that worked out really well with the theatre design course.'

Annie was trying hard to keep focused, but she felt a little squiffy. So long as she kept Charlie talking about safe topics, then she wouldn't make a fool of herself. When the time was right, she would mention Henry. Just drop his name into the conversation. She took another sip of Saki. It went down far too easily. 'Did you start at the Golden Globe straight from Uni?'

'No. I worked in an architect's office for a few months and then I travelled around the States. I wanted to see my favourite architect's work. Frank Lloyd. Have you heard of him?'

'The chair designer?'

'He's known for a lot more than furniture design. Organic architecture. I'll have to show you one day.' Annie was imagining them on a motor bike tearing across the wild prairies of America when Charlie said, 'I've got some books at home. I stayed away too long.'

'Why too long?'

He gazed into the distance. 'Because I lost touch with what was happening back here. My responsibilities. Now I'm back, I'm going to put that right.'

'Your career?'

'Family. What's your story?'

Annie wanted to know more. Who did Charlie feel responsible for? He cupped his face in one hand. It felt as though they were the only two people in the room. 'I don't have much of a story. If I do, then I've lost my place in the book. I live at home with my parents and sister. Work in a travel agent.'... *tell him about Henry...* 'Until Jojo moved in with Nico, we spent most of our free-time together.'

'And now?'

Annie wrinkled her nose. 'Not so much. They seem happy together, so that's good.'

'Maybe. It could just be that Jojo is at that age.'

Annie cocked her head and frowned.

'I have a theory.' Charlie straightened up and Annie realised their heads had come so close together they had almost been touching. 'Sometimes you meet the wrong person at the right time, like Jojo. Other times, you meet the right person at the wrong time. You want to be with them but can't because you have other commitments.'

It sounded profound, but with a muggy head, Annie couldn't quite grasp the meaning.

'Oh. You don't think Nico is right for Jojo? Or are you saying…' It had almost made sense, but then she lost the thread.

Charlie laughed. Then the soundtrack to Van Morrison's Brown-Eyed Girl played. He covered his face with his hands and groaned.

'Come on up Mr Brown-Eyed Girl.'

It suddenly reminded Annie of where they were, that they were not alone.

'Why did this seem like a good idea?' Charlie grimaced. All the staff clapped, and he stood up.

Annie squirmed. Surely, he wasn't going to sing? Yep, he was. She peeked through her fingers. He sat on a bar stool and took hold of the mic. Could she sneak out without him noticing?

Then he sang. A rich, deep voice that was incredibly sexy. The man up there was no longer Charlie, the boy next door, everybody's friend – he was gorgeous, a superstar. And he was looking directly at her as he sang. If only she had brown eyes.

24

Starlight Night had finally arrived. In the changing room, Jojo tried to create a little personal space amongst the hot bodies and flapping feathers of head-dresses and bustles. The air was charged with a heady mix of adrenalin, nervous tension, and excitement. Heads bobbed up and down as the girls struggled into their extravagant costumes.

'I swear I saw John Jenkins in the second row,' Sly squealed.

'He's responsible for bringing magic back onto the TV. I heard that Annika Riley's here too,' Bobbi said.

Jojo was sick with nerves. Tonight meant everything to Nico. He deserved to be discovered and stood a good chance. The only thing that could let him down was her solo performance. She had to get the rabbit trick right. It was the build-up to his finale. It had gone well in rehearsals that week; there was no reason it wouldn't go smoothly. She just had to stay calm.

'I'm looking forward to seeing Kai Keisler's act. I've

been a big fan since I discovered him at a little club in Brixton. Clever of him to keep it under wraps,' Bunty said.

Jojo tried to tune out the conversation and keep focused.

'How are you feeling, babe?' Bobbi said in a sympathetic voice, which increased Jojo's anxiety.

'Fine. Great. We couldn't have worked harder than we have. Nico is amazing. Even John Jenkins will realise that.'

'I hope so, darling. What about your solo?'

'It's been going really well in rehearsals.' Her hands were sweaty.

'And if it doesn't when you're out there?' Bobbi spoke softly, her voice full of concern. 'Have you got a plan B?'

'I can't. Nico told me to do it exactly as he instructed. There's no way I could improvise.' Jojo hadn't told Bobbi about the alternative act she had worked up with Charlie. Best forget that crazy idea.

'Oh, I don't know. Those adorable gurning faces you make will have the audience eating out of your hand.'

'So long as Pixie and Muffin are eating out of my hand, or at least sitting still in my hands, I will be more than happy.' The last call was announced. 'Wish me luck.'

'Break a leg,' the women said in unison.

'Come on, girls!' Charlie called from the door. A line of beautiful showgirls, each at least six feet tall in their heels, taller with their headdresses, streamed past him.

'Keep your tongue in, Charlie! It's not polite to drool!' Bobbi quipped.

'Just wait until we've finished and we come and find you,' Sly winked.

Jojo and Charlie watched a vibrant pink bustle sashay away from them as the girls prepared to make their entrance. An electric blue feather hovered in the breeze. It drifted then fell as weightless as falling snow. A sound of applause. The Starlight show had begun.

'Ready for action Bat Girl?'

'Could we sedate Pixie and Muffin? Just a little to make them more pliable?'

'The girls are fine. I just visited them in their dressing room and they're looking forward to their big night. Let them have a couple of Martinis after the show.' He frowned. 'You look as though you need one now.'

Jojo sighed. 'I don't think I can pull it off, Charlie. What if it goes tits up?'

'Then we have a plan. As soon as you say the word, I'll set things in motion.'

'I can't. Nico told me to follow his instructions to the letter. It's fine. I can do this,' Jojo told herself more than Charlie. She had to get it right.

'I know you can, Bat Girl. I never doubted you. How did Nico take the change of order?'

'What change? He didn't tell me.' Jojo's heart sank. Nico's act was to be the last that evening. The prestigious position that they had worked so hard for.

'A last-minute change to the line-up. Kai Keisler now has the top spot.'

That explained Bobbi's sympathetic tone. 'Why change at the last minute?'

'Nico has known for a couple of days. It was always close between the two of them. Don't worry Bat Girl, you will wow them.'

That Nico had kept this news to himself meant he minded a lot. They just had to shine extra bright and show John Jenkins and Annika Riley that they were the stars of the show. This did nothing to quieten the butterfly farm that had taken up residence; batting their wings against her ribs.

. . .

Annie loved the intimacy of the Golden Globe theatre. It may have been the smallest theatre in London, but as far as the world of magic went, it was the biggest. Annie read out loud from the programme. 'It was originally a private club for magicians and members of the Magic Circle, before Peter Walker turned it into a boutique theatre and showcase for new magicians. Theatrical magic is having a renaissance, with new and original approaches exciting audiences around the world. The Golden Globe leads the way, living up to its reputation of discovering future stars. This evening's show combines traditional with the Avant-Garde to bring you the very best in theatrical magic. Prepare to be stunned.'

Henry peered over her shoulder. 'I've heard of Kai Keisler. Wasn't he claiming to be the next Uri Geller or something?'

Annie hadn't, but she was pleased that Henry had found something to approve of after complaining that the theatre was 'a bit pokey' and 'there wasn't enough room for his legs.' Henry took the programme from her and, whilst he was reading, Annie scanned the auditorium, hoping to glimpse Charlie. She squinted at the boys in dark clothes who flitted in the shadows on the stage and glanced up when there was a movement in the aisles.

'If you're looking for the talent scouts, I can see Annika Riley over there — centre, third row.'

Annie nodded. 'Yes. And I think I saw John Jenkins when we first arrived. I'm so excited for Jojo.'

'I don't know what all the fuss is about. People get discovered on New Faces and then sink into oblivion. Magicians should stick to children's parties.'

Annie would not let Henry spoil her enjoyment of this performance. She had been looking forward to it for weeks.

The orchestra struck up, and Annie clasped Henry's hand. She was a child at the circus for the very first time.

A parade of beautiful girls accompanied Peter Walker as he introduced the show. Fireworks popped like champagne corks, sprinkling the audience with glitter. Catherine wheels, strobe lights, and fire in dazzling colours lit up the stage. Even Henry had to be impressed.

The rotund man with a moustache was on first. A back-drop told the audience that he was in a French restaurant. Annie wondered whether Charlie had painted it. She would have to ask if his job included scene painting, and if, as an architect, he enjoyed drawing and painting, or was it more about design and calculations? Max was seated at a table where he was served a roast chicken. The waitress put the cover back on the dish and left Max to enjoy his meal, but when he lifted the lid, a live chicken strutted across the table. The audience laughed they were enjoying Max's performance and Annie wondered why Jojo didn't use her quirky humour in their act.

'When's the Amazing Bongo coming on?' Henry muttered.

Max was taking a bow and so Annie checked her programme. 'Hocus Pocus and then Nico and Jojo. They come on again in the second half.'

The dancers Annie had seen at the matinee gyrated onto the stage, and Henry sat forward in his seat. 'That's more like it.'

Nico was introduced as being the most accomplished sleight-of-hand magician in Europe. When he came on stage with Jojo, who was dressed in a sparkly dress slit to the thigh, Annie's heart nearly burst with pride. She was stunning.

Nico made a show of removing his jacket and handing it to Jojo. He loosened his tie, and the women started whooping. Playing to his audience, Nico feigned shyness, and then he shrugged and removed his tie altogether. Jojo might as well have been a coat stand. Annie wanted to like Nico, but was finding it difficult. What did Charlie mean when he said that Nico was the wrong man at the right time? There was a lot that made little sense that afternoon. The jug of Saki they finished between them had something to do with that.

Whilst the women were making a collective groan of appreciation, Annie scanned the audience to see if she could spot a crazy fan. Her heart skipped a beat when she spied Charlie at the back of the auditorium. He must have seen her too, because Annie experienced a little frisson of something when he looked in her direction. This evening, he was bound to meet Henry. It didn't matter. It wasn't as though there was anything between her and Charlie, but she was embarrassed. She should have said something.

'Get on with it,' Henry said a bit too loudly.

Annie wriggled down in her seat to hide, but Henry had a point. Nico was milking it — all of that ridiculous flirtation with his adoring fans. Eventually, he produced a pack of cards and shuffled them. Annie strained her eyes. She was staring hard, but couldn't make out how he did it. With each shuffle, the cards became smaller. Smaller and smaller, until they were the size of a thimble. Then with one puff, Nico blew them away. A sprinkling of sparkles. Dust.

The sword trick was next. Nico closed each portion of an upright box on Jojo before thrusting swords into her. It would have been a dull act if not for the hilarious faces Jojo made whenever Nico's back was turned. Annie guessed that this was not an improvisation that had Nico's approval.

The audience clapped enthusiastically, and the curtain came down. 'That wasn't bad. A bit old hat but polished,' Henry conceded.

'Let's get a drink,' Annie said when the lights came on. She was worried that alone in an almost empty theatre, Charlie would spot them. At some point that evening, she would have to introduce Henry to him, but the longer she could put it off, the better.

'Is it worth moving? The second act starts in less than thirty minutes.'

'We have tokens for a complimentary drink. You can have a soft drink if you prefer.' Annie knew that this would persuade Henry and tried to suppress her irritation.

'Just the one then.'

Nico was in the bar, standing with a group of important looking people. They had a well-groomed, expensive look about them. She recognised John Jenkins, Annika Riley, and Adele Pearson, the woman that had been pointed out as a famous choreographer when Annie was waiting to go into the Hocus Pocus matinee show.

Annie steered Henry into earshot of their conversation, hoping to pick up any information that might be of interest to Jojo. A man in a collarless shirt and jacket was introducing Kai Keisler to John Jenkins. Nico and Kai made quite an impression, one with dark Mediterranean looks and the other blond and blue-eyed. Annie searched the faces of their fans, trying to find one who might have left the note, but it could have been any of them — or none. Nico and Kai seemed to get on well, patting each other on the back as though they were the best of buddies. Maybe they were. The first bell rang with a five-minute warning to return to their seats.

Nico met Jojo backstage. He rubbed his hands together and Jojo could almost imagine them igniting. His energy was palpable. 'This is it bella. My big moment. Walker has talked Kai Keisler and me up as the best the Golden Globe has to offer. I'll have my own show. Tour Europe. The world.' Jojo's knees turned to jelly. 'When you've finished assisting me with my next act, the stage is yours. I'm trusting you to keep the audience enrapt. I want them on the edge of their seats, full of anticipation. Follow the act *exactly* as I taught you. Okay? The escape act is phenomenal. Let's see Kai Keisler try to top that.'

And then they were on.

25

Jojo turned boxes around to show the audience they were empty, handed Nico a cylindrical tube, escorted a member of the audience to the stage and then back to their seat, put her arm out to receive two doves, and then everyone was clapping, and Nico was presenting her.

'Don't let me down,' he whispered, as he helped her into a spangled tailcoat.

The stage was all hers. There was a complete hush. The lights were too bright and hot. She couldn't do it. From the wings, Charlie gave a thumbs up and reassuring nod. Jojo took a deep breath and tried to ignore Pixie wriggling in her sleeve. The piano and string quartet went straight into playing the calming music, as instructed by Nico. She just had to hold the audience's attention. Keep them rapt.

Jojo opened up the doll's house. Inside, scrambling around the library, was Muffin. Unbeknown to Nico, she had secured a tiny pair of glasses on his nose. The audience gave a collective ah, when Jojo scooped him out of the study and gave him a kiss. Producing the second rabbit, Pixie, went to plan. She noticed people shuffling in their seats; one man looked as though he had nodded off. The trick was boring, even to Jojo. Now to push the two rabbits together to make one. Muffin lunged over her forearm and scampered across the stage. There was a ripple of laughter as Jojo gave chase with Pixie tucked away in her bodice. Then Pixie made her getaway. The audience roared with laughter.

'I'm switching to the back-up plan,' Charlie called from the wings.

Jojo ducked behind the curtain. 'No. I can't.'

Too late. Charlie had taken things into his own hands. Behind her, a fluorescent light show was projected onto the backdrop. As if prepared for this change of plan, the orchestra changed tempo.

Jojo had no choice but to go with the flow. If she was going to do this, then it had to be sensational. The audience was no longer laughing. She flung off her tailcoat and the harness was fitted in seconds, whilst lights and music created the effect of a lightning storm. Then Charlie raised her up into the fly tower.

Annie sat on the edge of her seat. Jojo hadn't prepared her for this. On stage, the storm had cleared and Jojo was tumbling and turning down a psychedelic rabbit hole. Violins increased the tension, and images flashed by, as Jojo stunned the audience with her acrobatics. When she landed, the errant rabbit took one look at her before running into the wings. Jojo had gone into acting mode. Her expressions were perfect as she considered the bottle with *drink me* and the cake with *eat me*. She took a sip from the bottle and a curtain dropped, hiding the doll's house; behind her, a much bigger version was projected. It was magical. Annie stole a glance at the people on either side of them, who seemed transfixed. Jojo stepped through an opening in the curtain as if entering the house and a second later, the curtain lifted to reveal the doll's house but no Jojo.

Just as Annie thought Jojo's act was over, her head and arms emerged from the windows of the doll's house. The audience went crazy. They had seen nothing like it. Pretending the act was over, Charlie wandered onto the stage and lifted away a portion of the house. He carried it off stage as though clearing the props with Jojo's hand, waving from a window. On the other side of the stage, Jojo made a horrified expression from a window of the house. Some members of the audience were laughing so hard they were wiping tears from their eyes. Charlie removed another portion. He carried it for a few steps and then put it down, rubbing his back. A leg popped out of the top and waved wildly. The audience was in hysterics.

When Nico stepped onto the stage, the audience thought he was pretending to be perplexed and then angry, so they laughed even more. Jojo made a face and then disappeared, leaving Charlie to remove the doll's house sections to the biggest applause Annie had heard all evening. There were wolf whistles, and a few people stood up to cheer. Nico smiled and thanked the audience by taking a bow on behalf of Jojo. There was a bit of confusion as some violins started a menacing piece of music and a couple of girls in leather shorts and chains strutted onto the stage. Nico waved them off, and the curtain came down.

'Wasn't she amazing?' Annie said to Henry as they waited in the bar for Jojo and Nico.

'It was pretty impressive. To be honest, your friends Alice in Wonderland routine and Kai Keisler saved the show from flunking. The way those doves changed colour was amazing.'

'Hush.' Annie looked furtively around the bar to check that nobody important could hear them. 'It was all good, but I know what you mean. I was worried when Nico came on the stage and the curtain went down. He looked a bit surprised to see Charlie carrying away a portion of the house with a hand waving from the window. Do you think Nico's reaction was part of their act?'

'I don't know, but his entrance fell flat. The Amazing Bongo in his boxers.'

Annie elbowed Henry in the ribs as Jojo approached, wearing a magnificent pewter dress. It rippled like a moonlit lake as she glided across the room. She couldn't wait to congratulate Jojo and left Henry's side to greet her.

'Oh Jojo, you are amazing.'

'It's gorgeous, isn't it? A present from Nico this evening. Have you seen him?' Jojo searched the room behind Annie.

'No. Come and have a drink with us. We can wait for Nico to change and then go together to the restaurant. You look gorgeous and that Alice in Wonderland routine was truly inspired. Did you hear the audience cheering? I thought they'd never stop. Then the curtain came down, and I thought the show was over.'

Jojo went white. 'What do you mean, the curtain came down?'

'When Nico came on the stage and Charlie was pretending to clear away the house with you still inside it. He acted confused. Then - the curtain came down.'

'He did his escapist act?'

'Yes, of course he did. It was good. A bit of an anti-climax following Alice. Don't look so worried. That's good, isn't it? You wanted your double act to be the best and between you, I think you have pulled it off.' Jojo seemed a little shaky, which wasn't surprising, an adrenalin dip. 'Say hello to Henry and I'll order some drinks at the bar.'

Feeling a little reckless – it was as though she had been on that stage herself – Annie ordered a bottle of champagne. They would soon finish it between the four of them. Henry was driving, but a small glass of champagne to celebrate Jojo's success wouldn't hurt. Annie was returning to the table when she saw Charlie talking to Jojo. She tried to gather her thoughts and emotions. There was a leap of joy at seeing him, followed by a dread in explaining Henry. He would wonder why she hadn't mentioned him, and Annie was embarrassed because she knew the reason.

Charlie was squatting alongside Jojo, holding her hand. The compassion and love in his eyes were unmistakable, and Annie's heart contracted.

'Hi Charlie.' Annie hoped she sounded blasé.

Jojo gave Charlie a long look, communicating something that Annie could not interpret. If Henry wasn't there, would they have included her?

'Charlie. I forgot to introduce you to Henry, Annie's boyfriend,' Jojo said.

Charlie looked from Jojo to Annie to Henry, and then back at Annie. 'I didn't know you had a boyfriend.'

Annie avoided his eyes and felt herself blush. She wanted to run away and hide. When did things get so complicated?

'Henry.' Henry's voice was warm and welcoming.

At that moment, the waiter arrived bearing a silver tray with a bottle of champagne on ice and four glasses. 'I thought we ought to celebrate Jojo and Nico's big night,' Annie said as the waiter distributed the glasses. Nobody spoke. 'It's okay, we'll pour,' Annie said, discomforted by the silence.

'I don't know that there's anything to celebrate,' Jojo said. Annie noticed for the first time that her eyes were a little red.

'Of course, there is. Your act was sensational.'

'That's what I was telling her,' Charlie said.

'Why don't you sit down and have a glass of bubbly with us,' Henry said.

Annie and Jojo shared a look which conveyed to Annie that Jojo wasn't happy and Annie could guess why. Nico didn't like being upstaged by his assistant.

Charlie had declined Henry's invitation, but they seemed to chat about football or something, so Annie moved her chair closer to Jojo's. 'How was Nico after the show?'

'I haven't seen him.' There was a tremor to Jojo's voice, and Annie wanted to wrap her arms around her.

'He'll be signing autographs. I see what you mean about the women getting worked up. When he removed his gown and was wearing only swimming briefs, I was afraid knickers would be thrown at the stage,' Annie said.

'I wanted to meet him when he came off, but Charlie told me to wait and give him some space. Now I know why. He must be furious.' Jojo wiped away a tear and then dipped her head to hide behind a cascade of hair.

Annie gently nudged Jojo, presenting her with a glass of bubbly in one hand and a tissue in the other. Jojo nodded. She wiped her nose and took a slug of champagne. Henry and Charlie were still deep in conversation and so Annie took the bottle and went to fill their glasses. Charlie shook his head, and Henry accepted only the tiniest measure as he was driving.

'Charlie's been telling me about his globe-trotting. That's where our future lies, darling, tailored holidays for the explorer. You know, Thailand, Australia, the USA.'

Henry made it sound as though he and Annie were senior partners that owned the travel agency chain when all Annie did was phone through booking requests for a week in the Costa-del-Sol, and Henry, as far as she knew, gave training presentations to the sales staff. He also gave the impression that their relationship was serious. It was the first time he had called her darling. Why now? Charlie would think that they were about to get married. Why did it matter so much to her, what Charlie thought?

'I'd better scoot. I just dropped by to let Jojo know Nico would meet her at the restaurant. He'll be wanting to talk to Walker and meet John Jenkins.'

'Thank you, Charlie. You'll let him know?'Jojo said.

Charlie nodded, his eyes full of concern. Annie loved him for taking care of Jojo, but she couldn't help feeling a little envious that the warmth of his gaze was for her friend.

When Henry and a tipsy Annie and Jojo arrived at Lee Chang's, it was busier than they had known it to be. Henry had refused his champagne and so Annie and Jojo shared the bottle. Annie had hoped that Nico would calm down and make Jojo's evening by joining them in the bar. She hadn't booked a table and was afraid that they might get turned away. It wasn't the celebratory meal she had anticipated. Jojo looked as though she were at a wake and Henry kept on about the cost of champagne.

'I am sorry, but we are very busy this evening. I might find you a table at ten o'clock.'

Henry snorted and looked at his watch. 'Let's go,'

'Is that your friend trying to get your attention?' the waiter said.

Charlie was waving them over from a table of eleven. The stagehands, Pedro, a few of the Hocus Pocus dancers, and other faces Annie didn't recognise had gathered at the same restaurant. Charlie suggested they squeeze on the end, and the rest of the party, who appeared more inebriated than Annie and Jojo, insisted, shuffling along to make room. Annie could tell from the set of Henry's face that he was displeased with this arrangement. Jojo, however, seemed to relax a little, and that was enough to convince Annie that they should stay. She would placate Henry on the drive home by thinking up a special date for him. When they had all settled around the table, Annie found herself at the opposite end to Jojo, who was sitting between a couple of the dancers. Charlie was on her right, and Henry to her left. They seemed to get on picking up on football again. Annie tried to follow the conversation, but football didn't interest her. Across the table, Jojo looked distracted. Why couldn't she celebrate her fabulous performance?

One of the dancers said something to Jojo and Annie watched her making an effort to engage. Only Annie would guess that she was miserable. A man in a silky bomber jacket and tight Levi 501s stood behind Jojo. Annie watched with interest as he tapped her shoulder. Then just as it got interesting, a waiter arrived with a tray of dishes blocking her view. By the time chicken egg foo yung, prawn chow mien, and pork won ton had been distributed around the table, the man was leaving. Annie noticed Jojo read a business card before slipping it into her clutch bag. She caught Annie's eye and beamed. It was so frustrating that they couldn't talk.

'So, where did you and Henry meet?' Charlie said to Annie.

'At work. I guess that's where most people meet.'

She was rescued by the special fried rice being passed to her by a girl named Coco. When they joined the table, Lenny had ordered several more dishes after checking for allergies. That didn't go down well with Henry, who would have preferred to keep their order separate, but in the party's commotion, his protests were unheard.

'Is it serious? I mean, have you been together long?' He concentrated on rolling the edge of his napkin.

Annie glanced at Henry, who seemed to be delivering a presentation on the travel industry to a girl whose attention was on anyone but him. 'He's the first man that I've been this serious about,' she answered honestly.

'Oh.' He released the napkin and it unfurled.

'When I say that, what I mean is, he's the first man that I've been out with for more than two or three dates. I'm sorry I didn't mention Henry before. It just kind of never came up and we haven't been seeing each other for long.'

Charlie nodded, but his eyes were still on the napkin as he folded in a corner. 'He seems like a decent bloke.'

'How about you? Are you involved with anyone?'

'There is someone. Someone special.' He looked straight at Annie, and her heart jolted. 'I can't tell her how I feel yet. There's something important that I have to do first. I just hope that I'm not too late.'

'Do you think she feels the same?' Annie's voice felt strangled in her throat.

'I don't know. I hope so.'

'Me too,' Annie said, and she meant it, although there was an unfamiliar ache below her ribcage. A feeling of loss, and regret, for something that she never had.

26

'Jojo Evans?' the man in the silky bomber jacket said, when he sidled up to her in the restaurant.

Jojo's stomach dipped as though she were on a roller coaster. Was this the person who had sent the anonymous note? Bunty and Sly sat on either side of her, but both were engaged in conversation, oblivious to her visitor. 'Yes?'

'John Jenkins wants you to call this number to arrange a meeting.'

Jojo took the card and gazed in awe at the man who had delivered a message from *John Jenkins*. 'I'm sorry Nico isn't here to meet you. He will be so excited when I tell him.' If only he were there. This was what they had worked for. A dream come true.

'Who's Nico? Never mind, it's you JJ wants to see.'

'Me?' It felt as though she was having palpitations; her heart was beating so fast.

'He liked your moves.' The man winked and Jojo caught him enjoying his view of Bunty's ample bosom.

She tucked the business card into her bag. Nobody seemed to have noticed, except for Annie, who was giving her the eagle eye. Her performance had impressed John Jenkins. That meant she really was good. If she sat there a moment longer, she would combust with excitement. Annie and Charlie kept on glancing across the table. They would sense something was up. Nobody must know until she had worked out how and what to tell Nico. There was no way he was going to join them at the restaurant. She had to go home and make her peace with him. What she had done was wrong. Nico had trusted her to maintain a certain mood to prepare for his grand finale and, instead, she had stolen the show. His act would have fallen flat. They were meant to be a team, and she had let him down badly.

Their apartment block was in darkness when the taxi drew up outside. Once inside, Jojo slipped off her heels and crept into the bedroom. The bed was made. The room just as they had left it. They had never been apart at night, not since Jojo moved in with Nico. She went from room to room, switching on the lights. No Nico. No note. Now Jojo was worried. It had been callous of her to leave without him. She should have found him and apologised.

Jojo slipped off her beautiful dress and hung it in the wardrobe alongside the other clothes Nico had bought for her. It was a week since he had hidden her dressing-up box. Before he presented her with the pewter dress, she had planned to wear her 1940s evening gown with the flounced underskirt — there were very few occasions when she could wear that beauty, but there was no denying Nico had chosen a gorgeous gown for her. All the dresses he bought for her were wonderful, but she was looking forward to the return of her cherished clothes. Snug in a pair of fleecy pyjamas, Jojo switched on the electric fire in the front room. The central heating had been off for some time and the flat was chilly. By the time I've made a hot drink, Nico will be home, Jojo told herself.

It was eerily quiet in the flat. In her Camden squat noise would have carried from the street. Drunken shouts as people left the pub, police sirens, breaking glass. Here, in the heart of the West End, everyone had gone to sleep. The kettle built to a throttle – noisy in the still of the night. *Where are you, Nico?*

When Jojo opened the fridge to reach for a bottle of milk, she saw the champagne that Nico had chilled to prepare for their triumph. They had left the flat that afternoon full of hope and a certainty that this was it – that Nico would be discovered and the road ahead paved with gold. She had sabotaged his dream.

The mug of tea cooled in her hands as Jojo watched the artificial flames flicker. She wished she had a blanket to wrap around her, but was too miserable to move. The fire element clicked and Jojo tried to stop herself from nodding off.

She woke up as Nico draped a tartan throw over her. 'Why didn't you go to bed bella?' He had dark shadows beneath his eyes. His lips pale and thin.

'I'm sorry Nico.' Her voice broke as she tried to control the emotion that had been building all night, even as she dozed.

'Hey, it's okay. Don't cry.' Jojo lifted the throw, and he climbed in beside her. 'I've been doing a lot of thinking.'

'Where did you go?'

'At first, I was so angry I had to be alone. I walked and walked. Along the embankment – all the way to the city. Watched the sunrise. It was beautiful. I realised that this isn't going to work.'

Jojo freed herself from his arms and turned to face him. 'What are you saying, Nico?'

'You and me. You are a free spirit. It's why I fell in love with you, but I can't live like this.'

'Like what? Until now, everything has been perfect. It still could be.'

'No, Jojo. I can't trust you. A magician has to trust his assistant. Her life might depend upon it. I have tried to explain this to you, but you do not understand.'

'Are you breaking up with me? What about our act?' This was worse than anything Jojo had imagined. She loved Nico. Her world was falling apart.

'Don't cry, bella. It's for the best.'

'I am really, really sorry. It was wrong of me to improvise. I messed up the rabbit trick and didn't know what else to do.'

'Your boyfriend, Charlie, seemed to know exactly what to do. Did he put you up to it?' Nico was angry now. This was what Jojo had expected. What she deserved.

'No. Okay, I had played around with some ideas. When I thought I wouldn't be able to master the trick, I needed a back-up plan. I was going to show you to see what you thought, but then I became more confident in doing the trick and you told me not to improvise.'

'So why did you?'

'I didn't want to but—'

'--Charlie?'

'I will never do anything like that again. I promise. You *can* trust me, Nico.'

'You humiliated me. They were laughing.'

'No, no, Nico. They weren't laughing at you. They were laughing at me. I was trying to make them laugh. I know that wasn't my brief and I am truly sorry. Please say we can work this out. I love you.'

Nico looked into her eyes and she saw her love reflected back. He pulled her to him and buried his face in her hair. 'I love you too.'

'Can you forgive me?'

'If you promise you will listen to me and do as I say.'

Jojo nodded. She was exhausted, emotionally and physically.

'Come on, let's go to bed.'

The last thing Jojo thought before closing her eyes was, *Nico must never know that John Jenkins's assistant approached me.* If she followed up the invitation to meet with him, then she would have to part from Nico and she didn't know whether she could do that. Nico would never agree to her meeting with him. If he found out she had gone behind his back, their relationship would be over. None of this kept her awake as she fell into a long, deep sleep.

27

On the way home from the show, Henry was in good humour. Instead of bemoaning the cost of the meal or remarking on the chaotic way that events had unfolded, he was full of praise for Charlie and appreciation of the Hocus Pocus dancers. His attentiveness towards Coco had not escaped Annie's notice. She stared glumly out of the side window, watching but not seeing the car lights that sped by.

'It's a pity your friend isn't dating Charlie. I would enjoy seeing more of him. Top chap.'

He was. Intelligent. Sensitive. Funny. Caring. Charlie's words came back to her. *You and Jojo have a warped idea of what is Annie-like. I am going to prove to you both that Annie Daley is every bit as adventurous and spontaneous as Jojo.* She smiled to herself. Singing Dancing Queen as a tribute to Jojo and then dancing with him whilst everyone clapped did kind of prove his point. But Annie had insisted on foul play as a result of the Saki. 'Which,' Charlie had said, 'you didn't have to drink.' It had been fun. The someone special that Charlie spoke of would be incredibly lucky to have him. She wished him well. She wished... Annie sighed and censored that thought. 'Nico's okay. Intense, but Jojo loves him.'

The car purred through the night as Annie replayed her meetings with Charlie. Had he given any indication of being interested in a performer? They all flirted with him. Surrounded by the most beautiful women in England, he could have his pick. She had to stop imagining him back in that karaoke bar singing Brown-Eyed Girl, and the feel of his hand in hers.

'Here we are.' Henry pulled up outside Annie's house. 'Thank you for an interesting evening. Do you want to join me for a gym and swim session tomorrow?'

'I think I'll just have a restful day if that's okay with you,' Annie said.

A phone was ringing, but Annie couldn't wade through the water fast enough to answer it. Jojo needed her, but the current was too strong. She awoke with a jolt. The phone was still ringing and then someone answered it. Ten-twenty. Annie rarely overslept, but it was Sunday and she'd had a late night. She plumped up her pillows and snuggled down to enjoy the luxury of a lie-in when Jessica shrieked. A pounding on the stairs. A door slammed. Then all was still.

The moment of relaxation had gone. Best get up and find out what had rattled her sister. Mum was roasting the leg of lamb and the delicious scent of Sunday wafted up the stairs. Annie knocked gently on Jessica's bedroom door.

'What?' came a bark from inside. Jessica sat at the dressing table with her head in her hands, beneath her elbows, and scattered around her were pamphlets, lists, and notes. Unable to help herself, Annie gathered them up into a neat pile.

'I heard the phone.'

'One thing. I asked Gary to do just one thing. I've arranged *everything*: wedding dress, bridesmaids' dresses, catering, cars. All he had to do was book the Fenwood Golf Club for the reception.'

Annie perched on the bed behind Jessica. 'Could they fit you in another day in September? I know it's only six months away, but maybe if they have a cancellation.'

Jessica closed her wedding planning journal. 'Nothing until 81. He thought his mum had booked it for him rather than doing it himself. Maybe it's a sign. If he can be that careless over something so important, can I trust him?'

'Do you love him?'

'Yes. Of course, I do.'

'Then you will forgive him and move on. Look at Mum and Dad, they're always having misunderstandings — Dad dropping clangers. Marriage isn't like in the movies.'

Jessica frowned. 'I thought you didn't believe in love. Henry must be something to have made you all mushy.'

Annie shrugged. 'All I'm saying is, if you love him, don't let him go. To find someone you love, and to have those feelings returned, is precious. Anyone can meet someone and get married — find a willing partner when they think it's the right time. Wrong person. Right time. But everything is aligned for you and Gary. Right person. Right time. Don't throw it away, Jess.'

Jessica hugged Annie. 'Thank you. You're right, marrying Gary is more important than where we get married. I gave him an earful this morning.'

'Are you going to put him out of his misery?'

'No, not yet. He can suffer a bit longer. Mum's offered to

put up a marquee in the garden.' They looked at each other and then fell about laughing.

'A marquee? It would have to be a tent.'

'A two-man tent. There's only a couple of metres of grass behind Dad's fishpond and crazy paving.'

'Don't worry Jess. We'll think of something.'

Sunday lunch was a little subdued as their mum made what she considered helpful suggestions to Jessica: the W.I. hall, the Scouts hut, and the Bell and Whistle pub. With each suggestion Jessica became more irritable and so the meal was eaten mostly in silence with their dad making random comments about the weather: good for March, it being such an unpredictable month weather wise, and his rhubarb — new growth looking good, must be because of the manure he used.

When the plates had been cleared, Annie dismissed Jessica's offer of help and washed up alone. It was soothing soaping saucepans, and it gave her time to reflect. The relevance of Charlie's words had made sense when she applied them to Jessica and Gary. Most of her peers got married in their early twenties, settling with their first steady boyfriend, but Jessica had never been one to follow convention. Neither had she limited her choice of suiter, having played the field — as their dad was fond of saying. Annie rinsed away soapsuds and turned the pan over to drain. Bubbles burst on her forearm and she delighted in the rainbows captured within the tiny globes. Henry was, as Charlie said, a good man. On paper, he was a perfect match. They got on well together. Just because it was the right time to be settling down, it didn't mean that Henry was the *wrong* man. What if... she popped a bubble, you followed your heart on a whim and then found out it was all an illusion?

Annie drained the water and washed away the suds. She didn't know how she felt. Unsettled? Expectant and disappointed at the same time. There was one person who she had to talk to right now. Jojo.

But their phone was engaged. Annie tried again throughout the afternoon but still engaged — as if it had been left off the hook. By early evening it did ring, but there was no reply.

28

They spent most of Sunday in bed, emotionally bruised and a little wary, they tiptoed around one another by being courteous, thoughtful and restrained. When it got dark again, they got out of bed and planned an outing to a Spanish restaurant a short walk from their flat.

'Can I have my clothes back, Nico?'

'They're in the wardrobe,' he said.

Jojo opened the door just in case he had returned her precious collection. Cream, beige, and taupe, clean lines, understated. No colour or pizzazz. 'I meant my dressing-up box.'

Nico tucked in his shirt and then scooped up his loose change from the bedside table. When he didn't reply, Jojo wrestled with her need to pursue the conversation and a dread that it would lead to more cross words. She didn't have the emotional stamina for another round.

'The week's up,' she said in a soft, upbeat tone.

Nico stood behind her in front of the wardrobe mirror. He

placed his hands on her shoulders. 'Do you really want to dress like a teenager from a squat? I thought you had grown up bella. That I had taught you about style and good taste.'

'You have. I love the outfits you bought for me. It's just that those clothes all mean something to me. The fox fur belonged to my granny.'

'They are just clothes bella. Old clothes. You have your memories here.' His fingers fluttered over her breastbone. 'Together we will make new ones. But we will make them with you wearing beautiful clothes that befit a woman of your sophistication and elegance. It is time to leave behind the little girl that lived in a squat.'

Jojo tried to ignore the lump in her throat, the tears pricking her eyes. She had always felt unique and glamorous in her vintage clothes. Now she realised with a burning shame that her appearance had been shabby. Maybe Nico was right. It was time that she grew up.

In the Spanish restaurant, Nico was as attentive and charming to Jojo as he was on their first date. There was no performance for the waiters or other diners.

'Do you have any idea how beautiful you are?' he said, holding her hand across the table. 'You had me under your spell from the moment I saw you sitting at a table with your friends. A parrot amongst a flock of pigeons. Everyone in that pub was looking at you.'

'They *were* when three doves came flying out of my handbag. The landlord went crazy.' Jojo covered her face with her hands as she remembered that afternoon. 'They crapped all over his customers.'

Nico laughed. 'We got thrown out.'

'You took me to a Wimpy bar.'

'And bought you a Knickerbocker Glory which you got all over your face and on the sleeves of your blouse.'

'A 1940s apricot pink blouse with Belgium lace.' She fell in love with that blouse after seeing it on an antique stall at Camden Market. The stall holder was persuaded to put it aside for her until she had enough money to buy it the following week.

Nico changed the subject. 'We are good together. A team.'

They had almost finished the seafood paella. It was an enormous plate and as they became full, they picked off the best morsels, leaving only rice. A waiter cleared their table and emptied the bottle of Rioja into their glasses.

'Have you ever been married?' Jojo tried to sound nonchalant.

'No. Have you?'

'Of course not. Did you ever get close to getting married?'

Nico laughed. He signalled for their bill. 'Are you angling for a proposal?'

'No. I just wondered.'

He gave her a knowing look and Jojo felt small. The subject was closed. He was a liar. Maybe he was still married to Meryl – a crazy woman who committed violent acts and had good reason to hate Jojo. Nico's conviction that Meryl would not dare to harm her did not reassure Jojo. What was in that film? A recording of their wedding, or something more sinister? A recorded death threat that Nico was keeping as evidence in case Meryl made another attempt on his life?

The next day when they arrived at the Golden Globe, Kai Keisler was signing autographs. Nico hesitated, waiting to be spotted, but they might as well have been invisible.

'We're earlier than usual. I expect your fans haven't turned up yet,' Jojo said.

They walked through the theatre and Jojo cringed, hoping

that Nico wasn't remembering how she had made a fool of him. Thank goodness he had forgiven her.

Max was in the corridor by the changing rooms. 'Have you heard old man?' he said, twirling his moustache.

'Heard what?' Nico barked, and Jojo hoped his mood improved before he practised throwing knives at her.

'Both Annika Riley and John Jenkins want the same act. Come on, spill the beans, is it you?'

Nico's jaw clenched, and a flush bloomed on his neck. 'You will hear soon enough,' he said, before striding away.

Bunty was massaging cream into her calves when Jojo pushed open the door of the changing room to a haze of steam. 'You surprised us all on Saturday night with your Alice act. Has Peter Walker recovered yet?'

'Why? What did he say?' Nico was right, she had let everyone down breaking with protocol.

'It's not so much what he said. I saw his face when the curtain came down on Nico after your solo. You, my darling, are going to have some explaining to do and a bit of grovelling, I should think. Women are not meant to show off like that! Didn't you know we are only capable of being dancers or assistants?'

The gushing from a shower slowed and then stopped. Bobbi emerged, wrapped in a towel. 'I thought I heard your voice, darling.' She left wet footprints as she padded across the room to flop onto the bench alongside Jojo. 'Phew. What we need in here is a lounger like the ones at the spa.' Her face was pink. She smelt of white musk.

'Or a spa. Right here. Wouldn't it be great to have a jacuzzi to relax in?' Bunty had finished dressing and was tugging a brush through her luxurious curls.

Jojo watched her own reflection between those of Bobbi and Bunty, drab and dull in her beige shift dress. The two of them didn't need fancy clothes to ooze glamour. They had natural style and confidence. Maybe she had relied too much on her clothes to express her individuality because now she felt as though her identity had been stripped away to expose Joanna Evans, the nuisance kid who was bullied at school.

Sly burst into the room, her arms full of shopping and dance kit. 'Sale at Hartleys. What's the news from the Starlight?'

'John Jenkins and Annika Riley are both bidding for the same act. Of course, that will attract other sponsors and agents. It's so exciting! Does anyone know if it's Kai or Nico?'

They were all looking at her. It definitely wasn't Nico, but she didn't want to tell the girls, besides he believed he could turn things around. 'It's still early days. Let's see after the Easter Gala.'

'I knew it!' Sly squealed. 'I saw John Jenkins's man pass you a business card at the restaurant.'

Bobbi gave Jojo a secretive look, pressing her lips together and signalling something with her eyes. Jojo took it to mean, tell me later.

'That was just some drunk guy trying to pick me up. Whatever made you think he had something to do with Jenkins?'

When Bunty and Sly had left for a coffee in Cake Presto, Bobbi said, 'Come on, tell all.'

'There's nothing to tell.' Jojo was afraid that word would get back to Nico.

'John Jenkins's business card? Is he interested in Nico?'

Jojo turned to hide her face. She was desperate to share her news. If only she could trust Bobbi. 'Will you promise to keep this to yourself?'

'Of course, darling. I'm the epitome of discretion.'

'Sly was right. A man working for John Jenkins asked me to ring his office to arrange a meeting. But...' Jojo bit her bottom lip, 'he's not interested in Nico. Only me.'

Bobbi's face was hard to read. Thoughtful. Perplexed. Jojo felt the same. 'Can I see the business card?'

'Sure.' Jojo retrieved it from her purse and then waited whilst Bobbi scrutinised it, much as Jojo had done in quiet moments.

She sighed and handed it back. 'It looks genuine. Did he say why he wants to meet with you?'

'No, but I assumed it was because he liked my act.'

'It was a brilliant act. But why is John Jenkins interested in you? No offense. He's looking for a magician that will transform the world of magic. This is big time. Your act was cute and sexy. You know Jenkins owns several nightclubs and, to be frank, has a bit of a reputation for seducing young wannabes?'

That thought had occurred to Jojo, but she had dismissed it. Now she felt stupid. 'So, you think that's all this is, a pickup?'

'I'm just saying be careful. Has Annika Riley contacted you?'

'No.' Bobbi was right. According to the Golden Globe's jungle drum, both teams of talent scouts were after the same act. They were looking for an exceptional magician, Nico or Kai. It was time to accept her reality. She was nothing remarkable or special. Her silly dreams were like the outfits she chose from her dressing-up box. She could dress herself up and pretend to be something else, but that wasn't real. It was as though she were back on the playground with Simon Pugh laughing at her for believing in an imaginary world. Annie had saved her then. This time, it was Nico.

29

Annie had tried Jojo again first thing on Monday morning. This time Nico picked up and, although he was polite, Annie could sense the irritation in his voice.

'I've been trying to reach you.' There was so much Annie wanted to share with Jojo. Talking to her friend might help to unravel the complicated emotions that were knotted in the pit of her stomach. 'You left without saying goodbye.' Annie lowered her voice. 'Was Nico okay when you got home?'

'Yes, of course.' Jojo sounded bright and breezy, as though it was a different girl who had shredded a tissue, her eyes puffy from crying, the night of the show.

'Good. I was worried. Could you meet me at Cake Presto later today?'

'I'm sorry I can't, Annie. Best not meet up at work until after Easter Gala. I can't really spare the time. You will both come?'

'Yes. Yes, of course.'

'Okay. I'll see you after the Gala show.' That was it. She hung up.

It was probably a good thing if she didn't bump into Charlie for a couple of weeks. Give her time to settle down and get some perspective. The Golden Globe was glamorous, with its colourful characters, a secret tunnel, magicians, and disappearing doves. She was getting swept up in the romance of the place, not the person. Henry kept her feet firmly on the ground, and that was what she wanted. Security. Certainty. Jojo didn't need her anymore; she had Nico. Annie was like a third wheel. It was time to step back and give them some space.

The travel agents were quiet that morning and so Annie offered to make Sarah a coffee.

'Hey, that's not fair!' Sarah scowled at the paper in her hand.

'I don't mind, but if you really want to make it, go ahead.'

'No – this. Don't tell me it has nothing to do with you dating the man from head office.'

Annie stood her empty mug on Sarah's desk and peered over her shoulder.

'Apparently, you've been picked at random for the Greek Islands jolly. If you believe that, then I'm Prince Charles's girlfriend. No doubt Mr. Bulletin Board will be joining you.' Sarah thrust the Head Office newsletter at Annie.

'I really didn't know, Sarah. You're right, if Henry put my name forward, then it's not fair. I'll find out and put things right, I promise.'

'I'm not begrudging you the holiday. You deserve it as much as any of us. It's just, you know?'

Annie nodded. 'I do know. I'll make some coffee.'

If Henry had pulled some strings, why hadn't he warned her? After a slow start, the shop became busy, leaving no time for speculation and comment from the other staff. She meant what she had said to Sarah. Unless she was awarded the place on a fair and transparent basis, she would have to turn the offer down.

Henry's Jaguar was waiting for Annie in a rare parking spot just down the road from the travel agents. She saw it as soon as she stepped out of the door and her heart lifted.

'What a wonderful surprise,' Annie said, climbing in beside Henry. She kissed him on the cheek. 'If you keep on spoiling me, I might come to expect it.'

'Nothing is too much trouble for my princess. Good day at work?' He pulled out into the traffic, the car gently purring, and Annie let herself sink into sumptuous soft leather.

'It was okay, thanks.'

'Just, okay?'

'Why?' Annie had a feeling she knew what was coming next.

'I thought you might have had some good news.'

Henry could have read about Annie being selected for the Greek trip in the newsletter. She gave him the benefit of the doubt. 'Maybe. It seems I was picked at random to do a recce on one of the new resorts.'

'Just one?'

'I don't know. We were busy and so I never really found out the details.'

'I think you will find it is the luxury holiday, visiting three islands. It includes transfers by yacht and excursions.' He turned to grin at her. 'Impressed?'

'So, you engineered it?'

'Perk of the job.'

Annie was uncomfortable. She would have loved the holiday under other circumstances, but it wasn't fair to the other staff and she was disappointed in Henry. 'Won't it be awkward when your colleagues find out that we are seeing each other?'

'They all do it. Mark and Fiona are going with us. They've been having an affair for years. Everyone knows about them.'

'Isn't Mark married?'

'Exactly. He's not going to squeal on me.'

They were out of central London, cruising on the road back to Fenwood. Annie closed her eyes. Was she being too prissy? Too judgmental? Henry's attitude to Mark's affair and his lack of integrity did not sit well with her. She thought she knew him. That he was reliable, solid, and honourable. 'It doesn't seem fair. I thought staff were rewarded with the opportunity of a holiday for their achievements, like the number of sales, length of service, or the recommendation of their manager. If I get picked for no apparent reason, it's going to look bad.'

'There is a reason. This manager recommended you. I thought you would be pleased. Our first holiday together.'

'Can't we just book a holiday to the Cyclades? Let someone else like Sarah have this opportunity?'

Henry drove in silence, breaking too hard at the lights. He swore at a driver who cut in front of him. Eventually he said, 'I'll say you have commitments and can't travel this year.'

Annie didn't want him to lie, but for now, it seemed best to let it go. 'Okay. It was a lovely idea. Thank you for thinking of me. Let's plan a holiday together, anyway.'

Henry didn't reply. He dropped Annie off at her house rather than driving to his flat as she had anticipated.

'Do you want me to come over later when I've changed? I could make us some supper?'

'Not tonight. Maybe later in the week?'

Annie knew Henry was sulking because his surprise had backfired, and maybe she was being too precious. If he had talked about the holiday with Mark, then he might feel embarrassed explaining Annie's refusal. If Henry was okay with Mark having an affair when he was married, what did that say about Henry's morals?

When Annie heard Jessica's key in the door, she waited for her sister to thump up the stairs and then bang her bedroom door shut. Jessica did nothing with a light touch. Annie had showered and changed out of her work suit. Jessica would be doing the same before supper and, Annie suspected, a night out with Gary or their friends. She knocked on Jessica's door. 'Do you mind if I talk to you while you change?'

Jessica peeled off her tights and threw them in a laundry basket. 'Go ahead.'

Annie sighed, not knowing where to start. 'You have more experience with men than me.'

Jessica snorted. 'Do you want me to tell you about the birds and the bees? You can't get pregnant by sitting on the same toilet seat.' She snorted again, enjoying her joke.

'Don't be daft. I'm serious.'

Jessica turned her back to Annie, who undid her zip. She let her silky dress drop to the floor and stepped out of it. 'Okay. I'm listening.'

'How did you know Gary was the right one?'

'Apart from having a perfect arse, and a season ticket for West Ham?'

'Yes.' Annie waited.

Jessica pulled on her jeans and then lay down on the bed and breathed in before zipping them up. Annie made a disapproving face. 'They've just been washed; they'll loosen up. I don't know. I kind of knew early on.'

'What was different about Gary compared to the other men you've gone out with?'

'We just hit it off. There was a chemistry between us.

When he looked at me, my stomach flipped. The touch of his fingers sent electric waves through me.' Jessica smiled, a faraway look in her eyes. 'He makes me laugh. And he's good in the sack.'

Annie had felt it, an electric current at the touch of his hand. She had tried to pass it off as static energy. She stood up to leave. 'Okay thanks.'

'Hey not so fast. Why do you want to know? Has Henry proposed or something?' Jessica held up two tops. Annie pointed to a short-sleeved blouse with a bold Hawaiian print.

'No. I'm just confused. What if you get all of those feelings that you've described, but it's the wrong man?'

'What do you mean, the wrong man?'

'I mean, they're not suitable. Isn't it better to find someone who ticks all the right boxes? Someone with similar interests and values?'

'Don't tell me you've got a checklist? Honestly, Sis, you make it sound like you're choosing a kitchen appliance not falling in love.'

'You know, I don't believe there is such a thing as falling in love.'

'If you say so. But I'm a thinking that is exactly what you *are* doing.' Jessica winked. 'I'm not stopping for tea. We're getting a pizza.'

A few days ago, Annie had received a letter inviting her to a holiday rep. recruitment day at a London hotel. She hadn't mentioned it to Henry because she had been in two minds about going. Now, it seemed like a good idea. This job in Spain might be exactly what she needed. A new start that wasn't dependent on a man.

30

'I'm going to change my finale,' Nico said, after watching Jojo perform the rabbit trick perfectly.

'Is that wise with only ten days to go?' Jojo settled Pixie and Muffin back in their basket. She was trying to handle them with authority and transmit a message: *Behave*.

'Keisler must be favourite because all the scouts are excited about one act and nobody has approached me.'

Jojo cringed at her naivety at believing John Jenkins was interested in her performance. 'The press may prefer your act. It's still very close. There doesn't have to be a winner. Isn't this all about discovering new talent?'

Nico ran his fingers through his hair. 'Maybe. It's just what you said about the act being dated. Jenkins was throwing around the phrase new-wave magic when we met at the interval. Keisler with his tie-dyed doves is original. Everyone has seen an escapist routine. I could make it more dangerous.'

'No! I was terrified when the lock got stuck. Please don't, Nico.'

'Let's see. I've been working on something. Sword trick next?'

Jojo nodded. 'I'll ask Charlie to fetch it.'

'No need.' Nico stuck his head out of the door. 'Phillipe. Be a good man and ask Charlie if he could deliver the sword box.'

'Why don't we have a quick coffee break whilst we are waiting?' Jojo said.

'Don't tell me you're meeting your friend again.'

'No. You asked me not to until after the show, but I really ought to phone her or try to see her after work. I'm sure there was something that she wanted to talk about when she phoned the other morning.'

'I'll buy you a coffee in Cake Presto, but no cake. You'll be seeing Annabelle and Henry after the Easter Gala. Until then, you need to focus one hundred percent on our act.'

It was the first time Nico had agreed to take a break with Jojo. He usually said that he didn't need a midday meal and grabbed a coffee in the resource library when Jojo was at Cake Presto. Heads turned when they walked into the café. Jojo was aware of a couple of women whispering together. She doubted she would get much of Nico's attention after all.

Mrs Brew wasn't star struck; they had to wait in line for their coffees and carry them to the table.

'Nico, why do you call Annie, Anabelle?' This bothered Jojo because it seemed to create another barrier between her best friend and partner, as though Nico was keeping Annie at a distance.

'Annabelle is a beautiful name. Annie is a child's name, like Jojo.'

That stung. Jojo tried to make light of it. 'And Nico is more grown up?'

'It's my stage name. What were you christened?'

Jojo took a sip of coffee. She would like to ask Nico the same thing. Remind him that his name was Nicholas Brown, but he must never know that she had opened his safe. 'Joanna.'

'Joanna. That is much better than Jojo. From now on I will call you Joanna.'

As Nico hardly ever used her name, it did not bother Jojo too much. It was good sharing a break with Nico. Maybe she had been neglecting him to spend time with Annie and Charlie. The only problem was his fans. 'Get ready to sign autographs,' Jojo said as the two women approached their table.

Whilst Nico was busy doing his stuff, signing and conjuring, Jojo took their cups back to the counter. Mrs Brew received them with a smile. 'Nice to see you come in with your man for a change.' Then Mrs Brew looked past Jojo and shook her head a fraction, her eyes sending a message. Jojo spun around to see the back of a woman with a similar hair style to Meryl leaving the café.

'Who was that?'

'Who?' Mrs Brew frowned. Then she wiped over the counter, and Jojo wondered if she was just being paranoid. There were lots of women with cropped hair, it was fashionable. Why would Meryl visit Cake Presto?

The sword-trick box had been delivered to their studio, whilst they were in Cake Presto, but they needed Charlie or someone else to assist. On stage, it would be a member of the audience. 'I'll get him,' Jojo said.

Charlie was at the end of the corridor. He came when Jojo called, but there was none of his usual banter. He had seemed a little subdued since the Starlight show.

'Ready to go?' Nico asked as he surveyed the box of swords.

'Not yet, I have to limber up.' It wasn't just her body that needed to be prepared; Jojo had to mentally psyche herself up for this trick. It was dangerous and every time they performed it; she was afraid. Today, images of Meryl going on a killing spree jangled her nerves. What if that had been her in the café? Was she watching them, waiting for an opportunity to take her revenge? When Nico finished thrusting swords into the box, she would warn him that Meryl might have been in the café, but not now it would distract him and it was crucial they both got their timing right.

Jojo closed her eyes and tried to imagine that she was alone in a bubble. She focused on her centre and visualized herself rooted to the ground. A stretch of her hamstrings, a twist of her torso – this way and that. Then her neck, bending her head forward to stretch the tendons. Mentally moving through her body, finding the tension and relieving it. She took a deep breath and, satisfied that her body and mind were ready, focused on the room and task.

'Ready?' Nico asked again and Jojo nodded.

His face was set in concentration as he drew the first sword.

Jojo stepped into the box.

'Shut her in Charlie.'

Charlie left an opening, a window for Jojo's face.

'No. Shut the window. It helps me concentrate better.' This was Jojo's signal. She had ten seconds after the window was closed to make her escape.

She counted down. Nine. Eight. It wasn't a hard trick. She just had to slide open the trapdoor beneath her feet. All it needed was a little nudge. Seven. Six. okay, a bigger nudge. Five. Four. Nothing. Nothing. She was running out of time.

'Help, help!' She knew it was hopeless. Nico wouldn't hear her. What was she meant to do in an emergency? She couldn't remember. She pushed again. Come on, come on! 'Help!' Nothing. Three. Two. One more second and it'd be too late.

'What are you doing?' Nico sounded annoyed and then his voice rose in panic. 'What's wrong?'

Jojo pounded on the door. 'Stop Nico! The floors stuck.'

The door opened and Charlie was there. Her legs weak, she fell into his arms.

'Joanna.' Nico pushed Charlie away and held her tight. 'What happened? Why didn't you move the floor? My God. I nearly put a sword in you. Are you okay, bella?'

Jojo wasn't okay. If Charlie hadn't heard her cries for help, she would have been seriously injured or killed. Her legs were weak as Charlie helped her into a chair.

'I can take it from here,' Nico snapped at him.

Jojo kept her head bent over her legs. 'I'm just a bit dizzy.'

Nico threw open the doors to the sword box. 'These bloody props. Victorian like the theatre. Nobody looks after them. Someone should properly check them before use. Very convenient that Charlie was on hand to rescue you.'

'It's okay. I'm not hurt.' Jojo couldn't deal with Nico's temper right now, his feud with Charlie. 'Let's call it a day. I'll get changed and meet you in the theatre.'

Nico sighed. 'I'm having a word with Walker about Charlie's incompetence. That boy has the hots for you and it's getting in the way of his work.'

Jojo didn't bother arguing with Nico. She just wanted a bit of quiet time to recover from the scare. 'Meet you at three?'

Bobbi met Jojo on her way to the changing room. 'I just heard. Are you okay, darling?'

'Yes. Sort of.' Bobbi hugged her and Jojo's body relaxed. Then came the tears. A big loud sob. 'I'm sorry.' Jojo shuddered and pulled away to wipe her nose.

'What you need is a stiff drink. Get changed and I'll find a medicinal shot.'

Jojo gave a watery laugh. 'I'm okay.'

'Trust your Aunty Bobbi,' she winked.

A hot shower helped. Accidents happened. That's all it was.

'Here you are darling, a double Scotch, courtesy of Max.'

'Does he know too?'

'Everyone does. To be honest, we're all a bit spooked by these unexplained accidents. Sly's convinced it's the wrath of Molly May, but I'm afraid it might be something far more sinister.' Bobbi put a hand on Jojo's arm. 'Whoever sent you that anonymous note obviously means business.'

'I thought you said it was from one of Nico's frustrated fans.' Jojo took a sip of Scotch and screwed up her face.

'Maybe it was. I'm just saying, be careful.'

'The floor of the sword box got stuck. It's no big deal. It just needs oiling to loosen it up.'

'You're much cooler about it than I would be. Maybe you should consider who would want to harm you. Have you got any enemies?'

Jojo took a bigger glug of Scotch. This time it went down easier. Maybe it was an acquired taste. 'No, of course not.' But her thoughts were on Meryl. If it was her in Cake Presto, then she could have sneaked into the rehearsal room and tampered with the trick. Meryl would know her way around.

'Maybe it *is* Molly May. Stranger things have happened. If you look up the history of this theatre, you'll find reported sightings of her in the forbidden tunnel and stories of unexplained accidents similar to yours.'

'Why me?'

'You're new. A magician's assistant. The first one since Meryl and you know how that ended. She disappeared without a trace.'

Jojo went to take another glug and realised that she had drained the glass. It hadn't made her feel better. Bobbi's dire warnings and the high alcohol content had made her woozy. 'I'd better find Nico.'

Charlie was hanging around outside the changing room. 'Are you okay Bat Girl?'

It felt a little as though she was under water, but Jojo held her act together. 'Yes. Thanks for rescuing me.'

Charlie was looking at her oddly, as if he wanted to ask her something. He coughed. 'I haven't seen Annie since the show.'

'No, I've told her I'm too busy rehearsing to meet for coffee. Charlie, did you work with Meryl?'

'Who's Meryl?'

'She was Nico's assistant before me.'

'No. Must have left before I started.'

They walked together towards the theatre. 'Nico and I were in Cake Presto earlier. I thought I saw her, Meryl.'

Charlie stopped walking. 'I didn't think you knew her.'

'I don't, but I've heard about her.' Jojo wondered whether she should confide in Charlie. Maybe tomorrow, when she wasn't under the influence. If she spoke now, her tongue might just run away with her.

Charlie leant in. 'Have you been drinking?'

'Just a medicinal shot. Charlie, do you think someone might have got into the rehearsal room and tampered with the box? I mean, how long was it left unattended?'

'It's possible, I suppose. I delivered it as soon as Nico asked and so it was there until you got back and asked me to assist with the trick.'

Nico joined them. He glowered at Charlie. 'This is what I mean! If you spent half as much time doing the job we employ you to do instead of flirting with Joanna, then accidents wouldn't happen. I've spoken to Walker about your conduct.'

'Joanna, huh?' Charlie shook his head at Nico.

'Can we go home?' Jojo said. She was afraid. Bobbi was right, the falling gantry, anonymous note, and then another near miss. It wasn't a coincidence. She had to talk to Nico about Meryl, admit to opening the safe. If Meryl was mentally unstable and held a grudge, then she was dangerous.

31

Annie sat in the back row, feeling a little detached from the other applicants who seemed to have bonded over lunch. She had arrived just after the complimentary buffet. If she had been serious about the job from the outset, she might have taken the day off and would now be pointing things out in the information pack, or making jokes, like the boy with quiffy hair and the two women in the next row. As it was, she first went into work to get permission from Lisa. Then, before she could change her mind, she hopped on a bus headed for Victoria. It was a wonder that she had found the hotel and arrived in reasonable time, given the lack of planning. Why was she here? A job in the sun with accommodation. Annie turned the pages of the recruitment brochure. *Every day an adventure. Creating memories. Part of a team.* It sounded wonderful, but as a dream. An idyll. If this became her reality, she would live in Spain on her own. Maybe with some of these people. She cast her eyes around the conference room. Most of the applicants were close to her in age, early twenties. There were a few older women, thirties and forties. One who looked as though she was sixty, but her face was weathered by the sun and she was very thin, so maybe looked older than her years. A man in his forties and several young men. Annie wondered what was happening in their lives and why they felt the need to uproot, to succumb to the promise of sunshine and adventure.

A man in a suit strode into the room a sheaf of papers under one arm. As each back straightened in sequence, it reminded Annie of a breeze through a field of corn. According to the programme, group-work would follow the presentation, then a test paper and interview.

'Today we hope to recruit six to eight holiday reps for four of our resorts in the Andalusian region of Spain. Working for Thomaston Holidays is like joining a family.' There was an appreciative murmur.

Annie's attention strayed. She had a family, a job, a life. Why did everything have to change? Mum's pink camellia came to mind. Every year it flowered and Mum would look out on it from her kitchen window and announce that summer was on its way. Then one day, Dad moved it to a sunny spot in the garden. Annie had been eating Coco Pops when they discussed it.

'You can't move my camellia,' Mum had said.

'I thought we agreed to put down crazy paving. You said that you wanted a patio.'

'Can't you work around the camellia? It could die of shock if you transplant it.' It was those words that made six-year-old Annie pay attention. She imagined a plant crying out unheard before withering away in the night.

'Or it could thrive,' her dad said.

Would she thrive or die uprooted from Fenwood and replanted in Spain? Living in Fenwood, working at the travel agents in Trafalgar Square, suited her perfectly. She was content. It was the people around her that were changing. Jojo settled with Nico. Jessica getting married in September, even if they had to have their wedding reception in the Social Club. Mum and Dad were moving to Scotland. Maybe she was too cautious, afraid to take risks. Charlie didn't think so. Annie smiled to herself. There it was again, that bubble pushing up into her chest. The camelia, she now remembered, had died.

The presentation had finished and there was a stir of activity around her as people reached for their bags and consulted the paperwork. 'What's happening now?' she asked a woman sitting to her left.

'Group-work. You should have a letter on your badge telling you which group you're in. This paper tells you which room.' The woman's badge said that her name was Shi Yanyu and her group C.

Annie hoped they were in the same group so that she could follow Shi Yanyu, but her group was B the Wordsworth room on the first floor. As she followed a trail of people up some stairs, Annie had a stern word with herself. She may have arrived a little after the other applicants, but she was just as serious. It was no good going through the interview half-hearted and then being disappointed when she didn't get the job.

Five empty chairs formed a circle in the middle of the room. Three people, one man and two women, sat in corners of the room nursing clipboards and observant expressions. Annie sat with her back to the door so that she could see all three of the people watching her.

'You have twenty minutes to plan a one-day excursion in London. The time starts now.'

The only man in their group jumped up straightaway and grabbed hold of a marker pen. He removed the top purposefully and stood in front of the white board. 'Let's start with a brainstorm.'

'Tower of London.'

'Trafalgar Square.'

'Houses of Parliament.'

'St James's Park.'

They all reeled off the obvious tourist attractions. Annie needed time to reflect, to come up with something original. What would Jojo do? She opened her bag to find a pen, keeping one eye on the whiteboard. Her hand closed around a biro. In the right-hand corner, a woman with thickly framed glasses was taking notes. Her head popped up. She stared at Annie, then scribbled some more. Annie needed a scrap of paper but didn't want to appear disengaged.

'What about a theatre matinee?' she threw in. Then, when her suggestion was being noted, she dived back into her bag. There was a neatly folded sheet of white paper. Annie retrieved it and then unfolded it, all the time keeping her eyes forward. She wanted to scribble down a timetable before suggesting it to the group. Annie planned to take the marker pen out of bossy boy's hand and write up a proposed schedule.

She smoothed the paper out on her information folder and clicked the top of her biro. If the excursion started at ten and finished at four, they should be able to fit in two or three major attractions, lunch and a bus tour. Annie bent her head to jot this down. It was only then that she saw what was written on the paper. Her heart missed a beat. A nausea swept over Annie and she stood up, knocking over her chair.

'I'm sorry, I've got to leave.' Everyone was looking at her.

Outside the room, Annie gasped for breath. She covered her eyes and felt the room sway.

'Would you like a glass of water?' The woman with thickly framed glasses had followed her out.

'No, thank you. I'm okay, but I don't think I can continue with the interview. I'm sorry.'

Annie was glad that she wasn't expected anywhere. She needed to be alone to think things through. Sitting on a bench in St James's Park, Annie felt as though her roots had been ripped from the ground because there was nothing solid, nothing that she could rely on. What was written on that paper had shaken her.

If you don't want to

If you want

If you value your life

That was all. Three lines of incomplete sentences, but Annie knew what the final note would say because it was in her dressing table drawer. The page must have been inside one of Charlie's books when she carried them in her bag. How it got there was easy to deduce, but why had he sent an anonymous message to Jojo?

32

Nico was moody on the way home from the Golden Globe. Jojo had suggested he stay at work. It was still early, but after the sword trick incident, Nico seemed reluctant to let Jojo out of his sight. She was in the kitchen making coffee when Nico joined her. She felt his anger before she turned to see his scowling face.

'You encourage him. I've told you before. Now this. Can't you see what he's doing? Then you — throwing yourself at him.'

Jojo needed to drink a mug of coffee before opening her mouth. She was still a bit intoxicated.

'I could have killed you! I don't think you understand the risks involved in magic. You think it's all white rabbits and stardust.'

Jojo, about to pour water into the coffee peculator, set down the jug. 'Don't patronise me, Nico. It wasn't my fault the floor stuck. Why are you shouting at me? It was you who nearly killed me. You could at least be sympathetic.' *Like*

Charlie, she was tempted to say, but knew that would light a touch paper.

Nico raked a hand through his hair. 'You're right. I'm sorry Joanna. Go and sit down. I'll bring in the coffee.'

And then we need to talk, she thought. But not until I've downed a good half a mug and can think straight.

Five minutes later, Jojo passed Nico a coffee and sat beside him on the sofa. She had rehearsed in her head what she needed to say. It was time to come clean about the anonymous note and her suspicion that Meryl was responsible. But something else was eating her and hard as she tried to put aside that grievance for another day, it would not be buried.

'I don't like being called Joanna. It's not me, and neither are these clothes.'

'Fine. Go back to your little squat and childish friends. I thought you were more than that. Obviously, I was wrong.'

The stress of the day caught up with Jojo, and she annoyed herself by crying. They were hot, angry tears. 'I will. Just give me back my clothes and I'm out of here. I've had enough!'

Nico left the room. Then the front door slammed. At first, Jojo thought he had gone to get her clothes, but as time passed, she realised he wasn't coming back in a hurry. That's great. Way to go Jojo. Meryl could be stalking her. She needed to let Nico know so that he could protect her. She tried the front door, and it opened. At least she wasn't locked in. A clock ticked loudly; one she hadn't noticed before. Nico's coffee was cold. Why couldn't she have kept her mouth shut? Maybe he was waiting for her to pack her things and leave. Where would she go? The thought of life without Nico was unbearable.

Jojo took their mugs to the kitchen and washed up. Her head was pounding from the Scotch and caffeine. If only she had gone with her first instinct and refused the whisky. Jojo checked her watch; Annie would still be at work. As she dialled the number, Jojo felt calmer. Her friend would help to put things into perspective.

One of Annie's colleagues picked up. 'Sorry, Annie took the afternoon off. I can leave a message.'

Jojo hoped Annie hadn't gone to the Golden Globe, hoping to see her. Annie has a life other than you, she berated herself. 'Please, could you tell her Jojo called? Is she in tomorrow?' Jojo left a message that she would be in touch, planning to visit the travel agent's when she could get away.

A key turned in the lock. Jojo held her breath, relieved that Nico had returned, but afraid he might still be angry with her.

'Are you there, Joanna?'

Jojo peeked around the door.

'Oh, thank God bella. I thought you had left me.' He was holding a bouquet of roses and lilies. 'I'm a jerk. I don't deserve you, my beautiful butterfly.'

Jojo took the flowers from him. They smelt of summer. 'They're gorgeous. Thank you.'

'It is to say that I am sorry. Sorry for nearly killing you. And sorry for throwing away your old clothes.'

Distracted by the flowers, it took two heart beats before Jojo fully comprehended. 'All of them?' Her voice broke.

Nico nodded. 'I'm sorry bella.'

'Freddy the Fox? My Dior gown? *Everything?*'

'Afraid so.' Nico looked sheepish, as though he had been caught with his finger in the buttercream. Didn't he know those clothes meant everything to her? Jojo was afraid to speak. Eventually she squeaked, 'Is there any way we can get them back?'

Nico shook his head. 'Are you going to put those flowers in water?'

There was nothing else to be said. Her clothes had gone.

'Could you put on more coffee, Joanna? Mine went cold.'

Jojo nodded and went through the motions. He didn't mean to hurt her. She swiped away the tears, afraid that Nico would see.

It wasn't until they had finished supper, a simple dish of spaghetti in an olive oil, lemon and garlic sauce, that Jojo felt strong enough to bring up the anonymous note.

'Nico, we need to talk,' she started.

Nico reached across the table and took both of her hands in his. 'I didn't mean it bella. I don't want to lose you. I love you so much.'

The knot of misery in her chest loosened a little. 'I love you, too. This is about today.' She held up a hand to stop Nico's interruption. 'I haven't told you everything. It's important you know, because I'm afraid.' She took a deep breath. 'The day after the accident on the stage, I received an anonymous note. It said, *if you value your life, keep away from him.*'

'Who?' Nico puffed out his chest. His jaw tightened. 'Keep away from who?'

'I think they meant you. It was addressed to Nico's assistant.'

'Why didn't you tell me?' A nerve in his cheek twitched.

'Nico, please try and stay calm. I've got more to tell you, but you need to listen. I didn't tell you because I knew you would react like this and I didn't want to wind you up before the show.'

'And so why now?'

'Because three things have happened.' Jojo waited for him to register. When he continued to frown, she marked them off on her fingers. 'The falling gantry. The letter. Then, this afternoon.'

Nico took a deep breath and let it out slowly. 'I have another confession to make.'

'Go on.'

'The falling gantry was me. I didn't want you to go out with Annabelle and I thought that if you were a little shaken up, you would send your apologies and spend the evening at home with me.' He grimaced and then made a childlike gesture covering his mouth.

'Why would you do that? What if it had hit me?'

'I knew it wouldn't. I was just playing around. A joke.'

'But you blamed Charlie! *Nico*.' She didn't see the funny side. It had scared her.

Nico folded his arms and sat back in his chair. 'I still blame Charlie.'

'How can you? You just said that it was you.'

'I blame Charlie for this afternoon and for the note.'

'Now that's ridiculous.'

'Is it? Can't you see? Charlie is in love with you. He's trying to turn you against me and make himself a hero. Every time I leave you alone for two minutes, he's at your side with all that ridiculous banter about superheroes. He's just trying to get into your knickers.'

Nico's coarse remark repulsed Jojo. He was wrong about Charlie. There had been nothing sexual between them. She trusted him. 'There's something else you don't know.'

Nico went a little pale. 'What's that?'

'I too have a confession to make. When you locked me in the flat and threw away my clothes.' There was no harm in reminding him of his shortcomings before she admitted hers.

'I didn't do it on purpose.'

'Anyway, I was looking for the caretaker's phone number so he could let me out and I found the code to the safe.' The air between them felt charged, but she had to continue. 'I saw the safe when I was looking for my clothes. I thought that there might be a spare key in it and so I opened it.' Nico stared at

Jojo without blinking, and she felt her stomach cave. 'I saw your marriage certificate.'

'I told you about Meryl. I'm not hiding anything from you, Joanna. You've let Charlie and his nasty suspicions get into your head.'

She didn't remind him he had denied ever being married. 'This afternoon when you were signing autographs, I think she may have come into Cake Presto. I couldn't be certain, but I saw Mrs Brew signal to someone behind me and her eyes kind of slid over to you. I turned around and saw a woman with an elfin cut leaving in a hurry.'

'Why didn't you tell me?' Nico threw his napkin across the table. 'That bloody woman. I should have got her locked up. I'm too soft.'

Jojo was relieved that Nico now knew everything. 'I'm scared, Nico. What if she's trying to harm me? She could have tampered with the trick and sent the note. What will she do next?'

'Nothing, because I won't let her. You were right to tell me bella. From now on, I'm not letting you out of my sight.'

'Are you still married?'

'No. Well, on paper – yes, but that's a technical detail.'

'What's on the cine film Nico? I saw Meryl written on the tin.'

'It's my insurance against any claims that bitch might make. If a court of law sees what's on that tape, Meryl will get locked up for good.'

'Surely, if she's dangerous, you need to tell the authorities? For her own good as well as ours. I'm afraid Meryl wants to kill me Nico.'

'Meryl knows that I have the power to take away her freedom. So long as I am at your side, she won't come near you.'

33

Annie could think of two explanations for the anonymous note: Charlie was in love with Jojo and wanted her to leave Nico. Or, and this seemed much more likely to Annie, he knew something about Nico and feared for Jojo's safety and well-being. She'd had her suspicions about Nico from the day they had met him outside the hidden tunnel, and Charlie's opinion had been obvious even then. When she first read the three incomplete lines, Annie's reaction was a stab of pain — Charlie was in love with Jojo. A tide of grief and loss had her stumbling out of the assessment centre. It had taken a couple of walks around the lake, noticing a scattering of primroses and a bird carrying a twisty twig to build its nest, before Annie's mind calmed and she was able to think rationally. Charlie would never send a note like that for his own gain. That's not who he was. As the sun sank lower in the sky, Annie had forced herself off the bench, said goodbye to a mallard who had been keeping her company, and made her way over the little footbridge and out of the park.

By the time she got the train back to Fenwood, Henry would be home.

The Jaguar was in his parking space at the back of the flats. It was six fifteen. Henry would be getting ready to go out with her later that evening. She took a deep breath and pressed his buzzer. He sounded surprised but pleased to hear her voice and told her to come up. His front door was open, so Annie went in.

'Hold on, won't be a minute.' Henry's muffled voice came from the bathroom. He stepped out, a toothbrush clamped between his teeth. He took it out of his mouth and waved it at her before grinning and disappearing back inside. 'You weren't at work this afternoon,' he called out.

Annie sat down, hands in her lap. This was why she didn't like going out on more than one date. She had given Henry the impression that they had a future together, and now she was going to hurt him. It was unkind and Annie didn't do unkind. She had no practice at breaking up.

'Well, this is a pleasant surprise,' Henry said, when he had finished in the bathroom.

Annie took a deep breath. 'I'm sorry to turn up uninvited. It's just that this couldn't wait.'

'Oh bugger. You're not pregnant, are you?'

His assumption threw Annie. If she had been pregnant, then his reaction would have been no comfort. 'No, I'm not.' Indignation helped Annie deliver the next line. 'I've really enjoyed the time that we've spent together, Henry, but I think that it's time for us to go our separate ways.'

'Oh, I see. This is about the trip to the Cyclades. It's okay. I'll make up an excuse for you. I know I was pissed off, but there's no need for you to go off on one.'

'It's not that. I enjoy being with you, but I'm not in love with you, Henry.'

'We like the same things. We have fun. I can give you a comfortable future. You and I could set up our own company. We have everything going for us, Annie.'

'But we're not in love.'

'That's just for films and books. I like you a lot and I reckon we could have a prosperous future together.'

'That's not enough for me, Henry. I thought it was, before I understood what it was to fall in love, but not now.'

Henry frowned. 'Are you telling me you've been seeing someone else behind my back?' Now he was angry. His pride hurt.

Annie stood up to go. 'No. I would never do that. That's why I'm ending it now. I didn't mean to lead you on. I thought I wanted what you did, but this afternoon I realised I wanted more. There is someone. I don't know how he feels about me, but to carry on seeing you now that I know I'm in love with another man would be wrong.'

Henry nodded. He hung his head. Annie got up to go. 'I'll see myself out then?'

She had done the right thing. Now that she knew what love was, she couldn't settle for anything less. But what next? How was she going to tell Jojo about the note? Should she confront Charlie, give him an opportunity to explain himself? Annie didn't know whether she could listen to Charlie declaring his love for Jojo. It would break her heart.

34

True to his word, Nico followed Jojo to Cake Presto at lunchtime, and then back to the studio to watch her eat a salad.

'I don't know why you need to eat during the day, Joanna. We always have a substantial evening meal.'

'Because my work is strenuous. I burn off more calories than you. Besides, it's good for both of us to have a break.' It didn't feel like a break. They had been in the same room all morning and Jojo had seen no one but Nico. Phillipe had delivered their props silently. The lack of a window added to Jojo's feeling of confinement.

'Finished?' Nico stood over her.

'Yes, but I need time to digest my meal before contorting my body.'

'Then you can watch me work the card trick.'

'I have to freshen up.' Surely, she could go to the toilet unaccompanied.

'Joanna, you went on the way back from picking up your lunch. Do you really need to go again?'

Who was this woman, Joanna, dressed in lycra? Jojo didn't recognise herself. Maybe in time she would get over the loss of her beloved clothes collection. She could start again — track down similar treasures, but they would hold different memories. Nico meant well. He had her best interests at heart. She had asked for his protection, and that was what he was doing. If Meryl was stalking her, she wouldn't get past Nico.

'I won't be long.'

Jojo was on her way back to the studio when Peter Walker called her name. It surprised her he even knew it; they had never spoken before. He beckoned her to follow him and strode ahead to his office, which was above the front of house. It was like being called in to see the headmaster. Jojo pulled her woollen wrap down to cover more of her body. Could he fire her for doing an improvisation that he hadn't approved? Jojo wished now that Nico *had* accompanied her.

Walker didn't sit down when she entered his office. 'Why haven't you called John Jenkins?'

'I. Um.' She was lost for words as her brain tried to process what was going on. 'How did you know?'

'JJ has been giving me merry hell. Accusing me of favouring a competitor. Thinks I'm playing him. So, what are you up to? One week until Easter Gala. If the press gets hold of this story, you'll steal the limelight, and it will all be about Jojo Evans instead of the Golden Globe's Easter Gala. Maybe that's your plan?'

Jojo felt for a chair and sunk into it. 'No. No, it's not. I'm sorry. He's really interested in our act?'

'Why do you think he gave you his card? Any other performer would have been overjoyed. It's what this is all about: The Starlight Show, Easter Gala. I'm sorry it's not Nico. He deserves a break, but the world of entertainment is changing. Traditional is a dirty word. How about you phone JJ now?' He picked up the phone receiver, and stretching the cord, handed it to Jojo.

Jojo's heart was racing. Blood rushed to her head. 'Now?' Her hand shook.

'You've kept him waiting long enough.'

'I don't have his ...' Walker was already dialling the number.

John Jenkins PA made an appointment for Jojo the following afternoon. When she put the phone down, she felt sick.

'I don't know how to tell Nico.' That was an understatement. How was she going to get to the meeting without him following her? He would be furious. Disappointed. Angry. 'I can't.'

Walker cupped his chin in one hand. 'Let me handle Nico. I'll call him to a meeting tomorrow afternoon and keep him busy until you get back. You'll have to tell him before the show.'

Peter Walker was a softie, like a cuddly uncle, not the scary figurehead she had imagined. 'Thank you,' Jojo said. 'Can I tell Nico that you wanted to talk to me about something just now?'

He frowned. 'I did.'

'I know, but about something else?'

'Tell him I wanted to talk to you about wearing lycra and woollens. What happened to those whacky outfits that made me smile?'

Jojo giggled. She liked Peter Walker.

Nico fell upon Jojo as soon as she walked from the front of house into the theatre. 'Joanna. Are you alright? Oh my God, you gave me a scare. I've been looking everywhere for you.'

'Sorry. Peter Walker called me into his office.' Jojo hung her head to hide her smile. 'He wanted to have a word about my choice of dress.'

Nico gave a smug laugh. 'What did I tell you? Really, Joanna, it's a good job you've got me to keep you in order.'

Later that afternoon, when she was getting changed, Bobbi joined her in the dressing room. Jojo was bursting with her news. If only she had got away from Nico to visit Annie at the travel agent, but it was impossible.

'You look as though you've won the Pools,' Bobbi said, meeting Jojo's eyes in the mirror.

Jojo tried to stop smiling, but her facial muscles seemed to have set. It had been like that all afternoon and so she had just pretended to be really happy and Nico believed it was because of his attention. She gave a half laugh in response to Bobbi's observation and tried to hide her face as she gathered up her makeup and hair brush.

'You can't hide anything from me, darling. Do tell. Has Nico proposed?'

Jojo sighed. It would be good to tell someone. Bobbi would understand the significance of what Peter Walker had told her. Tomorrow's meeting with John Jenkins could change her life. 'If you promise to keep it a secret.'

Bobbi clasped her hands together. 'He has! Nico's proposed.'

'No. better than that.'

Bobbi threw up her hands. 'Don't keep me in suspense. What's happened?'

Jojo relayed her meeting with Peter Walker, how he had insisted she phone John Jenkins there and then. 'He didn't want me to audition as an exotic dancer. He's really interested in me as a serious performer. Oh Bobbi, I'm so excited. But I'm meeting him tomorrow. I've got nothing prepared.'

Bobbi took several deep breaths. 'Wow. That's amazing. I'm stunned.'

'So was I. I couldn't believe it. I still don't.' Jojo pinched herself. 'His PA said it was just a meeting, but what if he asks me to perform? What should I wear? Should I have something prepared?'

Bobbi shook her head as if trying to settle her thoughts. 'If his PA said it's a meeting, then that's what it will be. He's seen your performance and will be at Easter Gala. I'm so happy for you, darling. I'm not sure how Nico will take the news.'

'Promise me you won't mention this to anyone? I will tell Nico before the Gala, but not yet. First, I have to find out what John Jenkins is proposing.'

Bobbi hugged her tight, and Jojo felt lucky to have Bobbi as her friend.

Nico must have tired of waiting outside the changing room because he had disappeared. Jojo guessed that he had popped up to the resource room and took advantage of his absence to seek Charlie. She wanted to know if he had acquired the length of strong silk. If she could rig it up safely, she could use it to roll her body up and down, and to secure her feet, enabling her to stand mid-air. Nobody had done anything like this before, but Jojo had spent years thinking it through and believed it was possible. Could she practice in the week before Easter Gala? Only if Nico gave her some space.

Charlie wasn't backstage, or in the props room, but Phillipe was. 'Is Charlie at college today?'

'No. Your boss asked for me to assist instead of Charlie.' He shrugged.

Jojo was irritated that Nico was referred to as her boss, but it explained Charlie's absence. 'Do you know where he is now?'

'He is with les animaux.'

Jojo had to stop herself from running to pets prop. She burst through the door and caught Charlie cradling Muffin against his chest. He looked as if he had been caught out.

'Your secret is safe with me. I won't tell anyone that I found you petting the rabbits. How is Muffin?'

Jojo couldn't see Muffin because Charlie turned his back. The hutch was empty. 'Where's Pixie?'

Charlie seemed to do a better job of concealing the rabbits than Jojo had on stage. 'Maybe you should do the rabbit trick; you're good at this. Talking of which, have you got the silk yet?' She wanted to tell Charlie about her afternoon, but she didn't have time. Nico would be looking for her.

'Yes. Where shall I leave it?' Still, he did not face her.

It was then Jojo knew something was wrong. A coldness spread from her neck to the tips of her fingers. 'Let me have Muffin.'

'Jojo.' His voice was barely audible, but his face a plea. His body protecting what was in the circle of his arms.

She pushed his shoulder, and he turned to reveal a tangle of ears and paws. 'What's happened? Are they okay?' Jojo knew the answer, but wanted to preserve a precious minute of ignorance.

'I'm sorry, Jojo. I didn't want you to find them like this. I was going to take them home and bury them. That bastard.'

'Give them to me.'

'Don't put yourself through this Bat Girl. Let me—'

'—My name's Jojo.' She held out her arms.

Muffin's body was stiff but warm, his head at an awkward

angle, eyes glazed over and empty. Pixie felt like a child's soft toy, her ears silky as in life.

'I trusted you, Charlie. I thought you were my friend. How could you do this?'

Confusion and then anger flitted across Charlie's face. He glared at Jojo. 'I was trying to protect you.'

'Protect me? By scaring me and then pretending to be my saviour? You were going to blame Nico for this. He was right. Get away from me.'

Charlie threw a cylindrical prop out of his way as he headed for the door. It crashed. The door slammed. Jojo collapsed over the dead rabbits and sobbed. Pixie and Muffin were babies. They hadn't enjoyed a summer meadow or felt the sun warm their fur. She rocked back and forth to still the pain in her heart. That was where Nico found her.

He righted the cylindrical prop which had rolled close to the door. 'This place is a mess. Couldn't even throw this in a bin. Hey, what's up?'

Jojo raised her head and held out the corpses.

'Blast. Now we'll have to buy and train another couple before the show. Disease?'

'No. Murdered.'

'Don't handle them. Throw them in a black sack or better still, leave it for one of the stagehands. You over excited them. Their hearts can't take it. I told you not to play with them. What were you even doing in here?' Nico held a ball of screwed up paper. 'I'll get Phillipe. Here, this can be thrown with them.'

Jojo lay Pixie and Muffin down in their hutch for the last time. Then she opened the ball of paper. 'Look at this.' She handed it to Nico.

He read the note out loud. '*You have been warned. Why don't you listen?* I told you not to go anywhere without me!' He was angry, but Jojo knew it wasn't with her. She was angry too. Nico put his arms around Jojo and stroked her hair. 'My poor baby. I'll find out who's threatening you. I promise.'

'I already know. You were right. It was Charlie.'

35

'They've got some smashing swimsuits in Miss Selfridge. Perfect for your jolly,' Sara said, as she stowed a couple of bags under her desk. 'Don't take any more walk-ins and then you can go to lunch early. Lisa won't be back until two. I won't tell.'

Annie would have loved to do a bit of shopping. Easter was next weekend, and she hadn't bought any chocolate eggs. 'I can't leave the shop because I'm expecting an important call.'

'Let him wonder where you are. I'll take it.'

Sarah had forgiven her for being awarded the Cyclades holiday. She was a supportive colleague, but Annie wasn't ready to confide. Henry's pride had taken a hit, and the least she could do was spare him from office gossip. 'I'll eat my sandwich out the back. Would you mind finding me if I receive a private call?'

Annie had no regrets following her break up with Henry. She had enjoyed spending time with him and until she got to know him better, how was she to know that he wasn't the one? There was an ache beneath her breastbone. A hollow filled with expectation, dread, and fear. All she could think about was Charlie. Laughing as they chased through the forbidden tunnel. Singing like a Rock Star at the karaoke bar, totally relaxed and unaware of his magnetism. He had likened her to a babbling brook and then blushed like a school boy. Was she expecting too much, imagining that he might feel the same way about her?

Jojo could call at any minute and Annie didn't know what to say. She had tried to rehearse a speech but, in every scenario, Jojo defended Nico and was furious with Annie for suggesting he was anything other than perfect. Dread trumped expectation.

What if she was wrong? Annie's first reaction to the note had been dismay and disappointment. Misery. If Charlie's motive was to win Jojo's affection, then he would never be interested in her and he was not the man that she thought he was. The pain was fear.

'Call for you, Miss Daley,' Sarah called through the door.

Annie brushed away the crumbs from her ham sandwich and tried to prepare mentally. *Jojo, I have found out who left your anonymous note. I don't think it was a threat, more a warning from a well-meaning friend.* She took a deep breath. Why did Charlie have to use such dramatic wording? Couldn't he have just dropped subtle hints? If only he had told her, Annie, about his concerns they could have watched out for Jojo between them. Annie smiled her thanks over to Sarah and picked up the phone on her desk.

'Hi.' Annie was still thinking about her opening sentence when the caller spoke.

'Am I speaking to Annabelle Daley?'

'Yes. I'm sorry. Who is this?'

'Thomaston Holidays. It disappointed us you had to leave

before completing the assessment centre as you are a strong candidate. I trust you are now feeling better?'

Annie hadn't given another thought to the interview. 'Yes, thank you. I don't know what came over me. A twenty-four-hour bug. I had to walk out because thought I was going to faint.'

'You looked very pale. We should have sent someone to stay with you. The reason that I'm calling is to give you the opportunity to take part in another assessment centre. We are holding one in the Midlands next week and could accommodate you if you are still interested in the post.'

Annie didn't know what to say. It would be good to work for a different organisation to avoid any awkward encounters with Henry. The holiday rep job was exciting, an adventure, and accommodation was provided — *in Spain*. But if the note meant what she thought it did, then she couldn't leave the country. Jojo needed her. And then there was Charlie.

'That's a really kind offer. When do you need to know by?'

'Now?'

'In that case, I'll have to decline. I'm sorry to have wasted your time, but things are uncertain in my personal life right now.'

'Oh, I see. Well, better for us to find out now. That's the problem with employing women of a certain age. These little surprises catch us all out.' The caller gave an awkward giggle. 'I hope everything works out for the best.'

Annie frowned at the receiver when the line went dead. Whatever was she talking about? Then it dawned on Annie. Why did everyone assume she was pregnant just because she was in her early twenties?

When Lisa returned to the office mid-afternoon, Annie asked if they could meet in private.

'Thank you for letting me have yesterday afternoon off at

short notice. I had an interview for a holiday rep job with Thomaston Holidays.'

'Please don't tell me you're giving in your notice?' Lisa frowned.

'No. But I'm afraid it might be awkward for me working here.' Annie twisted her hands in her lap. 'The thing is, I was seeing Henry Clarke, but we've split up. This holiday assignment to the Cyclades shouldn't have been awarded to me. It's not that I'm not grateful, but I suspect strings were pulled. I can't accept the offer. I'm sorry.'

Lisa let out her breath. 'Phew. That's a lot of information. I don't approve of relationships between staff. Our policy is that one or the other should leave. In the past when we have discovered a couple are dating, the woman has left, but both times that I'm aware of the couples got married and so the woman would have left work, anyway. It would have been a pity to throw away your career as you have so much promise. Is this why you applied for another job?'

'Partly, but I'm also interested in the job.'

'Because?'

'It's different. A bit of an adventure. I'd be working in another country and learning new skills.'

Lisa looked thoughtful. 'Don't do anything rash. I have an idea.'

'About the Cyclades. Please could you recommend that Sarah goes in my place?'

'Now that you've told me it was a set-up, then I'd be glad to. I can't abide favouritism. But don't you worry, I've an idea that you will have something else to look forward to very soon.'

Annie left Lisa's office, relieved that she had sorted out at least one problem that was weighing her down. She had no idea what Lisa was talking about unless she too thought Annie was pregnant. Maybe she'd better keep off the Black Forest Gateau.

'Did I get a private call?' she whispered to Sarah, who was collecting brochures from a stand for her customers. Sarah shook her head.

36

'I don't want to leave you on your own all day. Why don't you stay at home and lock the door?' Nico was attempting to knot his tie in front of the bedroom mirror. 'Blast. I always end up with it too short.'

'Here. Let me.' Jojo unfolded the collar of Nico's shirt and removed his tie. 'You look sexy in a suit.'

Nico grabbed her wrists and laughed. 'Don't tempt me, you seductress. Walker was insistent that I represent him at this Magic Circle meeting. It may take all day. I'd be happy if I knew you were safe, Joanna.'

Jojo tied a perfect knot. 'Ta da. I'll be fine. Now that we know Charlie was responsible for the note and everything else that followed, there's nothing to fear. He wouldn't have hurt me, anyway.'

'I told you not to encourage him. It was obvious to me what he was up to. You don't understand the way men think, Joanna.'

Jojo sighed. 'Okay. I know now. But what I'm saying is, there's no need for you to keep a close eye on me anymore. Go off to your Magic Circle thing and I'll spend the day rehearsing so that my Gala performance is perfect.'

Nico gave his appearance a final check in the mirror. 'Okay. You're right. I'm really sorry about your rabbits. I'll see if I can get another couple while I'm out today. Someone at The Circle might be able to supply us. There's an excellent library and museum at HQ. A restaurant too.'

'Take your time and enjoy yourself.' Jojo kissed him. 'I'll be fine. Don't worry. See you back here this evening.'

When Nico had left, Jojo gave consideration to what she should wear to the meeting with John Jenkins. If only she had her dressing-up box. Beige blandness did nothing for her confidence, however chic. One shift dress was much the same as another. Nico's theory was having a co-ordinated wardrobe took the stress out of deciding what to wear and saved time. Jojo had always enjoyed taking her time selecting an outfit; it had been a highlight of her day.

She was tired from a lack of sleep. How could she sleep knowing that Charlie had deceived her? Pixie and Muffin would have trusted him, just as she did. He must have twisted their little necks minutes before she caught him. *Oh Charlie, how could you?* Thinking about the rabbits and Charlie's betrayal brought a lump to her throat. She wondered if she had any tears left to cry. On waking, her pillow had been damp; a silent tear trickling into her ear. Now was not the time to dwell on this heartbreak. In a few hours, she would be meeting with John Jenkins and needed to sparkle. If he really did like her act, it could transform her life. Jojo couldn't get her head around that possibility. Peter Walker's insistence that she was the act they were all talking about still seemed unbelievable.

It was time to go. Jojo switched off the hall light and tugged the front door. It was locked. 'No! Not today,' Jojo wailed. *Bloody Nico.* How could he make the same mistake again, today of all days? Unless he had done it on purpose. She felt nauseous and her head swam, making her dizzy. Nico wasn't cruel. He loved her. What if he had found out about her audition? *Bobbi.* Jojo closed her eyes and took deep breaths. No. If Nico knew, he would have confronted her. He was a good actor, but he wouldn't have been able to contain his anger and disappointment. There was no time to go into an emotional tailspin; she had to get out of the flat. Jojo hauled herself up on legs that felt as weak as Bambi's, to look out of the bay window onto the street. It was a quiet road despite being in central London. On the opposite side, a big Arab family of women in black hijabs was getting into a limousine. Fascinated, Jojo watched and waited until the car pulled away. All was quiet.

Then she saw Sid the caretaker park outside their block. She pulled up the sash window and leant out. 'Sid! Mr. Sid! Sid the Caretaker!' He disappeared down the steps into the basement flat.

She had to get a message to him quickly. If the car was parked outside, it meant he was planning to go out. A woman with a pushchair had turned into their street, her progress slow as she waited for a little boy who was trailing behind. Jojo ran to Nico's office to get some paper. All of his desk drawers were locked. Jojo's hands shook, not moving quickly enough. *Paper. Paper.* In the kitchen, Jojo seized a paper bag filled with plump tomatoes. She tipped them onto the weighing scale and looked around frantically for a pen. Nico was the writer and, being meticulously tidy, he left nothing lying around. *His jacket pocket.* Jojo ran to their bedroom and, on Nico's side of the wardrobe, found what she was looking for. Inside his jacket pocket there was the inevitable notebook and pen. She took only the pen, afraid that if she delved any deeper paper flowers, and other surprises would appear.

My boyfriend accidentally locked me in flat D. I have to get to an important meeting. Please, could you knock on the basement door and ask the caretaker to let me out? Jojo

Back in the kitchen, she grabbed a Tupperware box with a lid. She pressed the note inside and rushed back to the window. The woman had passed by and was now at the other end of the street. Jojo leant out and shouted, but was unheard. Then Sid came out with his wife. A handsome woman wearing a deep blue cloche hat. Excited at seeing the hat, which was similar to one that Nico had thrown out, and her last chance to be rescued, Jojo filled her lungs and shouted at the top of her voice. 'Help.'

Sid's wife looked up; one hand clamped to her hat.

'I'm locked in.' Jojo threw the box, which was miraculously caught by Sid.

He read the note. 'I'll be with you in a tick.'

Jojo hugged Sid when he opened the door to her flat. 'Thank you so much.'

They walked down the stairs together. 'You just caught us; we were off out.'

'I was admiring your wife's hat. It looks like a Molyneux.'

They stepped into the sunshine. 'Martha, this is Jojo, our maiden in distress. She was asking about that hat of yours.'

Martha beamed. 'Isn't it gorgeous?'

The hat was identical to the one in Jojo's collection. A blue feather trim draped around the middle. Faded and ragged now; it was a 1920s original. 'I collect antique designer clothes and accessories,' Jojo said, resisting the urge to snatch the hat from Martha's head to check the label.

'This was being thrown out, would you believe?'

Jojo's heart quickened. 'I would! Nico threw out my

beloved clothes by mistake. It was in my grandmother's old trunk.' Jojo clasped a hand over her mouth, afraid to believe she might have found her dressing-up box in case she was disappointed.

Sid and Martha looked at one another. 'Told you,' Martha said.

'Did you find it?'

'I couldn't throw away those beautiful clothes. None of them fit me, but I love this hat and an adorable green bag.'

'Would you mind terribly if I asked you to return them to me? Not the Molyneux hat or the green leather bag; you're welcome to keep them, but I would dearly love to have the other things. I didn't know Nico had thrown them out until it was too late — or so I thought.'

'That's very generous of you. Of course, you can have the trunk and clothes back. I was only going to donate them to the church jumble sale.'

'I'll make a donation,' Jojo said. 'I know you're in a hurry, but would you mind if I found something to wear now? I'm going to an interview and I would love to wear my polka dot fifties skirt.'

'Ooh, I love that! I used to wear a skirt just like it when I met Sid.'

'I'll be quick. And one more favour. Please, could you look after my things until I'm ready to pick them up? It shouldn't be long.'

Martha had put the polka dot skirt in a carrier bag for Jojo, along with a white blouse and red ribbon Jojo had picked out. She would change at the Golden Globe before her meeting. Bobbi had confirmed it was unlikely they would ask her to audition, but there was no harm in practicing. Besides, she needed to talk to Bobbi to find out how much Nico knew.

Outside the Golden Globe, Jojo mentally prepared herself

for meeting Charlie. The first time after the incident would be awkward. She would be polite and friendly, pretend it was nothing but remain aloof. No more Bat Girl and Spidey. It hurt, knowing his friendship had always had an ulterior motive. Charlie wasn't front of house or in the auditorium. Jojo was about to push through the doors to exit the theatre when Lenny swung himself down off the stage. 'Hey Jojo.'

'Lenny.' Jojo kept her voice formal.

'I've got something for you,' he said.

Her heart sank. What now? Another note? She couldn't take any more surprises.

'Here. Charlie said I was to give it to you.' Lenny handed Jojo a big package wrapped in brown paper.

Jojo guessed what it was and couldn't wait to open it. 'Thank you. What are you doing right now? Could you spare an hour or so?'

'Sure.'

The changing room was empty. Jojo left the unopened package on a bench and changed into her dance kit. Every few seconds, her eyes strayed to the parcel. She was certain that it was the silk banner. If it worked, it would be incredible. Like a child on Christmas morning, Jojo peeled open one side of the package and peeked in. There was fabric inside. She slipped her fingers between the folds, paper thin silk, masses of it. Charlie had come up trumps. It would have been good to share this triumph with him, to work with him in rigging it up. Instead, she would have to work with Lenny.

Lenny was sitting on the side of the stage fiddling with a transistor radio. 'Y'okay?'

'I am.' Jojo explained what she wanted Lenny to do. 'The silk has to be securely attached so that it can take my weight. It's got to support me whilst I do aerial acrobatics, so *very* secure.'

'Should be okay. Have you seen anyone do this before?'

'No. That's why it's so exciting. I've given it lots of thought. I can't practice my moves today, but if we could just check out that it's doable, that would be great.'

It worked. They tested and retested the strength of the hold. There was no way that it would come loose.

'I'm just going to try a few simple moves,' Jojo said. She had time and it would be great if she could confidently tell John Jenkins about this innovation.

Leroy hoisted her up. 'Okay. Ready to go.'

At first, Jojo was cautious. She tried simple glides, following a similar routine to the one she practised for the matinee. Then, feeling more confident, she rolled herself up in the silk and gently let herself down as it unrolled. There was so much she could do.

'Bravo.' A voice called from below.

Jojo came down to land. 'Did you see that, Bobbi?'

'Absolutely. It was incredible.'

'Did you say anything about John Jenkins to Nico?'

'Of course not, darling. I told you my lips were sealed. Why, has he got wind of your assignation?'

'No. I will tell him myself, but not yet. It may come to nothing, although I think it will impress Jenkins when I tell him what I can do with this parachute silk.'

'Are you sure it's wise to pursue this, what with Nico and then the curse?'

Jojo laughed, and then she saw Bobbi was serious. 'I can handle Nico. Why should I be spooked by the myth of Molly May? It's silly nonsense.'

'Are you sure? I heard about the rabbits. You've more pluck than me. I'd be terrified.'

37

Annie paused outside St Martin in the Fields church to enjoy the choir practicing within. Easter weekend was one week away. Mum would prepare roast lamb on Easter Sunday, much the same as every Sunday, and working days would remain the same. Easter weekend meant Easter Gala and Annie was excited for Jojo.

She turned left into the Strand and was caught up in a stream of backpackers and pushchairs negotiating their way to Charing Cross Station. Lisa had accommodated Annie's request for a late and extended lunch hour, although she had raised her eyebrows. Annie wanted to reassure her it wasn't another interview, but that would mean explaining herself. Would an hour be enough to convey her concerns to Jojo? Charlie's draft note was in her handbag. Annie stopped abruptly. A man bumped into her and grumbled. It felt as though she was being disloyal to Charlie. Maybe she should speak to him first. Annie's heart did a little palpitation. She had been walking too fast — was sweaty and probably looked a mess. This wasn't a good idea. Charlie was three minutes away. She had crossed this very road with his hand in hers. Annie rubbed her palm. What if she had got it all wrong and Charlie was in love with Jojo? He had said that there was something he had to do before declaring his love. She was standing in a shop doorway and caught sight of her reflection in the window. Hair a little damp, flicking up instead of under. Cheeks flushed. She gave her armpit a discreet sniff. The floral deodorant was more pronounced, but otherwise okay. There was no time to freshen up. If only she could warn Jojo of her visit and arrange to meet her privately. Charlie couldn't be the messenger today.

Cake Presto was busy as usual, but there was nobody Annie recognised from the cast. She waited in queue and when Mrs Brew was ready to serve, asked if Jojo had been in for her lunch.

'No love. Not seen her today. Earl Grey for you?'

'No, thank you. Have you seen Charlie?' She was asking so that she could avoid bumping into him. A flutter beneath her sternum.

Mrs Brew pursed her lips and frowned, then shook her head as if in disapproval. Was Annie's infatuation so obvious?

On the afternoon of the matinee Pedro had sent a message to Jojo, just as he had with Charlie's note and so Annie visited the front of house hoping to find him. There was no matinee that day and the box office was closed. 'Pedro?' she called, tilting her head, hoping it would carry her voice down the carpeted corridor beyond the twisted rope and brass barrier. 'Is anybody there?'

Annie was beginning to despair when she heard footsteps on the stairs, which led to a staff only section of the theatre. It was a middle-aged woman carrying a pile of documents. She was reading the top copy as she descended.

'Excuse me,' Annie said.

The woman looked up, startled by Annie's voice. 'There's no performance this afternoon. The theatre door should have been locked.'

'I'm a close friend of Jojo Evans. We arranged to meet, but I must have got the time wrong because I can't find her. I was looking for Pedro to see if he could pass on a message to say that I'm here.' Annie hated telling lies, but she couldn't leave without seeing Jojo.

'You won't find Jojo here this afternoon. I know for a fact that she has business elsewhere. I'm sorry that you've had a wasted journey.'

'What about Charlie?'

The woman's eyes darted to the outside door. 'Just missed him.'

'Where was he going?' One foot was ready to chase after him, but the other kept her grounded just long enough to hear the reply.

'He's taking some leave as of this afternoon and was in a hurry to get somewhere.'

Annie called out her thanks as she pushed through the theatre doors. Pedestrians moved quickly on both sides of the road. Annie tried to scan the heads methodically, looking for Charlie's curls, but whilst she was standing still, he would be getting away. She had to find him. An instinct led her in the same direction as the one they had taken together the previous week, and she was rewarded by a glimpse of his hair bouncing and a walk that could only be Charlie's. He moved as though he was trying to stop his feet from dancing, or playing an imaginary game of basketball.

Annie crossed the street, trying to keep one eye on him and the other on the traffic. He was almost out of sight when she had crossed the road and so Annie quickened her pace, weaving in and out of a Chinese tour group. He turned left into a side street. The same one they had taken together. He must be going to the karaoke bar. Convinced that this was Charlie's destination, Annie allowed herself to slow down and catch her breath. She was going to be late back from her lunch break, but she had to find out why Charlie had sent the note, especially if he was going on leave as of today.

Annie remembered that the karaoke bar had been in an alleyway, but she couldn't find the street it came off. They all looked similar. Annie took her time walking slowly down each one in case she missed it. There was an alley, but she had no idea if it was the right one. She stood in the middle of the road and looked up. What had Charlie seen that confirmed the location? Ah, there was an illuminated sign on one window. Her heart was racing. It would surprise Charlie to see her. Maybe she shouldn't have followed him. Annie couldn't turn back but was afraid to go in. She had to do this for Jojo. Annie took a deep breath and climbed the fire escape stairs.

The Japanese man at the door did not greet her with the warm familiarity he had shown Charlie, but he did ask her if she was expecting anyone else or would like to sit alone. Annie tried to see past him into the dimly lit bar. She couldn't see Charlie. A woman with a cute elfin cut was sitting at their table sipping what looked like a glass of Coke.

'I thought my friend might be here.'

'Come in and see.' He showed her in to the bar. Charlie definitely wasn't there, but as the manager had pulled out a chair for her, Annie thought she had better sit down. She needed a few minutes to recover from her charge across town.

Annie opened the song menu and smiled to herself, remembering how Charlie had suggested they sing Summer Nights together. He had mimicked Olivia Newton John and suggested she sing John Travolta's lines. Her head was bent when she heard Charlie's voice across the room.

'Oh, you should have ordered me a Coke too.'

Suddenly, she was embarrassed to be there. He was with someone. Annie raised her head slowly and saw Charlie sitting at their table opposite the woman with an elfin cut. Thank goodness there was little light; she could leave unnoticed. The woman could be anyone, a fellow student, a colleague. Annie didn't recognise her from the Golden Globe. Charlie was leaning across the table, maybe trying to get his voice heard above the music – something in Japanese with a funky beat. Now he was holding the woman's hand. She had to get out of there. If Charlie saw her now, she would die of embarrassment. If only she could crawl past their table.

A waitress stood in front of Annie, blocking her view. 'What would you like?'

For you to act as a screen and walk with me to the door, she thought. 'I was hoping my friend was in here, but I was mistaken.' Annie spoke softly.

'I am sorry. What you say?'

Annie repeated a bit louder.

'Annie?' It was Charlie's voice.

'I'm sorry I have to go.' Annie jumped up. She took one look at Charlie's bemused face and ran out of the bar.

Down the fire escape, out of the alley, and along the street, Annie ran. When there were enough people to camouflage her, she dared to look back. There was no sign of Charlie. So, he had sent the note to warn Jojo, but he wasn't in love with her. The woman he had talked about, the *someone special*, was with him now. His feelings towards Annie were platonic. She had been better off not knowing what it was to fall in love, because now she knew and it hurt like hell.

38

When Jojo burst breathless through the door of Jenkins Productions, she hadn't expected to be greeted like a celebrity.

'Jojo Evans?' A statuesque woman with Farrah Fawcett hair extended her hand. 'I'm so glad you came. They're all waiting in there. Can I get you a mineral water or something stronger?'

Jojo would have liked a coffee, but was afraid that wouldn't sound cool. 'Water would be fabuloser,' she said and then regretted it. Nico had warned her about using childish language and making up ridiculous words. 'I mean, that would be perfect. Thank you.'

'I'll let them know you're here.'

Jojo wiped her palms on her skirt and rejoiced at the way it sprung back. *Thank you, Martha.* She wondered who was waiting for her behind the double doors.

'You can go in now. I'll fetch your water.'

Six people stood up to greet Jojo. She recognised John Jenkins and was more than a little in awe. He was a celebrity in his own right, as the Sunday supplements often featured him commenting on his latest date or his views on a new TV show or act.

He shook Jojo's hand. 'You've met Annika Riley?'

Jojo hadn't noticed the diminutive woman with a halo of blond curls and turned to shake her hand. 'No, but I'm pleased to meet you.' *Annika Riley is here, too.* She wanted to step outside of the room, to squeal and jump up and down.

'Sebastian Faber, Children's BBC. Warren Fox, Moon Bay Films. Let's sit down and the others can introduce themselves.'

TV. Film. Jojo anchored one hand over the other to stop herself from trembling. Assistants, managers, PAs, the names and roles went over her head. She tried to regulate her breathing.

'I thought it best to bring everyone in from the outset. That's how I work. We've been working on a collaboration for some time, but until Annika and I saw your act at the Golden Globe, we didn't have our star. Now…' he rubbed his hands together. 'Well, this is all very exciting.'

'Slow down JJ. I think Jojo needs to hear our proposal from the beginning. Shall I?' Annika took over. 'I heard about your aerial acrobatics from Adele Pearson, who caught your act with a dance group. A matinee at the Golden Globe. I'd already marked you down as someone I was interested in.' She shot a look at John Jenkins. 'However, your performance at the Starlight show was stupendous. Mixing fantasy, magic and acrobatics. It was charming. Funny. Highly original. The effects were incredible.'

'We're thinking big.' John Jenkins interlaced his fingers. 'Stage, TV, film. A children's show.'

'We'd start with a TV pilot,' Sebastian said. 'Have you done TV before?'

Jojo shook her head.

'If – *when* the TV show takes off, we'll do a tour. Moon Bay is here with an interest for film rights, but that's way down the line. What do you think?'

Jojo was thankful a glass of mineral water had been set down in front of her. She took a sip to coax her voice out of hiding. 'I'm very excited by your proposal, but you haven't seen what I'm capable of yet. This afternoon I tested out a banner made from parachute silk. I can do so much more using that to support my aerial acrobatics. I can't wait to show you.'

Annika almost leapt out if her seat. 'I heard Cirque Solei had hired someone to investigate something along those lines. This is tremendous Jojo. When can we see you perform?'

Everyone started talking at once and Jojo tuned out. How was she going to break this news to Nico? Easter Gala was next week; would she be ready to use the silk banner by then?

'How about Easter Gala?' Jenkins said as if he had read her mind.

'It's possible.' Jojo's heart was racing. She had to grab this opportunity, show them what she was capable of. Nico would be furious, but if he loved her… Jojo knew Nico would not be glad for her under any circumstances. He would see this as his failure.

'Great.' Jenkins slid his fists across the table and leaned forward as if astride a motorbike. 'Get Walker to make you the last act. We need to discuss press communications. Ingrid?'

Jojo sat through the rest of the discussion, feeling as though she was in a dream. How could this even be possible? A TV show? A film star? She suppressed a giggle. One of delirium. *She* was the act they were all talking about. Not Nico. Not Kai.

'See you on Saturday,' Jenkins said, shaking her hand.

. . .

Peter Walker had made sure Nico would be at The Magic Circle HQ all day and so Jojo went back to the Golden Globe to talk to Walker about the line-up. He was at his desk when Jojo was shown in by his PA. 'How did it go?'

At last, Jojo could share her incredible news. She didn't even try to stay composed, breaking into dance with each revelation.

'So, they liked it?' Walker said, his mouth lifted on one side.

'Yay!' Jojo stamped the floor and waved her hands.

'Then I had better let the cast know that Jojo Evans will be star of Easter Gala and the last act.'

Jojo sobered up. 'Could you say Nico and Jojo? We'll do our joint act and then I'll do my solo last?'

'I was going to put your solo after Kai. He got a better reception than Nico. I know he's your partner, but that shouldn't sway things.'

'Please, Mr Walker. I don't know how I'm going to tell him about my meeting this afternoon.'

'He's not going to like it.' He clicked the top of his pen on and off. 'I'll have to announce the running order. There's to be a press release. I'll give you until Monday.'

'Thank you.' It helped, but it was Friday and so she had to tell Nico that weekend. Jojo was more afraid of breaking the news than she was performing.

Jojo changed out of her polka dot skirt and stowed it in her locker. Then she put on a beige dress to go home. One more week of beige and then she was going to collect her clothes from Martha. If Nico didn't like it, he could lump it. She loved him, but if he didn't love her for being herself, then he didn't love her at all. This realisation liberated Jojo. Why had she ever thought otherwise?

'How did it go?' Bobbi burst into the changing room. 'I heard you were back.'

Jojo didn't need any persuasion to share her fantastic news. She jumped up and down and squealed. It was the best thing that had happened to her in her entire life.

Bobbi gasped and screamed in all the right places and when Jojo had finished, hugged her. 'I knew it! You are an absolute star, darling.'

'Oh.' Jojo covered her mouth. 'Don't tell anyone. Wait until Peter Walker announces it on Monday. I haven't told Nico yet.'

'Your secret's safe with me.' Bobbi did a zipping motion across her lips.

Jojo left the theatre on cloud nine. She grinned at everyone she passed in the street. If it had been any earlier, she would have dropped in at Annie's travel agency to share her news, but Annie would have left by now. Instead, she ran for a number 15 bus.

It wasn't until the bus conductor asked for her fare that Jojo opened her Gladstone bag to find three dead doves. It was a blast of icy water on her elation. She shuddered at the touch of stiff feathers. Who would do this? Not Charlie. He couldn't have accessed her bag when she was at the Golden Globe. Or Nico. The significance of three doves hit Jojo. Who had she told about her first meeting with Nico? Nobody at the Golden Globe.

Jojo felt sick. She scanned the bus looking for an elfin hairstyle. A woman was getting off now. She could be Meryl. Jojo twisted in her seat to get a better look, but it was impossible. The woman who got off had walked in the opposite direction. Maybe Nico made a habit of seducing women by mesmerising them with the doves in their handbag number. Meryl was crazy. She had to talk to Nico before she did something more serious. But not until after Easter Gala. If Nico knew Meryl was stalking her, then he wouldn't let her out of his sight, and she needed to practice with the silk banner. At least her mood would be more sober when she got home. Jojo found a discarded newspaper on the bus. As soon as she got off, she crouched over a garden wall and shielding the corpses from passers-by, wrapped them up like fish and chips before disposing of them in the first bin.

39

'I know I ought to go out and help him or at least show some interest, but what the hell is he thinking?'

Annie and Jessica watched their dad from the kitchen window struggling with a tent pole. 'He's doing it for you,' Annie said.

'But I said no thanks. Even if he can squeeze it in to 100 square metres, there won't be any room for outdoor seating, not unless our guests are prepared to share the rockery with the fishing gnomes.'

'No luck with booking the social club?'

'No. It seems Tiny Tappers take priority over my wedding. We've a mind to just get married at the registry office and then bugger off on honeymoon. I'd rather no wedding reception than this.' Jessica made a face of absolute despair as their dad crawled underneath the marquee which had been laid out, covering the length and breadth of their garden.

'I'll have a word.'

Annie was relieved to have something else to focus on other than Charlie. Why did he have to take his date *there?* He hadn't held *her* hand across the table or looked at her the way he did that woman. She had read too much into what was his natural warmth and friendliness. Well, time to get over it, Annie Daley. So you found out what it is to be in love. It only took you twenty-four years.

'I've made you a cuppa,' Annie said, to coax her dad out from beneath the canvas. The first tent pole had raised one corner of the marquee several times in the last hour, but it was once again flat.

Her dad crawled out after a few minutes. 'I think I know what I'm doing wrong. It really needs two people, one on each side.'

'Okay. Drink your tea and then I'll help.'

It was chilly in the garden and getting a bit late in the evening to complete the task. Apparently, Dad had been struggling with it since Mum went out to an Easter Bring and Buy sale at the church hall. They drank their tea in silence, each lost in their own thoughts — Annie's were about her future. Life in Fenwood suddenly seemed too small, as though she were the marquee being squashed into a tiny backyard. Jojo had no time for her anymore. She hadn't even phoned back as she had promised. Life was just work and home.

'We're going to spend a week in Edinburgh so that we can visit surrounding areas, see where we want to set up camp.'

Annie laughed. 'If it's camping you're after, I hope you have more success than this.'

They both surveyed the dormant tent. 'Set up home, you know what I mean. I'd better put this lot away before Mum gets back. Get to it again tomorrow, but thanks for your offer of help dumpling.'

'Have you checked the dimensions, Dad? It seems a bit optimistic.'

'There might be some slack.'

'A droopy top? I know you're trying to help Jessica, but I'm not sure that this is the answer.'

Her dad let out a long and weary breath. 'You're probably right. It seemed a lot smaller when I saw it at the McIntyre's garden party.'

'Dad, they have acres of land. It would have seemed small.'

'Me and your mum want the best for you girls. Jessica to have the wedding of the year and for you to have your own adventures. I didn't think that Henry chap was right for you – too dull. My Annie is a live wire, the fearless one. He would have stifled your free spirit, love.'

Annie nearly spluttered her tea. Who was this stranger Dad was describing? 'Aren't you thinking of Jojo?'

'What the little scrap of a girl you adopted as though you were her mum? No, I'm talking about my fearless Annie. You were always one for an adventure. From the day you learnt how to climb out of your playpen there's been no keeping you down.'

It would take Annie time to assimilate this image of herself. Charlie had said something similar to Dad. Maybe she had attributed her own characteristics to Jojo and then felt the need to balance this exuberance with an anchor to keep them both grounded. Now Jojo had set sail and there was nothing to stop Annie setting her own course.

'When are you hoping to *up sticks?*' Annie said as she collected the tent poles, continuing her dad's analogy of setting up camp in Scotland.

'Well, that depends.'

'On me finding somewhere to live?'

'No love, although we would like to see both of our girls settled. It depends on what's available and how long it takes to sell this place. We've got a wedding to get through first, although I'm running out of ideas for the reception venue. I'll finish off here love. Give you a chance to change out of your work things before supper.'

The next day at work, Annie tried hard to concentrate on what the middle-aged couple were saying. They wanted a holiday in the sun but didn't want to eat foreign food or be surrounded by people who didn't speak English. That part Annie heard and understood, lots of their customers unused to travelling abroad made similar requests. She had plucked brochures of Costa del Sol and Benidorm from the shelves. It was the other requirements that she was having difficulty following.

'We want somewhere that has entertainment: Bingo, contests...'

Her mind wandered at the mention of entertainment. It was the Easter Gala next Saturday. Annie hadn't bought a ticket. If she went, she might see Charlie and she couldn't. It would be too embarrassing. He had seen her at the karaoke bar. What on earth had he thought? That she was stalking him? That the bug had bitten her, and she was there to do another rendition of Dancing Queen? Remembering the spectacle she had made of herself, Annie felt a flush creep up her throat and blaze her cheeks. Then, when he saw her, she had run away! There was no way Annie could go to the Easter Gala. Charlie might have some time off work, but he wouldn't miss the show.

'Dressed me in her bra, she did.'

'What? Sorry, I mean I beg your pardon.'

'My wife. We won that competition, didn't we? She slipped it off under her dress and put it on me over my shirt. All the others were getting up the nerve while my Kate just did it.' The couple laughed together.

'Some hotels that cater for English tourists have entertainment. I'll circle the ones that do in your brochure. Were you thinking Costa del Sol or Benidorm?'

'We like a bit of life. Which has more going on?'

'That depends on what you're interested in.'

'Dancing…'

Dancing Queen. Twirling around, feeling free and deliciously drunk. Was she this reckless, free spirit that Dad and Charlie described? Dad was right about one thing; Henry was far too staid for her. Mum and Dad were planning an adventure. Maybe it was time that she did the same. Take the bull by the horns…

'Bull fighting.'

Annie jumped and felt her scalp prickle. Had she spoken out loud?

'Could we get to see a bull fight?'

Eventually, Annie booked a two-week holiday for the couple in Benidorm and wished them a holiday to remember.

'Could you spare a few minutes to meet with me in my office?' Lisa said.

This was going to be about her late arrival back at work the previous day. Annie had apologised to Lisa, and she seemed okay at the time. Maybe she had been planning how to address Annie's conduct with her.

Lisa rarely asked anyone to meet in her office most business was conducted in the staff room or shop. When Annie was seated in front of her, Lisa folded her hands on the desk. 'How did it go with Thomaston Holidays yesterday?'

Annie knew that her brain was a bit befuddled, but was bemused by Lisa's comment. 'Yesterday?'

'I guessed you had gone for a second interview.'

Annie smiled. 'No, I would have told you. It was another matter and I'm truly sorry. It won't happen again.'

Lisa appeared not to have heard as she continued what must have been a rehearsed speech. 'I understand why you would want to move. Breaking up with Mr Clarke could make things awkward for you. You've been working at this branch for six years and by rights should have progressed to manager.'

'That's hardly possible when there's no vacancy,' Annie said in a teasing voice.

'No, but you've remained loyal to this branch at the expense of your career development.'

'It's fine. Until now, I didn't want anything else.'

'But now you do?'

Annie realised that she did, very much.

'Okay. I have a proposal for you. Our company has a sister one in Australia. It's in its infancy but with a surge in packaged holidays for Australians to Bali, it's growing. We need senior staff we can trust to help get things off the ground. It would mean working in Australia, possibly Bali. Is that something you might consider?'

This was beyond her wildest dreams. Could she do something that big? Until Lisa called Annie into her office, she had been contemplating a holiday on her own and that had felt adventurous. This was mega. 'I might be, when I have more information. When? Where? For how long?'

Lisa grinned. 'I knew you would be up for it!'

'I just said I would think about it.' But Annie knew that this was the adventure she needed to help heal her broken heart.

40

'How did you get out?' Nico confronted Jojo when she opened the door to their flat. So, he had intentionally locked her in.

'I climbed out of the window and down the drainpipe.'

'I hope it wasn't the window looking onto the street. Really, Joanna, you should try and act with more decorum.'

'An apology for locking me in is the response I expected.'

'Of course. I'm sorry bella. My head is all over the place with Gala approaching. I don't know why you didn't just stay in the flat. There was no need for you to go out.'

That afternoon, she had realised her potential with a powerful rush of energy. Nico would not smother that fire within. She just had to hold things together until after Easter and then she would be free. 'I've been rehearsing all day. I'm going to run a bath and then you can tell me about your day at the Magic Circle.'

'Good idea. I'll see what we have in the fridge and prepare supper. What's that on your hands?'

Jojo flipped her wrists and was surprised to find green dye had stained one of her palms. 'Is this one of your tricks?'

'No. If you will go climbing down drainpipes.'

Jojo laughed despite herself. 'Do you really think I would scale down a couple of floors wearing a shift dress? Sid, the caretaker, let me out.'

'Anything is possible. You are full of surprises.'

Jojo didn't know how she was going to deliver the biggest surprise of all.

The opportunity came the following morning as they prepared to go in to the Golden Globe for a couple of hours.

'I couldn't source any rabbits when I was at The Magic Circle, but it's probably best we drop your solo. You're a competent assistant. I was expecting too much, asking you to perform a trick.'

Jojo cleared her throat, willing herself to speak up. It was now or never. 'Oh, I forgot to tell you. I have some exciting news.'

Nico was sitting on the edge of their bed, putting on his shoes. He did not pause or look at Jojo, and that made it a little easier. '*Our* act is going to be top of the bill.'

Nico threw down his shoe. 'Why didn't you tell me as soon as you got home? That is phenomenal.' He leapt off the bed and pulled her to her feet. 'Really? Are you sure it's top? After Kai Keisler?'

'Yes. The last act. But the thing is,' she hesitated. He was gripping both of her hands with a look of absolute joy. 'The thing is, Walker asked for my solo to be performed at the end of our act. I expect he didn't want it to disrupt your escapist routine like last time.' Phew. She had said it.

'Oh, we don't need to worry about your little act.' He

waved his hands as though sweeping her under the carpet. 'I'm changing my finale anyway, so there's no need for you to keep the audience entertained. Just be my beautiful assistant.'

'Mr Walker was most insistent. I said the same thing to him, that there was no need for me to have a solo slot, but he made it clear he wanted no argument. Maybe he just wants to demonstrate that the Golden Globe is keeping with the times by letting women magicians perform.'

'I'd hardly call you a magician bella.' Nico laughed. 'Still, if that's what Walker wants, he's the boss. I expect we'd better find you a couple of rabbits. Try not to scare them to death this time.'

Jojo could put up with his condescending manner, so long as he understood she was to perform last. Now, she had to find a way to practice out of Nico's sight. That too was surprisingly easy because soon after they arrived at work Nico kissed her cheek and said, 'Are you alright to practice without me for a couple of hours? I picked up a few ideas at The Magic Circle and I need to talk them through with a technician. I'll be in the resource library.'

'I'll manage the best I can,' Jojo teased. 'But I suspect you are doing a Max. If I were to creep up those stairs in a few minutes' time, are you sure I wouldn't find you with an empty whisky glass having a snooze?'

Nico laughed. 'I promise. Now go and do some stretching or whatever it is you do. No sneaking off for cake.'

'So, back here at midday?'

When she had changed into lycra, Jojo went in search of Charlie to make her peace.

'He's taken off for a few days,' Lenny said when Jojo found him backstage rearranging the backdrops.

Jojo was disappointed. She hadn't thanked him properly for the silk banner, or told him about her meeting with John

Jenkins. How could she have suspected him of killing Pixie and Muffin when he had obviously doted on them? 'Will he be back for Easter Gala?'

Lenny gave her a long look. He clicked his tongue. 'Expect so. Don't think anyone can have leave that night. You be careful.'

Jojo didn't know what he meant. Did he know about the threats? He was looking at her as if he knew something that she didn't. 'What aren't you telling me, Lenny?'

'Nothing. Just take care with your aerial stuff.'

This was the first time Lenny had shown any concern for her welfare. Maybe she was beginning to be accepted. 'Thanks. As Charlie's not here, would you mind helping me practice with the silk by operating the pulley?'

The meeting on Friday had boosted Jojo's confidence and now, soaring above the stage, she felt as though she had wings. As she got used to the silk's tension and its natural movement, she discovered moves she would not have thought possible. The silk flowed behind her as she swooped across the auditorium and alighted as if weightless on the stage.

Bobbi clapped. 'That was stupendous. I was holding my breath. So graceful. Honestly, Jojo, I got choked up. It was out of this world.'

'That's what they want to call my show. Wanda's World. Or, The World of Wanda. They're not decided. It's a play on magic wand and wonder.' Jojo tried to sound nonchalant, but she couldn't disguise her excitement.

Bobbi was staring at her with an open mouth. 'Your own bloody show!'

'I know!' Jojo squealed and then kicked off the stage to do a somersault in the air.

'Now, you're just showing off. Have you got time for a celebratory glass of Scotch?'

'I remember the last time you led me astray. No, thanks all the same. Nico is expecting to meet me at twelve, so just enough time to get changed.'

The two hours had been very productive. Even if she didn't get another stint before Easter Gala, Jojo was confident of her act.

On Sunday, the telephone rang. Jojo tried to get to it before Nico, but failed. 'Yes, she's here. Hold on one moment.'

'My mum?' Jojo asked. She hadn't spoken to her parents since telling them she couldn't visit for Easter as it was the gala. They refused her invitation to the show and hadn't phoned since. Really, Jojo should have phoned them.

'No. It's Annabelle.'

Jojo tried to grab the phone from Nico, but he covered the mouthpiece and hissed, 'Don't go making any plans. You can't afford the time.' After delivering a stern glare, he handed Jojo the phone.

'Annie...' Jojo stopped herself from saying Apple Cheeks. Nico was standing close and would not approve. 'Lovely to hear from you.'

'I expected you to pop into the shop after receiving your message.'

Nico pressed against Jojo's side and she knew he was listening in to both sides of the conversation. He kissed her neck, and she tried to brush him away, but he did not take the hint. 'No. Sorry, I didn't mean to give that impression. You know how busy we are preparing for Easter Gala.'

'I dropped in to the Golden Globe to find you on Friday afternoon, but you weren't there.'

Jojo gave an awkward laugh. 'Of course I was there. Unless it was when I popped out to the shop for some essentials. I'm sorry I missed you.'

'I have something important to tell you.'

Nico was pressing against her back, his arms tight around her waist.

'You can tell me after the show.' Jojo kept her voice bright and jolly. She did not know what Annie was going to say but had a feeling Nico wouldn't like it.

'That's the thing. I'm sorry, but I can't go to your show. We really need to see each other. There's something I must tell you. How about tomorrow? You don't practice on Sundays and it's my day off. Come to Fenwood, that way you can see your parents too. Mum said they're disappointed you're not going home for Easter weekend.'

'What do you mean you can't go to the show? You never miss one of my shows.'

Nico tutted. Jojo tried to pull away from him, but he clung onto her. 'I can't get to Fenwood for a couple of weeks. But I'll see you soon, right? You will come to the show? *Please,* Annie.'

Annie sighed heavily. 'I don't know. Look, in case I can't, I'll just have to tell you over the phone. I found evidence that Charlie typed the anonymous note warning you to keep away from Nico. But I don't think it was a threat. I think he was trying to warn you.'

Nico dialled his index finger in circles by his temple and rolled his eyes.

'That's crazy Annie. I expect it was Charlie's idea of a joke. I'll have it out with him when he next shows up for work.'

'Is everything alright between you and Nico, Jojo? I mean, are you happy? Does he treat you alright?'

Nico made an exaggerated gesture of disbelief and then astonishment.

'He bought me new clothes. Prepares most of our meals.'

'I know. But are you happy, Jojo?'

Nico tensed behind her.

'Yes. Of course, I am.'

'You don't need me to rescue you or stand up to any bullies anymore?'

'I'll always need you, but as my best friend, not to defend me.'

'Then I wish you both every happiness together.'

'You're going to see me soon. You make it sound as though you are saying goodbye forever.' Jojo wanted to cry.

'I'll tell you everything if and when we meet. But I'll wait for you to call me. I'm not being funny, Jojo. I know you have a lot on. I just don't want to become a nuisance.'

She wanted to say, *Don't go Annie. I need you.* Instead, she hung up.

'Finally, your friend seems to be getting the message. Yes, Annabelle Daley, you have become a nuisance.'

'No, she's not. Annie just cares about me. She is and always will be my best friend.'

'I thought I was.' Nico kissed her neck. 'So, we were right about Charlie.'

41

Annie held onto the receiver long after Jojo had hung up, as if by doing so she was keeping a line of communication open. Her mum came down the stairs, artificial roses, pink crepe paper, and an assortment of haberdashery blocking her face.

'Is that Jojo on the phone? Give her my love. Ask her when we're going to meet this handsome new boyfriend of hers.'

Annie hung up. 'It was. I'm worried Mum.'

Her mum continued through to the kitchen and Annie followed. 'Jojo hasn't seemed like herself the last few times I've seen her. Everything about her is different, the way she dresses, and even how she acts.'

'Hmm.' Annie wasn't sure if that was a response to her statement or the array of flowers, paper, glue, and paints that her mum was arranging across the table. 'She's in love.'

'I don't see how that would make you act differently,' Annie said, although she had been behaving out of character herself. 'I know it makes you a little crazy, but that's not what I mean. It's as if Nico is suffocating her, putting out her light.'

'Has Jojo complained?'

'No. She says that she's happy.'

'Well, there you are. What do you think would work best? Should I cover my hat in this seersucker or crepe? I want a pink ribbon around the middle and lots of these pink roses. I'm just not sure if the material will stick and I don't want it bunching up. There again, crepe is a devil for showing glue marks.'

Annie sighed. 'I've got a straw hat that I don't wear. You could experiment with that. What's this for?'

'WI Easter bonnet competition next Thursday.' Her mum put down the hat. 'Is that all that's bothering you? Jojo? You're not getting upset because your dad's been going on about Scotland? We wouldn't think of selling the house unless we knew you and Jessica were both settled. It's a shame things didn't work out with Henry.'

'I'll get my hat.' Annie gave an apologetic smile before escaping her mum's scrutiny.

Dance Fever was playing full volume in Jessica's room. She would be getting ready for a Saturday night on the town. Annie closed the door to her own room and sat on the bed. Jojo had seemed unphased by her revelation about Charlie. Maybe she was overreacting. But why would he go to the trouble of writing and sending an anonymous note if it meant nothing? Charlie was trying to warn Jojo to keep away from Nico. Apart from being a conceited ball of slime, what was wrong with him? Married? A serial killer? Well, now Jojo knew, and she was going to talk to Charlie once he got back from leave. There was nothing else Annie could do. To accept the secondment to Australia would mean leaving behind Jojo, Charlie, her home. Her heart was heavy with loss, but she was already losing Jojo, and she had never had Charlie.

Her hat wasn't in the box for the charity shop, which was

where she had put it a few weeks ago after doing a spring clear out of her clothes. Annie slid the box back under her bed. Jessica. Anything that went missing from Annie's room ended up in Jessica's, although a straw boater wasn't her usual style.

Annie thumped on Jessica's door but couldn't make herself heard over the music. She pushed it open. Jessica's head was upside down as she blow-dried her hair. Annie wondered that her satin trousers didn't split; they were skin-tight. 'Jess!'

Jessica threw up her head. 'You could at least knock.'

Annie turned down the ghetto blaster. 'Have you seen my straw hat?'

'Yeah. I wore it when I dressed up as St Trinians. Thought you didn't want it. I came home without it so…' Jessica shrugged.

'I was offered a new job today.'

'Yeah?' Jessica squirted hair mousse into her palm and then threw her head down to lather her roots.

'It's in Australia.'

'Didgerydoo!' Her head whipped up.

'Only for six months to start with. I would work with the Australian office but in Bali making contacts for package holidays.'

'I'm so jealous. I'd love to go to Bali. You said yes, right?' Jessica fluffed up her hair until it resembled a candyfloss.

'I said I would give it serious consideration.'

'What's stopping you? Henry's history.'

'Jojo. You.'

'Last I heard, Jojo was in honeymoon heaven with her Italian stud. Why me?'

'Because I'd miss your wedding.'

Jessica grinned. '*Or* I could have my wedding in Bali. Just me and Gary, with witnesses at the local registry office here.

Then, we say our vows on a beach or something in Bali and have the wedding reception there. Romantic or what?'

Annie didn't know what to say. It could work. 'Would Gary's family and our mum and dad fly to Bali? It would be expensive.'

'Only one way to find out. So, you're taking the job?'

'Looks like it.'

Jessica turned up the volume and sang Dance Fever at the top of her voice. Annie watched with a smile. She couldn't join in; her heart was too heavy. If she accepted the secondment, it would mean leaving in ten days' time. The only opportunity she would get to say goodbye to Jojo was Easter Gala, and that would mean seeing Charlie. She didn't know if she could do that, even for Jojo.

42

'Congratulations.' Kai Keisler shook Nico's hand when they arrived at work on Monday morning. 'It was close. But you have this beautiful lady, so an advantage over me.'

Nico stood a bit taller. 'A good assistant is certainly an asset. It was, as you said, a close thing. No hard feelings?'

Jojo had to swallow her pride. Nico would find out soon enough that she was a great deal more than a pretty assistant. For now, it suited her to keep him in the dark.

'Do you want to practice separately again?' she asked when they were alone.

'No. I need you to run through my new finale with me. See you on the stage when you've changed?'

Jojo wasn't too concerned, as she knew the Alice act enhanced by her new aerial acrobatic routine would be sensational. Last time she performed it, Charlie had done an excellent job with the lighting and effects. On Saturday, she might have to rely on Lenny. Annie had made it clear that she thought Charlie had written the note to Jojo as a warning to protect her from Nico. It was possible, Nico could be a bit domineering, or Charlie had delivered the note for someone else, not knowing the content. Meryl.

Once Gala night was over, things were going to change. There would be no more Joanna in beige, and Nico would have to sort things out with his marriage, because Jojo was going to fly. No harness would keep her down. She was going to be Wanda of Wanda's World. Nothing was going to get in her way.

'This should be simple, even for you, Joanna,' Nico said when Jojo joined him on the stage. 'You will step into this transporter.' He indicated a circle marked out on the stage surrounding a trapdoor. 'Then, poof! I will do a spell and you will reappear at the back of the auditorium.'

'Using the tunnel?'

'That's right. It couldn't be easier.'

Jojo was suspicious. There had to be more to it than that. 'Not very imaginative for a finale. What am I missing?'

'Of course, I will be adding more techniques to the act, but that is all you need to know for now.'

'Where's the transporter?'

'Ah. Well, that's the thing.'

'What's the thing?'

'You will disappear from a ring of fire. And then a magnificent flash of light and sound will have the audience turning in their seats to see you emerge like a beautiful phoenix from the flames. You will change your costume in the tunnel. I've spoken to wardrobe they are designing something sensational.'

Even thinking about fire made Jojo's knees go weak. She shivered. 'I can't, Nico. You know that I'm scared of fire. Please don't ask me to do this.'

'There's no danger, I promise. Don't you want me to get a big contract? This will be the making of me, Joanna. Of us. You have to do this. For me. Please.'

Jojo took deep breaths to try to still her nerves. Would she overcome her fear if John Jenkins asked her to work with fire? Sooner or later, she would have to face up to it. 'Okay. I'll do it, but let me go at my own pace.'

'You are an amazing woman. Do you know how much I love you?'

The first run through was without fire, and that was bad enough. Jojo didn't know how she was going to open the trap-door without her costume catching fire.

'Your first costume can be skin tight with nothing trailing. Just use your feet like you do in the sword box trick.'

Jojo was unconvinced, but went through the motions. She slipped through the trapdoor into the chamber beneath the stage, out through the door and across to the tunnel. Jojo hadn't ventured into the tunnel before. It was pitch black. Phillipe had told her there was a light switch. She fumbled around the wall until she grasped its dome. When there was some light, Jojo entered the gloomy, dank space. Pipes ran along the walls on either side. There was just enough room to stand. Jojo wasn't claustrophobic — she couldn't have contorted her body into confined spaces if she was, but the tunnel was oppressive and Jojo feared what might lurk in the dark.

'Stopwatch is on. Now.'

Jojo covered her nose and mouth as a shield against the unpleasant smell, and stumbled onward. The tunnel rumbled. It hissed and spat. Jojo fell to her knees and scrambled up the incline. A scratching. Were there rats down there? There was a reason the tunnel had been out of bounds for the past few decades. The forbidden tunnel. The light flickered and then went out. It couldn't be much further. Jojo clambered to her feet and ran the last few metres. She burst through the curtain, gasping for air.

'No, that won't do. You took far too long,' Nico shouted from the stage. 'Could you at least try to resemble a phoenix rather than Worzel Gummidge?'

They went through the act several times without using fire. By the end of the day, Jojo had got used to the tunnel and Pedro, with some persuasion, had fixed the light so that it stayed on. 'The electrics need seeing to,' he grumbled.

Jojo had changed and was waiting for Nico when Bobbi pounced on her. 'How was Nico when you told him you were to be the star of the show?'

'Hush,' Jojo whispered. 'I'm playing it down, okay?'

Bobbi made a gesture of contained excitement, squeezing her fists and grimacing. 'I'm so proud of you.'

'I'm proud of me but for a different reason. I've been through the forbidden tunnel and survived to tell the tale.'

'How was Moll? Shaking her chains at you?'

'Not sure about Molly May, but I'm sure there are rats down there and it stinks of rotten eggs.'

'I wouldn't be so quick to dismiss Moll. What about all of your near misses? Don't forget the other girl who vanished.'

'When? Who?'

'I told you. Nico's last assistant. Maud. No, Meryl. She had a similar experience to you, unexplained accidents, and then one day she didn't turn up for work and nobody has heard from her since.'

Jojo was about to confide in Bobbi, to tell her that Meryl was alive and well and doing a good job trying to terrorise her with no help from Molly May, when Nico joined them.

'A good day's work, Joanna. Tomorrow we will practice using the ring of fire.'

'You promised to find a couple of rabbits tomorrow.' Jojo hoped to buy some more time to practice alone. Facing up to her fear of fire was harder than she thought.

43

'I thought I'd won the football pools, when Lisa told me I could have the Cyclades jolly, but now you've topped it. Bali! Bloody Bali. Annie Daley, you're a lucky cow.'

Annie was warming to the idea. Images of what looked like castaway heaven: palm trees, deserted beaches that seemed to stretch for miles, cerulean sky, and azure blue sea, were enough to have anyone packing a suitcase and heading for the airport. Her job would be to meet with hotel managers, identify possible resorts, and seek out potential holiday experiences. It would mean getting to know the local people and building relationships with future business partners. It was a daunting proposition, but one that excited Annie. She wanted to share the news with Jojo. And Charlie. Without them both in her life, the magnificence of this opportunity felt flat. Her mum had seemed to understand when they had a heart to heart at the weekend.

On the Saturday evening, after leaving her mum abruptly to avoid a discussion about Henry and her failing love life,

Annie returned to the scene of the haberdashery hat. Mum was draping her bonnet with a red polka dot fabric.

'Jessica took the straw boater. Sorry Mum.'

'Oh, that's okay. It was a different shape, anyway. The materials would behave differently. I think I'm going to go for the fabric rather than crepe. What do you think?'

Annie sat down at the table. She remembered years ago her mum covering it with newspaper and then pots of poster paint, and potatoes posing as lino cuts. It was a happy childhood. Mum was full of ideas to amuse them. 'Won't you miss all of this?'

Her mum put down the bonnet. 'I'll miss the house. I'll miss you and Jessica. I'll miss my friends. The W.I. *Everything.*'

'Then why are you going?'

'I know your dad says that he's glad of an early retirement, but the redundancy hit him hard. When he got all fired up about moving to Scotland, I was pleased that he found something positive to look forward to.'

Their heads turned simultaneously to observe Dad in the back garden, the marquee now fully erected, although it incorporated the fish pond, rockery, and garden shed. He gave them both a thumbs up.

'I may have found a venue for the wedding reception.'

Mum clapped her hands together. 'Why didn't you say? Where?'

Annie told her mum about the work opportunity. Her mum listened intently and then, when Annie had finished, she said that she would make them both a cuppa.

When the ritual of brewing a pot and pouring the tea was complete, her mum said,

'This sounds like the perfect job, so why am I getting the feeling that something is bothering you?'

Annie dunked a digestive biscuit in her tea. It gave her

time to think. She sucked on the soggy mess. 'No. Everything is fine.'

'Hmm. Like it is for me, starting afresh in Scotland.'

'Kind of. I *am* excited about a new adventure. It's a wonderful opportunity. It's just the things I would leave behind. The people.'

They both sighed.

'I read somewhere that new beginnings are always scary and endings sad. But nothing is going to get in the way of love. Not if you don't want it to. It's the people you love and who love you that count and you'll always have that. If your dad and me move to Scotland, and I'm not saying that we will, but if we do, then we'll still be here for you and Jessica. Nobody ever got anywhere by standing still.'

Now, back at work, Annie was trying to gather as much information as she could about the job. It would mean leaving in ten days' time. There was so much to do, briefings from head office, vaccinations, visa, shopping, packing, the list was endless. She had to tell Jojo her news. She couldn't just disappear without saying goodbye.

On Wednesday, Annie had a meeting at head office with some of the team who were being seconded to the Australian branch with her. Suddenly, it felt real. They were helping themselves to coffee outside a meeting room, introducing themselves to one another and comparing progress with visas and vaccinations, when Annie recognised Henry's diffident stoop from the corner of her eye. She was bound to come into contact with him at some point. Best to get it over with.

Annie knew Henry had seen her as she approached. He acted as though the notice board fascinated him.

'Hello Henry. It's good to see you again.' Her cup rattled in its saucer.

'Annie.' He acted as though startled. 'What are you doing here?'

She guessed that he would have been told of her secondment, but went through the charade, letting him express surprise.

'A tad more exciting than the Greek islands,' he said. His eyes and the slump of his shoulders belied the jovial tone.

'Not more exciting. Just different. It's what I need right now. A change.' Annie wanted to say more, to apologise for hurting his feelings, his pride, but she didn't know how. 'Anyway, it's good to see you.'

'They've gone in.' Henry nodded at the meeting room. 'You'd better not be late on your first day.'

By the end of the afternoon, Annie was exhilarated. She'd had so many questions, they tumbled out one after another, her arm shooting up and down. Everyone laughed and teased her, but in a friendly way. They swapped phone numbers so that they could share any tips they picked up before leaving and promised to make contact as soon as they were settled on the other side of the world.

Lisa didn't expect Annie back in the shop that afternoon and so she made a detour to the Golden Globe in search of Jojo. Charlie was on leave and so there was no risk of her bumping in to him. As she walked along the Strand, Annie cringed with embarrassment, remembering how she had imagined her meeting with Charlie the last time she took that journey. The woman he was with at the karaoke bar must have been the woman he had spoken of. She tried to be happy for him that things had worked out. They seemed happy together, and in love. Not goofing around like her and Charlie. How could she have danced and sung? *Don't go there,* Annie warned herself, before she lost her nerve and ran in the opposite direction. *Charlie will not be there today.*

Annie had written a note for Jojo and sealed it in an envelope. If she couldn't see Jojo in person, she could at least leave the note with Pedro. So long as the theatre door was open. Annie was in luck because a woman was coming out of the door as she approached. It was Bobbi, her long legs, and messy chignon, marking her out from a distance.

'Please, could you hold the door?' Annie called and caught it just in time as Bobbi left in a hurry. A clatter alerted Annie that she had dropped something, but whatever it was, she couldn't see it.

Pedro was sorting through some paperwork at the front of house. He was happy to pass the envelope on to Jojo, but unwilling to disturb her until after rehearsals. 'It's our busy time,' he explained. 'Easter Gala this Saturday. I've a few tickets left if you want one, but they're going fast.'

Annie hesitated. Jojo was right. She had missed none of her shows as long as they had known each other. 'Do you know whether Charlie, the stagehand, will be working that night?'

'All hands on deck for the gala. Doesn't matter that it's Easter weekend. It's the most important night in the Golden Globe calendar. So, do you want a couple of tickets?'

'No. No, thank you.' Jojo would understand. Annie wrote a note asking Jojo to phone her urgently. She just hoped that they could talk with no interference from Nico.

The light caught something on the edge of the pavement. Annie stooped down to investigate. It was a gold cigarette lighter. She turned it over in her palm. *Happy 21st Bobbi* was inscribed on one side. The door to the theatre had been locked behind her, so Annie could not hand it in. Instead, she slipped it into her bag. *I am going to see Jojo before I leave. I have to. I'll pass it to her and she can return it to Bobbi.*

A couple of buses went from the Strand to Liverpool Street station, but Annie wasn't sure which bus stop. She checked the timetable on a bus shelter, then glanced further up the road to see if there was another stop close by. That's when she saw Bobbi looking in the window of a shop. She took the lighter from her bag and, clutching it, ran after her as best she could in heels. 'Bobbi!' A bus to Liverpool Street sped past. Damn it. 'Bobbi!'

As Annie paused to catch her breath, Bobbi tossed a cigarette butt and then ground it with the toe of her shoe. 'Bobbi,' Annie gasped.

Deaf to Annie's cries, Bobbi scooted round the corner out of sight. When she reached the corner, Annie watched as Bobbi ran into the arms of a beautiful man. The pair of them belonged in Hollywood. It could have been the ending scene as the credits rolled. The man threw back his head to laugh and for a second Annie thought he looked familiar. Maybe he was a film star or someone she had seen on TV. She hesitated, unsure whether to interrupt the love scene.

'Um, excuse me.'

Neither of them acknowledged Annie. They linked arms and walked away. 'Bobbi.' Annie shouted. 'You dropped something.' At last, she had her attention. 'I found it outside the Golden Globe.'

Bobbi was effusive in her thanks, not realising she had lost the lighter.

'Oh, you just missed her,' Annie's mum said, when Annie arrived home that evening.

'Who? Jojo?' Annie couldn't believe her bad timing. If Jojo was visiting her parents, then she could catch up with her there. Annie kept her coat on, ready to run.

'No love. On the phone. She was worried about you, but I explained you had some good news to share. There isn't something else that I'm missing?'

Annie shook her head. 'I wanted to tell Jojo my news and say goodbye before leaving next week.'

'That's what I thought. Jojo asked me to tell you there's a ticket reserved for you for Easter Gala. She thought you could have a proper catch up after the show.'

'I already told her I couldn't go. I'll phone her back.'

'Jojo said not to return her call as they were going out. It was a pay phone.'

44

The day had finally arrived. Jojo peeked around the stage curtain as the auditorium was filling up. John Jenkins, Annika Riley, and Adele Pearson were seated in the second and third rows with some of their entourage. The Press and VIPs from the Magic Circle would fill the front row. Jojo was sick with nerves. So much could go wrong. The new rabbits were more docile than Pixie and Muffin, so she had no concerns about the first part of her act. She hadn't named them this time and did not let them out of her sight when she took them into the theatre. Nico had enjoyed cuddling them in the evenings after work, but Jojo had remained detached. The orchestra made a few exploratory sounds and Jojo's stomach fluttered.

'Ladies and gentlemen, this is your fifteen-minute call. Fifteen minutes, please.'

Annie wasn't seated. Jojo didn't even know if she was coming. Annie was always at her performances. Every single one since primary school. It was bad luck. An omen. If Annie wasn't there, she would mess things up. *Please Annie. I'll make it up to you. I'll value your friendship more. Be a better friend.* Somebody else was on the stage. Jojo let go of the curtain. Fifteen minutes. Hocus Pocus was on first and then Max. She turned to catch sight of Charlie about to climb up to the fly tower.

'Oh, you're here.' Relief and then shame swept through Jojo. 'I'm so pleased to see you, Charlie.'

He nodded and started to ascend.

'Charlie, I'm sorry. I was wrong. I should never have said those things. Whatever you did, I know you wouldn't have harmed Pixie and Muffin.'

He paused but didn't look at her. Then he continued to climb.

'Ten minutes to curtain-up. You need to get off the stage,' one of the stagehands said.

'Could you help with the lighting and effects of my act, Charlie?'

Charlie fiddled with a light and then came back down the scaffolding. He thumped lightly to the stage in front of Jojo. 'What do you think I'm here for?'

Jojo wanted to hug him. 'Thank you.'

'You'd better get off, unless you're planning to dance in the first number.'

Jojo was avoiding the changing room until Hocus Pocus was on stage. There wasn't enough room for them all, especially with all of those heels and headdresses. It was like being trapped in a cage of peacocks.

'Ladies and gentlemen, this is your on-stage call. Hocus Pocus, to the stage, please. Stand by stage management and technical staff.'

If Annie was coming, she would be seated by now. Jojo slipped through the door into the front of the auditorium. The rustle of programmes, a violin tuning, murmured conversations. The lights dimmed and Jojo felt the energy of expectation as though it was a living breath. But Annie's seat was empty. She wasn't coming.

An elfin cut. Jojo's heart bounced in her ribcage. It was definitely Meryl. She was alone and seemed to scrutinise the stage and all that was happening around it. When their eyes met, Jojo felt as though she had zapped her with a lightsabre. The words, *I'm watching you,* were loud in Jojo's head, as though Meryl was saying them. What was she doing here? Did Nico know?

The lights went out. The audience took a collective breath of anticipation and Peter Walker stepped onto the stage. The show had begun.

Annie would not go. She was watching a programme about The Eurovision Song Contest with her mum and dad. Girls in satin spacesuits and flicked-up hair were singing something in a language she didn't recognise. All the while, her head and heart were at the Golden Globe. In four days, she would fly across the world and Jojo didn't even know. If Jojo had put pride before their friendship, she would have disappointed Annie. The pain of unrequited love couldn't feel any worse than it did now. If she was honest with herself, it was the humiliation of having misread Charlie that glued her bottom to the sofa – not Terry Wogan's enthusiasm over the Irish entry, nor the backdrop of dewy pastures, and soft Gaelic music.

'What do you think, Annie?'

Had Mum been talking to her? What she thought was, the Easter Gala starts in two hours. If she got ready now and on a train within the hour, then she could just make it. As soon as Annie had made that decision, a weight lifted from her chest. It was the right thing to do. If she saw Charlie, then she would be polite and friendly; it wasn't as if he had intentionally misled her. He probably didn't even know that she had fallen head over heels and was now sprawled figuratively in an undignified mess.

When Annie arrived at the theatre, the show had just started. Pedro greeted her. 'Ah, Miss Jojo's friend. You can slip in now while the boss is doing his spiel.'

The auditorium was full, except for one seat in a row from the back L5. Annie manoeuvred her way between feet and bags, trying not to cause too much disturbance.

Jojo tried to blank the image of Meryl from her mind. If she was in the audience, in plain sight, then there was nothing she could do to harm her. Unless she had a loaded gun in her bag. What if she started firing into the audience or aimed at Jojo?

'Nico?' She had to tell him. Warn him.

'Ready?' he said.

Nico was psyched up for their performance. If she spooked him now, it would be a disaster. Maybe she was overreacting. Meryl was unlikely to get her hands on another gun.

But what if she had tampered with the props?

'What if the sword box is faulty?' Jojo whispered.

'It isn't.' Nico's voice was firm and even. Jojo tried to draw strength from him. Maybe she should have a plan, just in case.

'The Incredible Nico and Jojo Evans.'

It was the first time her name had been announced alongside Nico's. At the Starlight show, Nico introduced her as his beautiful assistant. The front row rippled with movement, the press taking notes. They would have learnt her name by now. Jojo prayed she wasn't front page news for the wrong reasons. *Magician kills assistant in failed sword trick stunt.*

45

'I know that the press and our distinguished VIPs are excited to see the Golden Globe's latest discovery. Remember, you first saw the act here. Another breakthrough in the world of theatrical magic. As always, you will have to wait until the finale. This Easter Gala is our best yet. I'm proud to present to you Britain's, nay Europe's, heck - the world's, finest magicians and dancers. The Golden Globe Theatre Easter Gala Show 1980.'

The audience clapped and cheered. Cameras flashed in the front row. The orchestra belted out Cabaret. Firework fountains spurted sparklers. The stage filled with colour and glitz as Hocus Pocus strutted their stuff. Sold out within days, Annie was about to watch a show that tomorrow morning would be featured in all the media's entertainment pages, but the only person she wanted to see was Charlie. Was he backstage now, watching the audience from the stage? A vision of him looking down at her from the scaffolding, that infectious grin daring her to follow him up into the fly-tower. He could be behind her in the sound and lighting box. Maybe he had seen her arrive late. They were bound to meet at the interval. What she would say, how she would say it, and what he might say in reply, occupied Annie's thoughts as the scene changed to one of a Parisian café.

That night, Jojo stepped onto the stage alongside Nico and the audience responded as though they were superstars. Standing on the stage, cameras flashing, Jojo was terrified. This was the biggest moment in her life. Top producers were there to see her perform. That was enough to have her heart racing but there was also the ring of fire. They had not pulled it off successfully in rehearsals; Jojo was too scared to practice and Nico refused to revert to the escape act. Meryl was in the audience – the woman who had stalked her, sent threats and warnings, and was known to be dangerous. And Nico believed that the act everyone was there to see was his. How was he going to react when he found out Jojo was the star of the show? She couldn't go home with him afterwards, but where else could she go? Shut down all other thoughts and concentrate.

When Nico opened the sword box to reveal she was all in one piece, Jojo's knees were like jelly. Never before had that trick felt so scary.

'Well done,' Nico said, off stage. 'I expect Walker will want to introduce me to the VIPs in the interval. I'll see you back here for act two.'

The buzz backstage was like a bottle of champagne waiting to pop. Jojo caught Charlie as he was about to go through the doors into the auditorium 'Charlie, can I have a quick word about the lighting and effects for my act?'

'It's all in hand, Bat Girl.' His voice was even, but the words were enough for Jojo to know that she had been forgiven.

'Thank you. I really appreciate you and everything that you have and continue to do for me. I'm really sorry that I didn't trust you. Your friendship means so much to me.' Jojo couldn't stop the tears. It wasn't just Charlie, it was everything.

'It's okay. If you stop crying, I really want you to meet someone who is special to me.' He gave her a concerned look and Jojo felt his warmth. Charlie was like the brother she never had, Annie the sister. How could she have shut out two of the most important people in her life?

'If this person is special to you, Charlie, then she's special to me. Your girlfriend?'

'Come and see.'

At last, it was the interval. *I am here to see Jojo. It is neither here nor there if I bump into Charlie. I'll be nonchalant. How do I explain running away from him at the karaoke bar?* Annie's resolve weakened and so she stepped into an alcove of the bar to compose herself whilst checking out who was there. It looked as though Nico was talking to a couple of reporters. The man who had introduced the show was standing with a square jawed hunk. Annie had seen him recently, and it wasn't on the stage. Shrieks of laughter, guffaws, exclamations. It was noisy and the air hazy with cigarette smoke. Waitresses dressed as Bunny Girls circulated with glasses of champagne. Annie plucked one from a passing tray. She should have sent a message to Jojo or at least arrived early so that Jojo knew she was there.

Annie left the crowded bar to sip her champagne in the foyer, and that was where she found Jojo. Excitement turned to dismay when Annie recognised Charlie and his girlfriend were sitting with her. Deep in conversation, they had not seen her and so Annie backed out of the room. None of the scenarios that Annie had rehearsed included Charlie's girlfriend. Of course, he would have invited her to the show. She was tempted to leave, to just go home and forget about him. *You are here to see Jojo, to tell her that in four days you will leave for Bali.* But not now, after the show. Annie abandoned her glass of champagne and returned to her seat in the empty theatre.

Jojo froze when she saw Meryl sitting in the foyer. 'Charlie, that woman. She's—'

'—My sister.'

Jojo looked from one to the other. 'I don't understand.'

'I wanted to tell you sooner, but I couldn't, not until I had evidence.'

Meryl cast her eyes down.

'Go on.'

Charlie took a deep breath. He clasped Meryl's hand. 'Although he doesn't know it, I am Nico's brother-in-law. I was in the States when they got married.'

'Nobody went to our wedding,' Meryl said. 'Just me, Nico, and a couple of witnesses he dragged — well, charmed — off the street. It seemed romantic at the time, but then everything Nico did was glamorous, exciting, magical.'

'It is,' Jojo said. She didn't trust this woman — Nico's wife.

'It was at first, but then he changed. It was so gradual I didn't notice. Choosing what I should wear, making fun of me in a light-hearted way. Then it got more serious. Nico cut me off from my friends and family. He would lock me in the flat if he needed to go out alone. He was driven by work and became more and more demanding of me. If he didn't get the audience reception he wanted, then it was my fault. There were punishments too.' Meryl's voice broke.

Charlie put a hand on Meryl's arm. 'It's okay. He can't hurt you anymore.'

Jojo felt woozy. She wished Charlie had kept this revelation until after the show. Soon, she would be back on the stage performing with Nico. 'So, that's why you sent an anonymous note to warn me?'

'I joined the Golden Globe just after Meryl left. I needed a placement at a theatre. It made sense to work here so that I could keep an eye on Nico. He wouldn't divorce Meryl and was making it impossible for her to work.'

'I had decided to leave him. I think he knew. It was as if he could get inside my head. Maybe he knew I wanted to shoot him. But I was a coward. I couldn't have done that, however much I wanted to.'

'I nearly let him drown in that tank of water myself. It's what he deserves.'

'You did that on purpose?'

'Just long enough to see him squirm, but I didn't want to frighten you, Jojo.'

'Tell me what happened.'

Charlie answered for Meryl. 'They were on the stage rehearsing. Nico asked Lenny to film the bullet trick to help him improve his technique.'

'The gun is loaded with a bullet that has Nico's name on it. I fire through a glass panel and he catches the bullet between his teeth. He shows the audience that it's the same one I fired.'

Jojo was impressed. 'That's pretty amazing. Not sure I would have the guts to pull a trigger. How does it work?'

'The bullet I load is wax. When it's fired, it's so hot it melts a hole in the Perspex glass. It looks as though it has gone straight through. Nico has the real bullet – which also has his name on it – in his mouth. He slides it between his teeth.'

Charlie took up the story again. 'The day that Lenny was

recording, a real bullet had been loaded. Meryl pulled the trigger and if Nico hadn't thrown himself to the ground, it would have killed him. Nico begged Lenny to keep quiet and to hand over the film so that he could protect Meryl. Instead, Nico used it to blackmail her and prevent her from divorcing him.'

'But now Charlie has evidence that Nico swapped the bullets himself,' Meryl said.

'Lenny took a copy of the film which he shared with me. I took it to a magician who lectures at my college and he pointed out how Nico had used his sleight of hand to swap the bullets. So, Meryl has nothing to fear. Let Nico do his worst and I'll tell the world how he terrorised my sister and held her to ransom.'

'I can't believe it's all over,' Meryl said. 'Charlie wanted me to come tonight so that I could face Nico without being afraid, but I'm not sure that's possible. Not yet.'

Jojo believed every word. She wished she didn't, but Meryl was voicing the thoughts she had been trying to silence since the day Nico took away her clothes and locked her in the flat.

'If it wasn't you, who killed Pixie and Muffin?'

'Honestly?' Charlie said. Jojo nodded. 'I think it was Nico. You didn't see his face when he came on in his speedos to an audience that was more entertained by you than him.'

Ladies and gentlemen, tonight's performance will restart in two minutes. Please make your way back to your seats.

In thirty minutes, Jojo would have to perform with Nico to a theatre of top producers and press. The Ring of Fire. She couldn't do it. The number one rule was magician and assistant had to have absolute trust in one another. 'I can't go on.'

Meryl grabbed her hands. 'You have to. Don't let him win.

If I can face up to Nico this evening, after all that he has done to me, you can.'

'All the VIPs in there,' Charlie nodded at the door of the adjoining bar, 'are here to see you — Jojo Evans. This is the chance of your life, Bat Girl. Don't blow it.'

'I wish Annie was here.'

'I thought she would be,' Charlie said.

'That's the other reason I'm here. Charlie wanted to introduce me to this woman that he can't stop talking about.'

'Annie?' Jojo wondered what else she had missed. It was as though she had been living in a different world. 'Does she know how you feel?'

'No. I couldn't tell her, not until everything was out in the open. I'm surprised she's missed your big night.'

'Annie doesn't know about my meeting with John Jenkins. We've barely spoken since the Starlight show.'

'Nico?' Meryl said.

'I could have made more effort.'

'He's clever. You don't realise you're being manipulated until it's too late.'

'They're coming out. If you don't want to run into the press, you'd better get going. See you back stage Bat Girl. You are going to dazzle them. Tomorrow, your face will be on the front cover of every newspaper.'

'Hardly. But I will give Nico and everyone else a performance they will talk about for days.'

'Decades!' Charlie grinned. 'Go knock 'em dead Bat Girl.'

46

The faded auditorium gradually filled as the audience returned to their seats. It seemed to expand with their breath. A breath that was held and then released as the curtain opened on the second act.

Now Annie had seen Charlie she knew she had been lying to herself because that *was* the reason she was there. It made her a poor friend. She was behaving like a lovelorn teenager. Well, now she knew. There was no doubt that Charlie wasn't interested in her and never had been. She had just one hour to get over it and then she would go out there with a smile on her face to congratulate Jojo on her performance, and Charlie on his new found love.

Kai Keisler was billed as the next act. Henry had enthused over his performance at the Starlight show. Annie hated to be disloyal, but she thought his act slicker and more original than Nico's. A handsome man too with his square jawline, and blue eyes like Steve McQueen. That's where she had seen him before. Bobbi and Kai made a dazzling couple.

The audience exhaled with a collective sigh as Kai released

a hundred coloured doves. Pink, green, lavender. They flew a rainbow over the audience and, with a tap from Kai, swept back to the stage in a glorious arc. Annie almost felt sorry for Nico, who was on next. Jojo was billed as the last act. Annie wondered whether Nico had engineered it so that Jojo didn't disrupt the audience before his escapist routine. She hoped Jojo would do the Alice act.

'What have you been saying to the Press?' Nico pounced on Jojo outside the changing room, clasping her upper arm in a vice-like grip. 'You're trying to make a fool of me.' Saliva glistened on his chin. He threw her away from him.

'Nothing. I didn't go out there at the interval.'

'You must have said something. Why else would they be asking for you? This is my big night. *Mine.* Don't you dare try to upstage me again.'

After this performance, she never wanted to see him again. 'Maybe they want to cover the female equality angle. That's why Walker's giving me more of a presence.'

That seemed to mollify Nico. 'Just don't get any ideas. You are my assistant. That is all you are and only if I deem you good enough. If not...' He clicked his fingers. '...then you are nobody.'

'I'll see you backstage,' Jojo said.

Bobbi opened her arms to Jojo when she escaped into the changing room. 'Darling. I couldn't help overhearing. Come here.'

Jojo let Bobbi hug her. She would have liked to stay there, enveloped in the heady scent of Opium and hair mousse. The adrenalin that had fired her up in the first half of the show had dipped, leaving her emotionally exhausted and wrung out.

'How can I go out there and perform with him?'

'You can't. The trust between magician and assistant has been destroyed. Without that magic, you're exposed. It won't work. I know.' Bobbi pulled away. 'Why don't I take your place? You stepped in for me. Now I'll do it for you. I've worked with Nico before.'

'That's really kind of you, but I've got to do the last act.'

'If you want my advice, I'd have a word with Jenkins now. Tell him you'll perform for him and a select audience another time. If you try to do it tonight, you'll mess up. Why don't you go home or to a friend's house? I'll cover for you.'

'No.' Jojo stood a little taller. 'I will not let him win. I've worked hard for this. Tonight is my night. I'm going to put everything into this. He will not take this away from me.'

'Are you sure?'

'One hundred percent.' Jojo was. Anger and determination had stoked an energy that was now coursing through her veins. She could do anything.

Nico and Jojo were welcomed onto the stage with great applause and a few whistles, which surprised Annie. Jojo looked a little pale. She ought to have swallowed her pride to be there for her friend at the interval. Annie hoped Jojo would see her sitting at the back of the auditorium.

Their act was disappointing. It was as though they were walking through the process, bored and disinterested. Jojo made her usual gurning faces, but Annie felt something was missing. The audience stirred, as though restless.

'Tonight, we are going to perform a trick that nobody has seen before. In fact, it will be the first time we have performed it. *Ever.*' The last remark raised some chuckles. Annie hoped Nico was joking.

'I am going to transport my beautiful assistant through a ring of fire to another time and place.'

Annie's heart lurched for Jojo — *fire*. The audience seemed to have sat up to attention like a dog waiting for a bone.

Jojo came back onto the stage dressed in a skintight silver suit. Annie would have advised her against silver; it would act like foil in the oven, increasing the heat. She looked stunning though, with her flame red hair. Nico drew a circle around her.

'I am going to summon the ring of fire. Keep focused on its centre. Are you ready Jojo?'

Jojo smiled at the audience. 'I am ready, Nico. See you in another time and place.' She blew him a kiss. Then, Nico pointed at Jojo's feet and flames leapt in a circle around her. Annie didn't take her eyes off Jojo, but when the flames died down, she had vanished.

'In a different time and place. My beautiful assistant will emerge a phoenix from the ashes.'

A cymbal heralded a flash of light from the back of the auditorium. Heads turned towards Annie. Behind her, where she had once emerged herself giggling with Charlie, there was a small explosion. But no Jojo.

Jojo was proud of herself. She hadn't so much as flinched when the flames licked the floor inches from her feet. Getting through the trapdoor unscathed had been achieved through years of practice contorting her body. Twenty. Nineteen. She had less than twenty seconds to run through the tunnel, slip on her costume and appear in an explosion of light at the back of the theatre. It was a simple act, but effective. Then the stage was all hers.

The door was jammed. Jojo pushed hard, but it didn't

budge. Ten. Nine. Nico would have to improvise; she would only be a few seconds late. Jojo hammered on the door.

Nico created another burst of fire. The audience gasped, delighted. Annie knew something was wrong. Then another. Someone shouted at Nico from the wings. Cameras flashed in the front rows.

Annie was glad she had a seat at the back of the theatre. Smoke screened the hidden door as she felt for the catch. If Jojo was trapped in the tunnel, she would find her.

47

Nobody came. The door had been locked from the outside. The trick would be ruined and if she didn't get out soon, then she wouldn't be performing the last act. Jojo hammered and hollered.

At first, she didn't notice the spark that had dropped from the stage. It was the smoke that aroused her attention. It smarted her eyes and tickled her throat. She thought it came from the fire now that it had been extinguished. A crackle and a heat against her thighs caused Jojo to turn and then she saw the flames. She was locked in a burning room.

'Let me out! Let me out!'

There was nothing she could use to cover her face and so Jojo lay on her stomach, hands shielding her nose and mouth. Bobbi was right. She shouldn't have performed with Nico when they no longer trusted one another. It was a trick they hadn't properly rehearsed and now it was going to end in disaster. Someone must have realised that she hadn't reappeared. Why wasn't anyone coming to her rescue?

. . .

Annie wasn't afraid of the hidden tunnel. It held a happy memory of Charlie running ahead, teasing her. It was the day she had fallen in love with him. Twenty-four years old and this was her first love. Annie wondered whether it would be her last. She couldn't imagine falling in love again. She didn't want to; it hurt too much. These thoughts distracted her and Annie was a little careless. The tunnel sloped as it followed the tiered seating down towards the stage, and she lost her balance. The heels she had worn, hoping to impress Charlie, were not suitable for this kind of escapade. She stumbled and then came over on one ankle. *Ouch.* Annie hopped around, holding onto a pipe that ran along the wall. She slipped off her shoe to massage her ankle. It was painful. She tried placing her injured foot flat on the floor. It was fine until she tried to take any weight. Annie lowered herself back down, hoping that the pain would ease enough to walk the last few metres out of the tunnel.

'Jojo, are you there?' she called.

The light flickered and then went out.

A dark tunnel was a different matter altogether. There was a hiss and a hum. The smell of rotten eggs. Annie was afraid. She couldn't just sit there hoping for someone to find her. Nobody knew she was there.

Jojo was relieved to hear Charlie shout from the other side of the door. 'Jojo?'

'Thank God. Let me out.'

'Stand back. I'm going to kick the door down.'

'I can't. There's a fire. Charlie, I'm afraid.'

'Okay. Just get as far away from the door as you can.'

The door fell in with a thwack followed by Charlie. Jojo

was grateful for his strong arms, which supported her and propelled her out of the burning room.

'We have to go outside.'

'Why? I'm on next. I can't go outside.'

'The theatre's on fire. We've got to go.'

Jojo stared at him. It made little sense. This was her night. The Alice act. She had to go on the stage. Charlie took her hand and, with some force and urgency, led her out of the fire exit and across the main street to the assembly point.

Jojo's teeth chattered. The theatre was on fire. Everyone was being evacuated. 'What happened? Where's Nico?'

'A spark of fire caught under the stage. I don't know where he is, but everyone's coming out. Just stay here.'

Bobbi ran over to them. Streaks of mascara stained her cheeks. 'Oh, my God. I am so, so, sorry. When I heard there was a fire, I went to let you out. You weren't there. I thought I had killed you.' Bobbi gasped out her confession between loud sobs.

'You locked me in?'

'I tried to stop you from doing your solo. It's not fair. First you stole my act — Adele Pearson sent a scout to see *me* at that matinee — then, Kai's. Kai is the star of this show, not you. I tried to warn you, but you wouldn't back off. This was *our* chance to get the recognition we deserve, that we have worked bloody hard for. You've been with the Golden Globe what — three months? — and you think you can just walk in and steal everything from us? Nico might forgive you, but I can't. If it wasn't for you, Kai would be signing a six-figure contract. You don't even need this, you're young. You'll have other chances, but I won't.'

Bobbi had lost it. She was shouting and screaming like a woman possessed. In the fug of her brain, Jojo realised Bobbi was responsible for all the threats and warnings.

'Why would you kill two baby rabbits?'

'Vermin. They're magician's props. You don't belong in theatrical magic or you would understand.'

'The doves?' Jojo looked down at her own hands, remembering the green dye. 'They were from Kai's act.'

'I hope you're satisfied now. The whole bloody theatre has gone up in flames because of you. Now all of us are out of work.'

They were attracting attention. A camera flashed. 'Jojo? Can I interview you for The Evening Standard?'

'Can't you see she's in shock? Jojo won't be talking to any reporters today.' Charlie stepped in to protect her.

'Where's Meryl, Charlie?'

'I don't know. We need to find her. Coming?'

They left Bobbi talking to the Press. No doubt, bad-mouthing Jojo, but finding Meryl was more important.

Sirens sounded. Three fire engines drew up, followed by an ambulance.

'Has anyone been hurt?' Jojo asked Charlie. Bobbi was right. This was her fault. Hers and Nico's. It was a tragedy the fire would damage the beautiful Victorian theatre, but if anyone died as a result, she wouldn't be able to live with herself.

Pedro was taking the register.

'Have you seen my sister, Pedro?'

Meryl ran over to them. 'Oh Charlie, thank God, you're safe. I heard you had gone into a burning room to rescue Jojo. Are you okay? You should go over to the ambulance and tell them you inhaled smoke.'

Jojo couldn't stop shaking. Her teeth chattered like a monkey.

'Here,' Charlie pulled off his rugby shirt, 'put this on. I'm fine in a T-shirt.'

'There's one person missing,' Pedro said. 'Let me count again.'

They huddled together, watching the drama unfold. Lenny came stumbling out of the building carrying the dove cage. He fell to the ground, and the cage opened, releasing the parrot, Kai's multi-coloured doves, and a chicken. 'Are there any other animals or birds in there?' Meryl asked.

'If there are, the firemen will rescue them. Lenny shouldn't have gone back in.'

'No. There's definitely one person missing. Seat L5.'

'Oh, that's okay. I bought that ticket for my friend Annie, but she didn't make it.'

'That's right. The young lady who took that seat arrived late, just after Peter Walker started his introduction to the show.'

Jojo and Charlie looked at one another in horror.

'Annie? Are you sure?'

'Seat L5. I'll report to the fire crew.' Pedro was already on his way.

'I have to go in and find her,' Charlie said.

'You can't!' Meryl clung on to his arm.

'I will,' Jojo said, but she was terrified.

'Let's just keep calm. Does Annie know about the tunnel?' Meryl said.

'Yes,' Jojo and Charlie answered together.

'I saw a woman in front of me make her way to the end of her row – the same side as the hidden door. It was when Jojo didn't appear at the back of the theatre.'

Jojo gasped. That was typical of Annie going to her rescue. 'I have to get her out.'

'No.' Charlie shouted. 'I do.'

They ran towards the fire, but were held back by a fireman. 'Keep away. The building could explode. There's a gas leak.'

'No!' Charlie roared. He fell to his knees. 'No!'

'Charlie, I'm scared. What if.... I couldn't bear it...'

'I didn't tell her I love her.' Charlie wiped an arm across his eyes.

'She's not dead.' Jojo was crying too. 'We have to do something.'

'Where did Meryl go?'

48

Annie gripped her ankle in both hands, willing the pain to ease, but if anything, it felt worse. She had to get out of the tunnel. The easiest way out was to continue down, either shuffling on her bottom or using the wall for support. As she was already seated, Annie tried a bit of bottom shifting. Her dress rucked up. The floor should have been cold, but was surprisingly hot. Too hot. Annie struggled to her feet. Progress on her bottom was too slow. The stage couldn't be much further ahead, she leaned her elbow and forearm against the wall, but she needed support both sides before taking any weight through her ankle.

'Help.' Her voice echoed. She prayed Charlie would hear her cries from backstage and come to her rescue. What if she didn't get out before the end of the show? She could get locked in overnight. Never mind the pain, she had to get out. Annie forced her foot to take her weight, allowing a tiny scream to escape. Then she laughed at herself. She was trying not to disturb the audience above her head when that's exactly what she had to do. Annie went to take a deep breath, but the air was thick and hot. Flames appeared at the end of the tunnel. Fierce, big flames. The scream came then, as if from someone else.

Annie forgot the pain in her ankle and the heat of the floor as she scrambled back the way she had come. She clawed the ground with sweaty hands, trying to find purchase. Her good foot levered her up inch by inch. Her life couldn't end now; it had barely begun. There were so many things that she wanted to do. With every excruciating haul upwards, Annie named something she would do if she survived. Tell Charlie she loved him. Travel the world, not just Bali and Australia, she wanted to see every continent. Have another Sunday lunch with Mum, Dad and Jessica and cherish every moment. Annie felt woozy. She would just close her eyes for a few seconds, take a rest. It was hard work. In her dream, Jojo and Charlie laughed at Annie because it had all been an illusion. A magnificent trick. The three of them were on the stage, taking a bow.

'Is anyone there? Make a noise if you're in here.'

In her dream, Annie was back in the tunnel. She was irritated by Jojo and Charlie. *It's not funny,* she tried to say and woke herself up. How long had she been asleep? It was getting hard to breathe. 'Help!'

There was a scratching sound. Annie imagined the rats clawing their way to freedom much like her but with more success. Then a louder noise, a banging. There was no time to dwell on what was making the noise. She just had to get out of there. Wasting no breath to shout, who would hear her anyway? Annie focused on crawling. When the slope became less steep, she heaved herself up to stand and gritted her teeth. A broken ankle, even an amputated foot, was better than dying; she had to ignore the pain and bloody well run.

A woman emerged from the smoke; a shawl wrapped

around her head. Molly May. There to lead her home, well she wasn't going anywhere with her, so she could bugger off.

'Annie?' the woman said.

Annie couldn't reply. She tried, but her mouth was too dry, her throat burning. Whoever this woman was — a ghost or real — then she was grateful. Even a respite break in heaven would be a blessed relief.

A damp cloth was being wrapped around her face. Firm arms supported her. 'You can do this, Annie. Just a few more steps. There's more air through here.'

They moved quickly together. There seemed to be a hidden wall in the tunnel. The woman slid back an opening and pushed Annie through. Here the air was lighter and Annie felt as though she could breathe if she removed the shawl wrapped around her face.

'Keep that over your nose and mouth.' The woman tightened the cloth. That was when Annie looked at her.

'You're that woman. Charlie's girlfriend.'

'Sister. I'm Meryl, Charlie's sister.'

Annie wanted to laugh. It was hysterical — a cliché from an old-fashioned farce. She was his sister. Her laugh came out as a muffled wail.

'We're not out yet. You're doing well. Just hold it together. Lean on me.'

Outside the theatre, Charlie and Jojo were examining the walls. 'I heard that there was an opening to the tunnel somewhere, but I thought it was just a rumour,' Charlie said.

'That's the only way Meryl could have got in. I checked with the firemen; she definitely didn't get past them.'

'Keep looking. Maybe we should split up. You go one way and I'll go the other.'

The explosion that ripped their world came with no warning. It threw Jojo off her feet and left her sprawled on the concrete yards away from the building.

'Get away now,' a fireman shouted. 'Everyone, clear the area.'

There was chaos as people ran and screamed. Annie and Meryl were in there. Nobody could have survived that explosion. Charlie was shouting at a fireman. Jojo closed her eyes. She had killed Annie. Behaving like a selfish child insisting that she come to her show, she had as good as murdered her friend. Bobbi was right, she was selfish. What did a TV contract matter now? Nothing was as important as Annie's friendship. She had meant more than a sister to her, taking the place of her mother, always looking out for her, putting her needs before her own. Annie was an angel.

The ambulance crew had gathered in a group around a stretcher. Something was going on within a cornered off area.

'Charlie.' Jojo interrupted his fight with the fireman. 'Over there.'

Annie felt the oxygen in her lungs and was grateful. If Meryl hadn't come to her rescue, she would have died. They got out a couple of minutes before the explosion. *Meryl. Charlie's sister.* She could hear Charlie now. Why was he so angry, shouting at everyone?

'I have to see her. Yes, I'm next of kin. Both of them. Now.'

An ambulance woman checked her blood pressure. 'Are you ready to see your loved ones?' she asked with a soft, lilting accent.

'Charlie? Jojo?'

'I'll get them for you. Your fella will start a fight if I don't let him see you soon. But only if it's okay with you?'

Annie nodded. 'Please. Is Meryl alright? She saved my life.'

'Meryl is great. She's a heroine, that's for sure.'

Charlie climbed into the ambulance where Annie was lying on a trolley wearing an oxygen mask. His beautiful face contorted with concern. 'Annie.' He took her hand and pressed it to his lips. 'If anything had happened to you… I love you, Annie. I should have told you. I love you. What if I never got the chance to say it?'

Annie's heart was so full of love it clogged her throat. 'I would have known. Would you have known that I loved you? It feels as though I've always loved you. As if I've known you forever.' She must have been given a tranquilizer or something because she was being most un-Annie-like.

'You love me?' Charlie said, as though it was a surprise. The best surprise ever.

'I love you.'

Jojo wondered how she had missed the romance between Annie and Charlie. It seemed that she had misread a lot of things. Now, she sat at Meryl's side and took her hand. 'I owe you so much. You and Charlie. If you hadn't gone back in to find Annie, she would have died in that explosion.' The tears came now. Thick and fast.

Meryl put her arms around Jojo. 'Everything's going to be okay.'

'What about Nico? You're still married.'

'Now that I have the evidence Nico loaded the gun, I'll be starting divorce proceedings. Even without his threats, I couldn't have done that before. He has a way of taking away your sense of self, making you believe you need him in order to survive. I did for a long time but that's all it was — surviving. The truth is, I thought of replacing the wax bullet with a real one. Maybe Nico read my mind, or put the thought in there. I know that sounds crazy, but he's clever – manipulative. I was planning to leave him. I just didn't have the courage. Are you going to be okay, Jojo?'

Jojo was aware of another presence. She looked up to see a young woman in a trench coat taking notes. Realising she had been spotted, the woman introduced herself, 'Hello Jojo. Howdy! magazine, celebrity news. Have you spoken to John Jenkins? Are we going to be seeing more of you? I hear that Children's BBC are interested in offering you a contract.'

Meryl steered Jojo away. 'Can't you see Jojo's in shock? She's also suffering from smoke inhalation.'

The woman followed them. 'How did you come to be locked under the stage, Jojo?'

They quickened their pace.

'Is it true you are Nico's estranged wife, Meryl? What was Nico like to work with Jojo?'

Meryl stopped a passing ambulance woman. 'I've been seen, but my friend hasn't. She inhaled a lot of smoke.'

'Thank you,' Jojo said when they were safely hidden inside an ambulance. 'I don't know how much she heard from our chat, but that reporter seems to have dug up a lot of information.'

'Sneaking around listening in to conversations.'

'I hardly think my story is newsworthy.'

'Are you kidding? Your act may have been cancelled, but you are hot news, Jojo. Tonight's drama is only going to boost your publicity.'

When Jojo had been given the all clear, the two women stepped out of the ambulance. Camera flashes blinded them. Until now, Jojo had managed to escape attention, but the young reporter's interest seemed to have triggered an onslaught of paparazzi.

Overwhelmed by the media's attention, Jojo shielded her eyes. Then she heard an authoritative voice. 'John Jenkins Productions will be making a statement. If you would like to make your way over to our communications unit.'

Jojo thought the instruction was meant for her, but a hand on her shoulder gently restrained her. 'JJ asked me to see that you were okay and if you were in need of anything. He suggested you might like a suite in The Savoy.'

'Oh, I couldn't afford that.'

The woman laughed. 'I'll book you a suite.'

Meryl was looking around as if trying to tactfully distance herself.

'Would you mind staying with me, Meryl? If Annie doesn't get admitted to the hospital, I expect she'll be staying with Charlie. It would be good to have your company.'

At that moment, Nico walked past, flanked by two policemen. He turned his head to stare at Jojo and Meryl before being led away. The girls let out their breath in unison.

'Yes please, although I doubt if we'll get any sleep after this evening's events.'

49

25TH FEBRUARY 1981

Twenty-eight million viewers had tuned in to watch the feature length pilot of Wanda's World. The show's success exceeded even John Jenkins's expectations. The party that evening, in St James's Palace Hotel, was to celebrate. Jojo adjusted her skirts so that they wouldn't crumple and found that she took up the width of the corridor where she waited, impatient to glimpse Annie and Charlie's arrival. A few reporters and cameramen had gathered at the hotel entrance, but Clarence House was the chief attraction that night. She hadn't seen them since they returned from their travels; they had so much to catch up on.

She heard Charlie's voice first. He was joking with the press because they were all laughing. Jojo peeked into the foyer, desperate to see her friends without the paparazzi spying her. She had already given a little speech on her arrival in a limousine accompanied by one of John Jenkin Productions communications staff. At last, Annie stepped into the foyer a vision of ruffles and bows. If it wasn't for the weight of her dress, Jojo would have run to greet her.

'Annie, Annie,' she cried, her arms open.

'There she is! Oh Jojo, I've missed you so much. Can I hug you? I'm afraid to touch.'

Jojo laughed and pulled Annie to her. They hugged one another tight.

'Shall I just go and get myself a beer or something?'

They pulled apart, both wiping tears from their eyes.

'Charlie!' Jojo kissed him on both cheeks, and then threw away any sense of restraint and hugged him too.

'If you're wearing 19th century now, I can't see you cramming many of those into your dressing-up box,' Annie said.

Jojo spread her skirts, and they admired the cascade of golden silk. 'It's a Vivienne Westwood. She's working on a collection of flamboyant historical clothing and I wanted something special.'

Annie gasped. 'Did she design it for you?'

Jojo laughed. 'No. Adele knows her and arranged for me to borrow a dress from her collection for the party. It's not a selfless act. This dress will be in all the celebrity mags. Well, it would have been if Lady Diana Spencer and Prince Charles hadn't announced their engagement yesterday.'

'Really? Surely, Wanda's World trumps a Royal engagement?'

The three friends took their time walking towards the party, eager to share all their news. As they got closer, the sound of laughter, cheers, and glasses clinking became louder.

'I've got a room booked for this evening. Shall we sneak upstairs for a catch-up before we join the madness?'

'If you're sure you won't be missed?' Annie said.

Jojo had to take a separate lift, as her skirt was so wide. When she stepped out two floors up, she heard Annie and Charlie laughing together as they raced one another up the stairs. She missed feeling carefree. The past ten months had been tough. She thought Nico worked her hard, but it was nothing compared to the demands of Wanda's World. But it was different. This was her dream. She was in control. It didn't always feel like it; there were tight schedules, and ridiculous demands on her time, but everything that she did was an expression of herself. She'd had to dig deep, and that meant facing up to feelings of inadequacy as a child, and struggling with her sense of identity. Now, Jojo knew who she was, and she was proud of all that she had achieved.

'You are so unfit, Charlie boy!' Annie gasped as she reached the top. Charlie pretended to be struggling behind her. Jojo had missed his grin. He radiated light, like a blast of summer.

When they had all admired the accommodation and settled down in Jojo's penthouse suite, she ordered champagne.

'Okay, but I'm keeping an eye on the time,' Annie said, reverting to her role as big sister. 'Half an hour, max. Any longer and you will be missed.'

'You see what I have to put up with, Bat Girl?'

Annie swiped him and Charlie pulled her in for a hug.

'I don't know what I would do without Annie looking out for me. This amazing woman planned our travels from Bali to Singapore and then Oz. It was the trip of a lifetime.'

'Charlie came out for Jessica's wedding and then we spent three months travelling.'

The champagne arrived and Charlie poured them each a glass. 'To friendship, adventure, and success,' he said.

'To being together.' Jojo clinked her glass with Annie's. 'I've missed you both so much.'

'To Jojo,' Annie said. 'Star of Wanda's World and ours.'

They sat in silence as they each took in how far they had come in the past year.

. . .

Annie's heart swelled with love and gratitude. A year ago, she didn't know what the future held for her. She thought she lacked imagination, but in her wildest dreams, she couldn't have envisaged how her life would unfold. Charlie was the love of her life; she couldn't love a person more and she was secure knowing that he felt the same. They had rented a flat in Islington on their return to London. Charlie was going to pursue his dream of working on the set design of a West End theatre and Annie was continuing her work as an expert on long haul holidays with an executive role at head office. Everything had worked out exactly as it should and at the right time. That night, when she thought the last bus had left without her it was just the road she had been travelling on, had come to an end. It was time to turn a corner and around that corner, a magnificent future awaited her. We can't always see what lies ahead, and that is when the most miraculous things happen, Annie thought to herself. And look at Jojo. She had become everything and more than Annie had expected her to be. Her vibrant, effervescent friend.

'Tell us about Wanda's World. When will it go on tour as a live show?'

'You'll hear all about that when we go down to the party. If we've only got thirty minutes, let's catch up on other things.'

'Fifteen, now,' Annie said.

'I heard the Golden Globe is reopening in the autumn,' Charlie said.

'I hope the Victorian features are restored in the rebuild. I loved that little theatre,' Jojo sighed. 'Has anyone heard what's happened to Nico?'

'I'm pleased to say that the divorce has gone through and my sister is free of that punk. I heard through the grapevine that he's back on the corporate parties' circuit, at least until the Golden Globe reopens.'

'Would Walker have him back after he burnt the place down?' Jojo exclaimed.

'It wasn't entirely Nico's fault. The Health and Safety Executive attributed the fire to faulty wiring and traces of gas in the old pipes. Walker didn't do due diligence in conforming with health and safety regulations.'

'What about Bobbi? She could have killed Jojo. Surely, she hasn't got off scott-free?'

Jojo interjected. 'I didn't press charges.'

'Why?' Charlie and Annie said together.

Jojo grimaced. 'I know. It could have been much worse, but Bobbi wasn't to know that the stage would catch fire.'

Charlie gave a half laugh. 'I haven't told you the best part. Kai is gay. He and Phillipe were seeing each other at the time of the fire. He thought Bobbi was loaded, living in that swanky flat. They were just after each other's money.'

'There were more illusions offstage than on. I guess we only see what we want to believe,' Annie said. This was something she had pondered on since the fire. At first, she couldn't forgive herself for not realising what was going on between Nico and Jojo, but Charlie had explained that Nico was a master of misdirection. As a magician, he drew the audiences' attention to one thing to distract it from another. 'I wanted to believe that you were happy, Jojo. I should have paid closer attention.'

'I wanted to believe it too. But I am now – deliriously happy and so are you. Let's finish this bottle and go party!'

When Jojo walked into the room, followed by Annie and Charlie, they were met with applause and cheers. 'May I present to you the amazing Jojo Evans, star of Wanda's World!'

. . .

The big revelation that the junior reporter had worked so hard to investigate was cut short. Lady Diana Spencer's engagement to Prince Charles was the top story that week. She had to fight for a couple of columns, as another reporter had snapped Jojo arriving at the party wearing a Vivienne Westwood gown, and that was the editor's preferred story on Wanda.

25th February 1981

Howdy! Magazine

Wanda's World Star – A phoenix from the ashes of The Golden Globe Theatre

Wanda's World took the country by storm with 28 million viewers tuning in to watch the feature length pilot. Who could not be enchanted by Wanda, the talented and beautiful Jojo Evans, whose acrobatics had us sitting on the edge of our seats?

Wanda has attracted a following of young women and girls who are inspired by her embodiment of independence, power, and strength. I was at the Golden Globe Theatre on the night that was to be the launch of this performer's career. Her last act was to disappear in a ring of fire and then reappear as a phoenix from the flames. Jojo certainly did that. Sadly, the Golden Globe theatre burnt down that night, but despite all this and more, Jojo rose triumphant.

The Golden Globe Theatre has a long history of discovering world-class magicians with the Easter Gala showcasing the top act tipped for stardom. Never before had a woman received this accolade. As a magician's assistant, Jojo, was little more than a coat stand, a spangled arm to receive the outer garments shed by heart-throb magician The Incredible Nico. But Jojo knew she was capable of more and with determination and ingenuity she surprised the audience and the Golden Globe's producer Peter Walker with her Alice Act — an unscheduled performance at the Golden Globe's Starlight show.

How did a woman rise to the top in a man's world? Everything was against Jojo. Her partner in love and magic, Nicholas Brown, was domineering and controlling. In the days leading up to Easter Gala, Jojo received threats to her life from a fellow artiste. On the night of the fire, Jojo was locked in a room under the stage in an attempt to stop her from performing. Nicholas Brown instructed Jojo to perform an act that was dangerous — the very act that led to the devastating fire. How did this diminutive redhead overcome adversity to burst onto our screens in her magnificent glory?

'Self-belief, determination, and using my imagination. Anything is possible. If you can't achieve what you want one way, there is always another way. But the most important thing — what makes me strong? Friendship. My best friend is always there for me, even when I stopped believing in myself.'

ABOUT THE AUTHOR

Deborah Klée is an award-winning author of page-turning, uplifting stories about friendship, community, and emotional courage. After a career in health and social care: an occupational therapist, health service manager, freelance journalist, and management consultant, she now enjoys writing happy endings for her protagonists.

Deborah lives on the Essex coast, where she loves to walk by the sea or the surrounding countryside, filling her pockets with shells, and acorns, and her head with stories. Visit her website at:

www.abrakdeborah.wordpress.com

or follow her on:

Twitter: @DeborahKlee
Instagram: deborahkleeauthor
Facebook: Deborah Klée Author

I hope you enjoyed reading The Last Act as much as I enjoyed writing it. If you did, please consider leaving a review. A book review introduces an author to new readers and is very much appreciated by the author. And if you do — thank you so much!

Praise for Deborah Klée

'Wow! this is a beautiful story, packed with emotional conundrums yet also tense and exciting. A lovely story, told with heart and humour and one which will hold you rapt until the end.'

'Deborah Klée has again created a story that draws you in immediately with fully rounded characters that you feel you really need to understand and want to get to know.'

'A lovely story, told with heart and humour and one which will hold you rapt until the end.'

'A heart-warming and emotional story that hits home a serious issue of today's society.'

'I am struggling to put into words how great this book is.'

'Such a clever, emotional read that entertains and informs. I was really impressed by this author and will look forward to reading more.'

'What an amazing read I really didn't want this book to end… A heartwarming read with romance, mystery and a reminder that we're all human. Deborah's writing is a pleasure to read and I cannot wait to read her future releases.'

ACKNOWLEDGMENTS

I completed an early draft of this novel in 2013. It was the first novel I had written. It never occurred to me I could write one, but my creative writing tutor at that time, Jenny Pêche, set an assignment for the group to write a five-thousand-word story using a writing prompt *Mirrors*. When I shared my short story, Jenny suggested it was the outline for a novel. I submitted the first version of this story to agents under the title Misdirection. Literary agent Hatty Grünewald loved the story and sent me pages of comments. A response like this is gold dust to a writer, but I did not realise this. I interpreted the feedback as 'not good enough,' so I put the novel aside and wrote another. Ten years and three published novels later, I rewrote the story, as Jojo and Annie were determined to be heard. So, my heartfelt thanks to Jenny Pëche, and Hattie Grünewald for their early encouragement and belief in me.

The early version of this novel also won me a place on a novel writing course with creative writing professor Sarah Dobbs. Sarah provided editorial guidance on my first drafts.

The Last Act has the same characters, setting, and premise as the original version, but is a different story.

Heartfelt thanks to: Beta-readers — Elizabeth Holland, Karen Heenan, Janet Bridger, Sue Chotipong, Ellie Holmes, Catherine Rendall, Lesley Kara, Anita Belli, Josephine Bowman, Collette Shuttleworth, Sue Smith, Janice Simmonds. The Frinton Writers' Group. Sally Freytag for assistance with copy-edits and proof-reading.

My amazing cover designer, Asya Blue Designs, has once again come up trumps with a fabulous cover.

I am particularly proud of this novel as it represents how far I have come in the past ten years and that would not have been possible without the love and support of my husband, Sherman and daughter, Laura-Jade.

Printed in Great Britain
by Amazon

25141083R00200